by
Cambria Hebert

#FINISH LINE
gearshark magazine

"A man is incomplete until he is married. After that he is finished."

—Zsa Zsa Gabor

#FINISH LINE

Arrow & Hopper

Chapter One

I once read somewhere that grief was just love with no place to go.

True and not true.

True because it hurts so much to love something and lose it. But not true because even after Matt died, I loved him; my love went wherever he was. To him.

Love isn't conditional on death. It supersedes it. Love has no boundaries. Therefore, I still loved Matt, even in grief. True, it was harder because our love became intangible. I couldn't see it or touch it... but I still felt it.

That was the grief. Giving love to someone who wasn't there.

Part of me still loved Matt, and I always would. He was my first love, my first relationship. He was also a friend, my best friend. Later, in death, he became a teacher. I realized he taught me the most important lesson I would ever learn.

Love and loss.

Because of Matt, I knew what it was to love and be loved. I also knew what it was like to lose it. The pain of being left alone.

I asked myself why for five long years. I punished myself, sank deep into despair and solitude.

The answer came not in words, but in a man.

The longer I knew him, the more convinced I became.

Arrow was the reason. He was my why.

I needed to learn how to love so I could love him.

I needed to learn how to break because he was also broken.

I succumbed to solitude only so I could really appreciate what it was not to be alone.

These were the hardest lessons I knew I would ever learn. I was remorseful Matt had to die, that something so extreme and permanent was the only thing that would get me to where I was today.

I couldn't regret, though.

To regret would be denouncing the connection I had with Arrow.

And though I loved Matt, I missed him far longer.

It hurt to know the person who taught me the most, the man who basically paved the way for the life I had now, was getting the short end of the stick. I wanted better for him, and it made me shamefaced to know I wouldn't ever be the one to give him that.

I knew now my infinity wasn't Matt after all, but Arrow.

Matt was my first love, but Arrow… he was my deepest. He was my last.

I just hoped wherever Matt was, he understood, because I couldn't stop it. And truthfully? I didn't want to.

Life is too frail to not make every day count— another lesson Matt taught me well.

I never thought I was the marrying kind. Getting married was something that kind of flew out the window when I realized I was gay.

Gay men didn't get married. Until recently, they weren't even allowed. Marriage wasn't that important anyway—at least not before.

A set of dark-brown eyes changed that. The tattoo just above where his heart beat proved me wrong.

Marriage was something I thought a lot about these days. It wasn't a piece of paper or a ring around your finger. It was more. So much more.

It was tying yourself irrevocably with another person.

An ultimate promise.

It was security, binding yourself in every way humanly possible to another person.

I wanted it. I wanted Arrow in every possible way. I wanted him to know I was always going to be here, and I wanted my name attached to his.

I had no clue what Arrow thought about marriage. I never asked him, and he never brought it up. Guess I was going to find out.

A few solid knocks in rapid succession on the apartment door made me belch. I was fucking nervous, which was fucking stupid.

Swallowing yet another eruption from my gut, I shoved back the thoughts and yanked open the door. Lorhaven stood there dressed in a leather jacket, despite the warm spring temperatures outside.

"What's wrong?" he demanded the second I opened the door.

"Nothing," I said and motioned for him to come in.

He pulled off his Oakleys and slid one earpiece beneath the neck of his dark-blue T-shirt so they were out of his hands and stepped into the apartment.

His eyes searched out his brother, wanting to be sure all was well.

"He isn't here," I said and shut the door.

Lorhaven turned. "Where is he?"

"Meeting," I replied.

"Why aren't you there?" He scrutinized.

"Because I didn't need to be." I cleared my throat. "And, I, ah, wanted to talk to you. Alone."

His eyes narrowed suspiciously. "Why?"

Arrow's big brother was an asshole. It wasn't anything new to me, and his constant suspicious demeanor didn't offend me like it used to. I understood his extreme overprotective nature when it came to Arrow (and Joey). I even respected it.

There was a time when I doubted we would ever get along. Hell, sometimes I still doubted it. But ever since the day I raced across the track to pull Arrow out of a multicar pile-up, things were different between me and Lorhaven.

Friendlier.

He welcomed me to the family that day, and since then, he'd backed up his handshake with actions. Arrow and I hung out with him and Joey regularly, something I knew meant a lot to A.

To me, too.

Joey was my first and only real friend since Matt died. The months we'd spent not really speaking had hurt. To have her friendship back along with a new one in Lorhaven gave me the sense of family I'd deprived myself of for so long.

"There's something I want to ask you," I said.

He made a sound, sort of an agreement, and shrugged out of the jacket to fling it over the back of the couch. "You called me down here because you want to ask me a question?"

"It's not something I could do over the phone."

He folded his arms over his chest and regarded me in a way that would probably make a lesser man piss his pants. Lorhaven didn't intimidate me. He never did, and he never would.

But, uh, yeah… I was anxious right now.

"I know how close you are to A." I began. "He told me you're more like a dad to him than The Fucker ever was."

Lorhaven's arms dropped to his sides. "He told you that?"

I nodded. "Yeah. And honestly, I'm fucking grateful to you for that."

Shock widened his very dark eyes. I committed the look to memory as I smothered a smile. I'd likely not see that look on his face ever again.

My voice dropped. "I think you were the one thing that stood between Arrow and total shutdown a few years ago."

"Until you came along," he replied, gruff.

"Thank you for everything you did for him, for everything you do. I know you already know how much he appreciates you, but now you know I do, too."

"He's my family," he said, like it was all he needed to say.

I half smiled.

"As touching as this is…" Lorhaven studied me. "Why do I get the feeling you want something?"

"Because I do." I took a deep breath. "I want Arrow."

He made a sound. "Pretty sure you already got that."

I shook my head once. "I want to marry him."

Lorhaven jolted like someone tossed a bucket of ice water over his head. "You wanna what?"

"I'm gonna ask Arrow to marry me, but before I do, I'd like your permission."

He swallowed like he had something lumpy in his throat. Then without a word, he went into the kitchen and pulled a beer out of the fridge. He took a long draw off the longneck and then glanced at me. "If I say no?"

"I'll ask him anyway, but we both know how much it would mean to him if you gave us your blessing."

"You haven't been together that long." He pointed out.

"So?"

"So why the rush?"

"I'm not rushing. I just know what I want."

"How well do you know my brother?"

I tilted my head. "You ask that like you think I don't know him well enough."

"He's been through a lot. I want to be sure you understand that."

I cut through the way we were about to talk around each other. "I know about the rape. And everything your father did to him."

He sucked in a breath. "He told you he was raped?"

I nodded, a little taken aback by the way he asked.

"In those words?"

"Yes."

"He never actually said it to me," Lorhaven murmured.

"I know. It's hard for him. Especially to say something he feels makes him so weak to someone he thinks is invincible."

"I'm not," he muttered, taking another pull on the beer.

"To him you are."

"He told you, though."

"He had to tell me. I wasn't there. I didn't see him the way you did. He might have not wanted to say it to you, but he never had to because you already *knew*."

"That was the worst night of my life," Lorhaven echoed, his voice haunted. He stared across the room as if he were reliving that night.

I shuddered because even though I hadn't been there, I was haunted by it, too. I couldn't imagine what it was like to have *seen* it.

"If it makes it any easier…" I said, trying to soften the blow that Arrow actually said the words to me and not to him. "It's easier to tell someone how broken you are if the person you're telling is equally as broken."

It was pretty fucking amazing actually. Here I was trying to soften a perceived blow to someone who once hated me, someone I wasn't that fond of at one point. Not only that, but I was requesting his blessing.

Lorhaven turned, leaning back against the counter, holding the beer by the neck but down at his side. All of his attention zeroed in on me. "What happens when your past comes back to bite you?"

"My past can't bite me." *It already did.*

"You sure about that, *Jayson?*"

My stomach lurched and my heart beat faster. It wasn't that I minded he knew about Matt and who I used to be; I just wasn't used to talking about it with people. People who weren't Arrow.

"Did Joey tell you about me?" I asked, low.

He made a rude noise. "No. I never asked her to. I'd never put her in that position. I assume what she knows was told to her in confidence."

It was more out of necessity. Both she and Gamble knew about Matt and my old career. But it was still in confidence. I respected him for that, for not expecting the woman he loved to fess up everything just because he wanted her to.

I began to smile, and he made a slashing motion in the air. "Don't get too pretty a picture in your head." He bitched. "If I had thought for one second you were up to shady shit with my brother or were bad news, I'd have made her tell me. I figured she said nothing because it wouldn't hurt Arrow."

"So how do you know?" I asked, because Lorhaven knew everything. I could tell just by the way he said my name.

"I hired a PI."

I made a sound. "I thought you didn't think I was up to shady shit."

He smiled, showing all his teeth. "I still would never let my brother live with someone I knew nothing about."

"How long have you known?"

He grinned again. "Almost from the beginning."

I felt my eyes pop wide.

Lorhaven laughed. "The second I saw my brother return one of those googly, longing stares with you on the track months and months ago, I made a call."

"So you know about Matt."

He nodded. "And that you were hell on two wheels."

My lip curled upward. "Something like that."

"I'm thinking Matt's death wasn't an accident," he deadpanned.

"You'd be right."

He digested that. "What happens when the press finds out who you are?"

"They haven't so far."

He tipped the bottle back again, drained the rest, then stared at me. "You and I both know they got a whole lot more curious when my brother was featured in *GearShark* and said he was in a relationship with you."

"I'll deal with it," I said, tight.

"Disappearing might have worked the last time, but this time you can't do that."

"I know," I said, harsh. "I would never do that to your brother."

"I hope the hell not, because it would kill him." His tongue ran over his front teeth. "And then I would kill you."

He didn't even say it as a threat; it was just the way it was. Lorhaven would kill me. There wasn't any doubt in my mind.

"I know my identity is going to come out, and when it does, it's going to be a media shit storm. Arrow knows it, too. I've told him everything."

He studied me a long moment. It sort of made me uncomfortable because Lorhaven was really hard to read. You just never knew what the guy was thinking.

"Have you had sex with my brother?"

See what I mean?

"What the fuck kind of question is that?" I growled.

"An honest one," Lorhaven rebutted.

I shoved off the island where I stood and paced away. "I'm not talking about my sex life with you."

"I don't want to have this conversation either. I don't want to think about it." He sounded horrified, yet he forged on. "But you called. You want my blessing? Answer the goddamn question."

I went to the fridge to get a beer of my own. I stared out the window over the kitchen sink as I downed some of it. I needed something stronger for this.

"Yes," I said, firm.

I didn't turn to look at his face when I answered. I didn't want to see his reaction.

"And he's… okay?"

A little of the awkward vibe left the air. I let out the breath I'd been holding. I understood why he was asking. When someone had been abused the way Arrow had, it wasn't a far reach to think they might have certain, ah, issues in the bedroom.

I turned around. "He's fine. I swear. I'd never do anything that would hurt him."

"You both have heavy pasts, haven't been together that long... Why do you want to marry him?"

Damn. This guy was like a fucking Vice detective. I thought I'd ask, he'd make some threats, and then shake my hand. I didn't expect all this.

Maybe I should have bypassed this convo and gone straight at Arrow with a ring.

Did guys propose to other guys with rings?

Oh my God, I didn't even know how to propose.

This was a complete disaster.

Lorhaven snapped his fingers at me.

I blinked and looked up. "I love him," I replied simply.

"Yeah." Lor agreed. "I can see that."

"It's not just that, though." My three-word response was enough, but still I forged on. "I want to give him that security. I want to give him somewhere he absolutely belongs, you know? I want him to have my name. I want to be legally bound to him so if..." I cleared my throat. "If anything ever happens to me, everything I have will go to him without fight."

"And everything he has would go to you…" He surmised.

I jolted and rushed forward to crowd his space. "Don't fucking talk like that," I growled. "He ain't going nowhere."

God, the fear I had about him dying on me was too real. It was my greatest weakness.

I jabbed my finger into the center of Lorhaven's chest. "I don't want anything of his, not his money or his cars. I'll fucking sign a contract that says so. It won't matter anyway, because if he dies, I'll follow."

Lorhaven's eyes flared. He knew exactly what I meant. He knew I was dead serious (literally). I knew what it was to live after someone you loved died. I barely survived it with Matt.

I knew without a shadow of a doubt I wouldn't survive a second time around. Not without Arrow.

"You love my brother more than him?" Lorhaven whispered, as if even he knew what sacrilege he spoke.

I sucked in a breath and removed the finger still drilling into his chest. Funny how he acted like he didn't even notice the way I pushed him.

"How dare you ask me that?" The words ripped out like a caged animal.

"It ain't nothing you haven't asked yourself."

Touché.

I stepped back, my shoulders slumping. "It's a different kind of love," I allowed. I couldn't say it outright. I wouldn't.

"How so?"

"Deeper. More…" My voice trailed away.

He held up a hand. "I get it. I shouldn't have asked. It was an asshole thing to do."

"I won't disagree."

He barked a laugh. "My little brother, married," he mused.

"So does that mean you're going to support us?"

The door to the apartment sprang open, and Arrow's voice cut through our conversation. "Hopp!"

"Here," I called out from the kitchen.

He appeared on the other side of the island, his keys dangling from his fingers. His eyes went from me to Lorhaven and widened. "Jace? What are you doing here?"

I glanced at him, hoping he knew this was a private conversation.

"Came by to see if you wanted to have lunch," Lorhaven answered without missing a beat.

Arrow looked at me, and I smiled. I hadn't seen him since this morning. I missed his face. "You have time?"

"Anything for you, babe." I tossed a wink at him.

I knew by the look in his chocolate eyes he wanted to kiss me. I wanted to kiss him just as much. We actually already had plans for lunch that didn't include food, but now that Lorhaven was here, those plans were going to have to wait until tonight.

Why couldn't he have just said yes and gotten out of the apartment? He was a damn cock-blocker.

"What about Joey?" Arrow asked.

"I'll call her in the car."

"I'm starving."

"What else is new?" Lorhaven and I quipped at the same time. We glanced at each other awkwardly, and Arrow laughed.

"I'm gonna grab a new shirt. I got oil all over this one in the garage. Then we can go."

"I'll go call Josie. I'll see you downstairs," Lorhaven called after him as he walked back to the bedroom.

I couldn't help but sneak a peek at his ass.

Lorhaven pulled out his phone and glanced at me.

"Thanks for not saying anything to him," I said, low.

Lorhaven lowered the phone, his eyes locked on mine. "You got my blessing."

I didn't think it would feel so good. I thought I was asking for this on behalf of Arrow and out of respect for his relationship with his brother. I didn't realize this was something I needed.

"Thank you," I said, meaning it.

He slapped me on the shoulder as he moved past. "You were already part of the family, Hopper, but I guess this will make it official."

"Hey," I whispered and glanced toward the bedroom.

Lorhaven swung around and arched a brow.

I stepped closer. "Am I supposed to give him a ring?"

Lorhaven sputtered. Then his face cracked into a wide grin. "I have no fucking clue."

"Lotta help you are," I muttered.

He laughed some more. "I'll meet you guys downstairs."

The door shut behind him, and the sounds of Arrow moving around in the other room beckoned. I took a step toward him, then stopped.

Holy shit, I was gonna do this.

I was gonna ask Arrow to marry me.

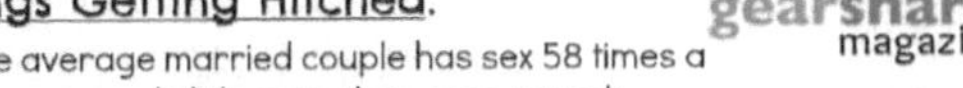

Chapter Two

I didn't tell him.

I didn't tell him how slightly obsessed I was with the way he caressed my lower back, how his fingertips whispered lightly over the dip above my spine. I thought of that moment more than once during the day. Some days I craved it. Some nights I rushed around getting ready for bed just to get to get there faster.

He never failed me. He always did it. My stomach always caved in when he did.

Still, I said nothing. I liked that he caressed me like that, not knowing how much it meant to me. If I told him, it would be like he did it because he knew how much I reveled in it. It was sweeter knowing he touched me this way, not because I wanted him to, but because *he* wanted to.

Would I ever get used to someone having full access to my body and heart? Probably not. Especially when it was so unexpected.

My stomach growled loudly as I rummaged for a clean shirt, the scent of soap wafting around me from my just-washed hands. It was only noon, but damn, the hours had dragged by this morning. It was probably because Hopp and I made plans to meet in the apartment for lunch. And not to eat.

As much as I loved my brother, I was a little bummed he picked today of all days to show up. But he did, and I wasn't about to tell him to get out. Family didn't do that. And I was partly shocked to see him and Hopp getting along. Alone.

What the hell was up with that?

"I'm coming in." Hopper warned as he approached me from behind. I glanced over my shoulder in time to see him swoop his arms around my bare waist and pull me against his chest.

When my back was turned, he always announced himself before he touched me. I never asked him to do that. He just did.

He just knew.

I think maybe I'd be okay with him just grabbing me. I mean, it was Hopp after all. But I never told him that. I think I was a little worried about it deep down, worried it might bring back some kind of flashback from that night over three years ago. The last thing I wanted was to flinch away if he wrapped his arms around me. I'd beat myself up for that forever.

"So much for our nooner," he whispered against my ear.

I leaned against him and sighed. His palm flattened over my stomach and rubbed lightly, making me groan and my hips jut out.

Warm, thick lips latched on the side of my neck, and I leaned my head to the side, giving him better access. With a low moan, he kissed a little deeper, stroking his tongue across my skin and making me quake.

The arms around my waist tightened, and I pushed my ass against his center. His body tightened, but he didn't thrust against my ass, something else he was careful not to do.

Reaching behind me, my hand curled around the back of his head and delved into his dark curls. He nipped at my skin, and I spun, matching our bodies up so we were pressed together.

At the same moment, we rocked our hips into each other, and my forehead dropped onto his shoulder. Fingertips grazed over my lower back, in that magic spot, and I sighed, sinking just a little more into his chest.

Filling my hands with his ass, I gave it a squeeze, pulling back and diving into his mouth. It was a slow kiss, considering how ravenous he made me. My thoughts turned fuzzy as our lips met again and again. Instead of delving deep with our tongues, they only grazed briefly as we made out, whispering caresses time and again.

Kissing him like this made my limbs heavy. Made my skin buzz with life and the outside world completely vanish except for his taste and feel.

With a deep moan, he pulled back. I licked my lips, and his eyes flared. "You don't make this easy," he grieved, rubbing his palm up my side.

I grazed my fingertips over his stubbled jaw and smiled. "I love you, Hopp."

"Not as much as I love you," he whispered.

I shook my head. "Not true."

"C'mon," he said, taking my hand. "Maybe if we eat fast, we'll have some time before we gotta be back down at the track."

I laughed, snagged a dark blue T-shirt out of the open drawer, and let him lead me toward the front door.

Before opening it, Hopper released my hand. "Put the shirt on, babe."

I laughed. "Yeah, 'cause there's gonna be a ton of people in the hallway just waiting for a glimpse."

He grunted but didn't budge. With a chuckle, I pulled on the shirt, but before I could yank it down over my chest, I felt his hand bunch the fabric.

Lifting my eyes, I watched him lower his head, pressing a kiss to the infinity tattoo on my chest. Too soon, the shirt was falling into place and we were heading toward the elevator, hand in hand.

"You and my brother getting along?" I asked.

He glanced at me swiftly. "Yeah, why?"

"Just making sure I don't need to kick his ass," I cracked, even though suddenly it seemed like maybe I did walk in on something.

Hopp rolled his eyes.

"Seriously, though, did I interrupt something when I came home?"

Hopper lifted our linked hands and kissed the back of mine. "No, babe. Everything is fine."

The elevator swung open, revealing Lor, who was standing there with his phone pressed to his ear. His body was rigid, and he was so focused on whoever he was talking to he didn't even hear us get off the elevator. "This is really fucking shitty timing," he intoned.

"Jace?" I worried, stepping toward him. "What's wrong?"

He jerked and spun. The phone slipped a little from his ear. He didn't look at me though.

He looked at Hopper.

My stomach clenched. "What!" I demanded.

"Be there in a few," he said, disconnecting the call. "Change of plans," he announced. "We're going to Gamble's."

"Why?" Hopper demanded, the hand in mine going rigid.

"I'll explain when we get there."

I made a harsh sound. "Or you could explain right now."

"I don't have all the details." He hedged.

"Just say it," Hopper snapped.

Lorhaven's eyes bounced between us, even glancing down for an instant at our clasped hands. A sour looked filled his eyes, twisting his lips.

"The press knows who Hopper is. The story just broke."

Oh fuck. His hand went limp in mine for a few seconds before stiffening again. My entire being went on high alert. Without letting go of him, I jumped forward, automatically placing my body in front of his.

"How the fuck did they find out?" I demanded.

"I don't know," he growled. "But we should go. Standing here where the press can find us isn't a good idea."

I didn't think about it. I just shifted, pulling my hand free to wrap my arm around his waist. "Let's go."

Lorhaven started toward the front entrance, and I made a sound. "I'll drive."

He didn't argue. The three of us moved to the side door that led out to the parking garage for staff and residents. I glanced at Hopper, trying to gauge the way he was feeling.

He sensed my gaze, returned it, and offered a smile. "I'm fine, babe."

But he wasn't, and I knew it.

At the Camaro, I opened the passenger door, and without a word, Jace dove into the back. Before Hopper could slip in, I fisted his shirt and tugged him back. He turned around, our stares colliding. He was waffling, caught between the present and the past.

"Hey," I said so low only he could hear. "Stay here with me."

He nodded, and I knew that was going to have to be good enough, at least for now. There was a sense of urgency surrounding us, breathing heavily on the back of my neck. The second Hopp was inside, my eyes scanned the garage, sweeping the space for anything out of the ordinary as I made my way around the hood to the driver's side.

The Camaro roared to life; the sound of the powerful engine gave me a burst of adrenaline and strength. I threw it into reverse and backed out of the spot.

Before driving forward, though, I hit the brakes.

The car jolted, throwing us all forward a little.

"What the fuck?" Jace spat, catching himself on the back of the seats.

My arm stretched across the back of Hopper's seat. I turned and glanced into the back. "You aren't surprised."

"What?" he wondered.

"Why aren't you surprised Hopp has a different identity?"

"I knew," Lorhaven replied simply.

I arched a brow. "You hired a PI to investigate my boyfriend?"

"Like you didn't know I would." He was unapologetic.

"No, Jace," I bitched. "I thought you might actually let me make my own decision."

"I did," he growled. "I didn't tell you what I found out."

"I already know," I growled back.

"Can we table this argument?" Hopper injected. "The vultures are circling."

I glanced over at him, but he was staring out the windshield at something else.

My stare followed his. "Fucking hairy goat balls full of piss," I cursed.

"What the fuck did you just say?" Lorhaven questioned from the backseat.

I ignored him and hit the gas. The tires squealed under the pressure, and my car shot forward with a roar. The large white news van heading straight toward us hit the brakes, trying to create a road block.

As if that were enough to get in my way.

I went on autopilot, my racing experience and training taking over. My car swerved around the van, then around a giant cement poll, narrowly avoiding a car parked in an embarrassingly shitty way, and straightened back out as we neared the exit.

A quick glance in the rearview, and I saw the van doing a three-point turn, which would likely be more of a ten-point when the moron driving got his head out of his ass.

I floored it and shot out of the garage like a bullet from a cannon. There were a few photographers on foot at the entrance. The second my car burst into sight, a frenzy to snap some pictures began.

I floored it. The car shot forward and left all those fuckers in my dust.

"Assholes," I spat.

"They work fast," Lorhaven muttered, disgusted.

"It's just the beginning." Hopper sighed, exhausted.

Reaching across the seat, I folded my hand around his.

We always knew this was a strong possibility. The more interested the media became in me, the more they would look at him.

It was only a matter of time before everyone found out Hopper was really ex-Motocross sensation Jayson

Hamilton. It was going to stir up a lot of shit for him. Shit I wished he didn't have to deal with at all.

Wishes were for stars, though, not flesh-and-blood men. I supposed now the time had come.

It doesn't matter how far or how long you run. The past always has a way of catching up. And usually at the most inopportune times.

The past is an asshole.

Happiness seems simple, doesn't it? Isn't being happy the goal for just about everyone on the planet? Happiness is portrayed as easy to attain, but in reality, it's hard to grasp. It's more of a façade, something people pretend to be because it's more socially acceptable. Sort of like being straight.

For me, being happy had become a myth. If I hadn't felt it at some point in my life, I might have labeled it an urban legend.

The past several months, I discovered happiness again. Not just happiness, though, something that went deeper.

Satisfaction, maybe. Contentment.

Love.

No. A *bone-deep rightness* that gave me newfound confidence. The kind of absolute truth I felt settle inside me, in my gut, as if it had grown there. Arrow was right. My life with him was where I was supposed to be. I loved him. I loved our life together.

I didn't want to look back, only forward. I only wanted to worry about if I should get him a ring, how I was going to ask him to marry me, and how soon I could get his sexy ass to the altar.

I didn't want this.

The press. The questions. The memories.

I didn't want to be dogged by the public and pursued by nosey-ass people who had no rights to the inside of my mind or the inner workings of my heart.

Unfortunately, I had to deal with this. I'd run too long. If my true identity had broken before Arrow, I might have run again. Packed up and walked. I couldn't do that now. He rooted me in place, and it didn't matter how forceful the wind blew, I wasn't going to move.

The only way to get to forever was to work through the present.

"Josie, we're here. Open the gate." Lorhaven's voice cut through my internal pep talk. I blinked and glanced into the backseat to see him disconnecting the call and tucking the phone in his jacket.

The Camaro slowed and was instantly swarmed by press. Arrow snarled and gunned the engine, which caused several reporters to leap back. A few of the more zealous ones didn't budge, though; they just kept aiming their cameras.

The gates opened slowly, and I watched, waiting for a few press to try and slip through. They didn't, though, likely because Gamble had security standing behind it who didn't look too friendly.

Arrow nosed through the gate the second the doors were wide enough for the Camaro, then pressed the gas to put as much distance as possible between us and the crowd. I breathed a sigh of relief as I watched the gate close and the reporters shrink farther away.

The huge white house came into view. Joey's yellow skyline was parked right up near the front door. She was pacing on the front steps. When she saw us, she jogged down and stood by her car, waiting anxiously.

Arrow stopped the car behind hers and threw it into park. When he turned toward me, I felt his probing stare. He was worried. I kinda was, too.

This news wasn't anything that would threaten what we had, but it wasn't going to make anything easier. Asking him to marry me seemed harder now. It wasn't just me he would be tying himself to, but the chaos my old identity brought.

Before we could say anything, my door was wrenched open and Joey's wild mane of dark curls filled the doorway.

"Jay," she fretted. "Are you okay?"

She was one of the only ones who sometimes called me Jay. Everyone else called me Hopper. I didn't feel like Jayson anymore, even though it was still my legal name.

A new vibe flowed off Arrow and smacked me in the back of the head. I began turning, but Joey grabbed my hand and tugged me out of the car.

In the driveway, she wrapped her arms around me in a full hug. I hugged her back, closing my eyes briefly. "I'm sorry," she murmured.

"It was bound to happen," I murmured against her hair.

She hugged me a little tighter. My eyes snapped up to A, who moved around the front of the car, watching us with a closed-off expression. My stomach sank a little. I didn't like that look.

Clearing my throat, I pulled away, smiling down at Joey. "Gamble here?"

She made a sound. "Of course. He's waiting inside, yelling at someone on the phone."

"Josie," Lorhaven said gruffly.

Her eyes warmed and lips curled up. I stepped out of the way so she could move toward him. He yanked her into his chest, arms closing around her like a vise. "The press give you any trouble?"

She shook her head and burrowed a little closer.

I took a step away from them and toward Arrow.

Lorhaven cleared his throat. "C'mon, Josie, let's head in."

They walked past, but Lor stopped to look between me and A. "You guys cool?"

"Yeah, we'll be right in." Arrow dismissed him.

The second the front door shut behind them, we met at the corner of the front end of the Camaro.

"Don't," he said when I opened my mouth.

I lifted a brow. "Don't what?"

"Don't try and tell me you're fine. I know better."

Palming the side of his waist, I smiled. "Wasn't going to."

His dark eyes searched, bouncing between mine. "Good, 'cause we aren't about that, Hopp. We don't pretend."

I let out a long sigh, shifting so we touched. My hand curled around his side to his back, tugging him right into my body.

"I'm transparent with you, babe. See-through. I don't want you freaking out, though, thinking this is going to somehow change us. It won't. I love you. The feeding frenzy of the media isn't going to change that."

Between our bodies, he raised his hand. Gently, his thumb glided across my lower lip. "I hate when she calls you Jay." I loved the growly, jealous tone his voice suddenly held.

He is totally jealous. Stifling a smile, I tilted my head. "You wanna call me that?"

"Honestly? I thought about it. Jayson is a sexy-as-fuck name."

I wagged my eyebrows. He'd never told me he thought so.

His chuckle filled my mouth when he leaned in for a fast kiss.

"But?" I asked as he was pulling away.

"Matt called you Jay, didn't he?"

My chest took a hit, like a fist pummeling me. Sometimes I thought I could still recall the sound of Matt's voice when he'd yell my name. And sometimes I wondered if it was really his voice I remembered or a version I'd fabricated because it was too painful to admit I'd forgotten.

Gazing downward, I nodded. "Yeah, he did."

"I think I'll stick with Hopp. It's who you are now, who you are to me."

I nodded, unsure what to say. I wanted desperately to tell him he could call me whatever the hell he wanted. Whatever I am was his. But I wondered if it would somehow take away from what I'd shared with Matt.

Sometimes I still felt I was caught in the middle, even though I'd already firmly decided with my heart and head it was Arrow's side I was on.

"You're the only one I've ever called babe," I murmured, lifting my head.

"That makes me kinda happy," he confided.

I grabbed his hand, knotting ours together.

"It's gonna get harder when we go inside," Arrow said. "When we see some of the stuff being vomited by the media."

"We're gonna have to lie low for a while." I agreed.

"Long as we're together, it won't matter."

"I'm keeping you right here with me." I vowed, tugging him toward the house.

"You're my favorite place, Hopp," he whispered, almost as if he didn't want me to hear.

The vulnerability Arrow sometimes showed was something that always hit me hard and fast. It endeared him to me, made me want to shield him from everything.

My feet bumped his when I turned, curling my fingers around the nape of his neck. Lowering my forehead to his, I stared deep into his chocolate eyes. "You're my favorite place, too, babe."

His eyes closed.

Lifting my head, I brushed a slow kiss over his forehead, then started for the house again. I couldn't put this off forever. The sooner I dealt with the past, the sooner I could get on with my future.

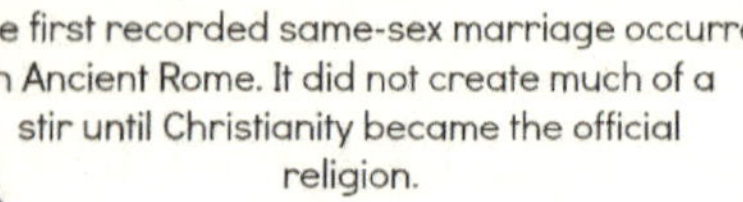

Chapter Four

I'd never been the jealous type. I guess because I never really cared enough about anything to be bothered. I learned a long time ago I didn't need much to survive.

I needed Hopper, though, and frankly, the longer I was with him, the more possessive I became. He was mine, dammit. Everyone needed to fucking recognize.

The sound of a television reached us before we even stepped into Gamble's large study. It was the news, or the sports channel, and they were talking about Hopper.

Everyone's attention was on the large flat-screen across the room, exactly where Hopper's went, too. We were hand in hand, but he stopped abruptly, which almost tore our fingers apart. Swiveling around to look at him, I tightened my grip.

His body was rigid, skin scary pale. The icy tone of his eyes was bleak and fastened on the TV like nothing could drag it away.

I wanted him here with me.

Following his suddenly haunted stare, I glanced at the screen. My stomach clenched so tight it made me want to double over, but I held stiff.

A picture of Matt filled the screen as the reporter went on and on. I didn't hear what she said because of the low buzzing between my ears. I'd never seen a picture of him until this moment. It crossed my mind a time or two to look him up online, but I never followed through.

I wasn't sure I wanted to see who had Hopp's heart before me. What if I couldn't compete?

The choice was out of my hands as of this moment. The image on screen would be one I wouldn't forget. I knew it was him; the look on Hopper's face told me. Even if I hadn't understood, I wouldn't be able to miss the headline across the screen.

He was good looking. No, *better* than good looking. He was bigger than me, about the same size as Hopper, with the same wide shoulders and narrow waist. The short hair on his head was dark and thick, cut close so it was never messy. In the picture, he was smiling bigger than my lips probably could stretch.

I could tell just from one look he was the kind of guy everyone liked. He'd been open, outgoing, and probably the life of the party.

From what I knew, he was also pretty selfless, at least when it came to Hopper. He'd basically helped Hopp build his career, putting his own in standby.

He had blue eyes, bright sky-blue ones. Kind of like Drew's. There wasn't a single cloud in them, as if he never knew what it was to be broken into a million tiny pieces.

A pit opened in my stomach. It was like a sudden sinkhole that erupted into a rumbly mess and began trying to suck me down. I resisted, but it was hard. It hurt. I felt like I'd eaten a plate of bad fish, spent four days puking, and was left in that weak, empty state where it hurt to even breathe.

How long was the stupid screen going to show his picture? When would they move on to something else?

As if the universe heard my plea, the giant image of Matt faded out.

Only to be replaced by another one that was much, much worse.

An image of Hopper and Matt together.

I swallowed down the rising bile but was unable to turn away. He looked different as Jayson. Leaner, younger. His face was clean shaven; there was no rough stubble giving him a more jagged appearance. The messy hair that sometimes curled up against his neck was super short, buzzed even. In the photo, his smile was more carefree than I'd ever known him to be.

It hurt.

It hurt a whole fucking lot.

Their arms were around one another.

Don't touch him. He's mine.

He was someone else's first.

I didn't hear what the reporter was saying. I didn't notice anything else going on around me at all. I was trapped, held prisoner by an image I never wanted to see again.

Thankfully, a large wall came forward and blocked out the TV. I blinked, looking up. Jace was staring at me with a concerned expression. He stood close, so close I could smell his aftershave. It was a nice scent; I should get some.

"Here." His voice was guff as he thrust a crystal glass of dark liquid toward me.

Good idea.

I took it and knocked it back in one swallow.

He observed me, slightly amused, until I grabbed the other drink in his hand, the one that was likely his.

I downed that one, too.

Jace snatched the glass away, held both at his side, and slapped his large hand over my shoulder and squeezed. "Look at me, little brother."

Narrowing my eyes, I stared at him. I hated when he called me that, which was likely why he did it. He knew it would get my attention.

"It's tough. I get it," he murmured.

I shook my head. He didn't get this.

His fingers squeezed me a little harder. "I know for a fact he loves you."

"He loved someone else first," I whispered.

Jace strained to hear, but when he did, his head jerked back. "Don't matter. You more."

He spoke so confidently. I knew my brother. I knew him very, very well. He wasn't lying. He truly believed Hopper loved me more than Matt.

How could he be so sure?

My heart wanted desperately to believe it. My head wasn't as quick to follow.

Did it really matter? He loved me now. We were together now.

Oh shit, I wish it didn't matter.

Somewhere in the room, a phone rang. Gamble made a sound, went to his desk, and picked up the landline. I didn't even know people used those anymore.

"What!" he barked.

He was silent only a few heartbeats. Then he made a sound as if cutting off whoever was on the other end.

"That's asinine!" he snapped. "If they want it, then they have to come up. That's final."

Lorhaven, who had been watching me up to this point, turned to stare at Gamble.

"And you tell that rag if they print so much as one headline, I will sue the whole company and then buy it out from under them! All the scumbags on staff will be out of a job!" he roared.

The phone slammed down with a finality that practically screamed death.

"Fucking morons," he muttered.

"Dad!" Joey admonished.

"Don't dad me," he muttered. "The press is full of leeches." Gamble glanced up and saw me. "Oh good, you're here."

A small frown pulled at his mouth when his eyes found Hopp. Peeking around Lorhaven, I saw Hopper had moved closer toward the TV and was sitting in a chair adjacent to it, eyes still riveted on the screen.

Holding my breath, I glanced back up, only to be hella relieved Matt no longer dominated the picture.

"Family meeting," Gamble announced.

I think that was the only thing he could have said in the entire universe to pull my attention off Hopper.

"What?" I said, bewildered, turning around.

"Up until now, we've managed to keep Hopper's life out of the press, but that's no longer an option." He stopped, cleared his throat, and looked over to where my boyfriend was staring at the TV like he was lost. Gamble lifted his voice. "Unless, of course, Hopper wants to run and avoid it all again."

I stiffened. "He's not going anywhere," I growled, lunging past my brother toward Gamble's desk.

Gamble's face was unreadable when he turned to me. "I'd like to hear that from him personally."

Dropping my hands onto the edge of his desk, my fingers curled under the edge and squeezed until my joints ached. But I said nothing.

That hole inside me was back, trying to suck me in again. The pain created a hollow iciness in my middle.

Then a warm, sure presence wrapped around me. Sort of like the sun when it comes out from behind a dark storm cloud. With it came touch—a touch I knew so well it was almost an extension of myself.

Hopper's hand wrapped around my waist and his arm slid forward as he stepped up beside me, pulling me against his side. "I'm not going anywhere, Gamble. I'm sticking this out."

My breathing hitched and my chest burned. I didn't say anything, though. Too many emotions and feelings warred inside me.

"I thought as much," Gamble declared. I felt his eyes but didn't bother looking up. "Then it's time for a family meeting."

"If you wanted to have a family meeting, why did you call me and Arrow down here?" Hopper asked, blunt.

The edges of my mouth turned up, and I bit back a laugh. Hopper tapped the side of my waist like he knew I was amused.

"You two are basically my daughter's brothers," Gamble barked. "You've been like a son to me for over five years, Jayson. Albeit a son who's annoying as shit sometimes, but a son no less." He went on. "You're family."

My whole body straightened. I rose to my full height and stared across the desk at Gamble. I knew most of that was directed at Hopper, but not all of it. "You consider us family?"

"Of course he does!" Joey insisted, rushing over to back up her father. "You're like the three sons he never had!"

"Makes me glad I had a daughter," Gamble muttered. "You three are pains in my asses!"

Joey giggled gleefully.

"I feel the love," Lorhaven quipped.

"Enough out of you." Gamble pointed at him. "You have yet to make an honest woman of my daughter."

"Dad!" Joey yelled, appalled.

I grinned, glancing over my shoulder. "When you gonna make my sister an honest woman, Jace?"

He gave me the finger. "She's not your sister. *Yet.*"

Joey gasped and wrapped her arm around my waist, just above Hopper's. I was basically a sandwich between them. "Yes, you are! Don't listen to him. He's being an ass."

I leaned closer to her ear. "You guys didn't get married when I wasn't looking, did you?"

"No." She moaned, totally exasperated.

"Enough nonsense. We have things to discuss." Gamble insisted.

His phone rang, and he snatched it up. "I'm busy," he exacted and put it back down.

Hopper and I glanced at one another. He snickered out of the side of his mouth. My heart clenched. I couldn't live without him. I just couldn't.

"Sit down," Gamble ordered.

Everyone found a seat.

I thought longingly of Hopp's lap but figured that would make me look like a clingy bastard. I wasn't clingy or needy. I spent a long time on my own. I knew I could survive alone…

Okay, fine, I needed Hopp. But I couldn't just go plop down in his lap, not right now. Instead, I sat in the chair beside him. His gaze beckoned me, but I didn't look. I was afraid he'd see the stupid vulnerability I felt.

He didn't need to see it.

He already knew it.

I should have fucking known. Sometimes the way we'd bonded was annoying because even when we wanted to keep something to ourselves, it was nearly impossible.

Reaching over, Hopper took my hand and pulled it to him. It wasn't done with a lot of show, as if he were making a statement. It was just a quiet gesture by a man who loved someone and wanted to make sure I knew he was still here with me.

I tightened my fingers around his with an inaudible sigh.

"The story broke out of New York," Gamble announced. "Some reporter did some digging, found some pictures, put two and two together, and then unearthed the rest."

"This is because of my cover feature," I said.

"It was bound to happen at some point." Hopper assured me.

I wasn't sure that was true. He'd been doing a damn good job of keeping a low profile before I came around.

"He's right." Gamble nodded. "Which is why I've had an official statement drafted and prepared for a long time."

"What?" Hopper sat forward.

Gamble laid his folded hands on the top of his desk. "This is business. I take care of my business." With that, he produced a piece of paper and held it out to Hopper, who stood to retrieve it.

I stared at him as he swept his eyes over the page. He was dressed in lightweight black pants with a dark-gray stripe down each leg. The material was silky smooth, and I knew my fingertips would glide right over his ass if I grabbed it. The muscles in his bicep bulged slightly as he read, causing the sleeves of his white T-shirt to pull taut.

When he was finished, he looked at me. "It's basic. Just a confirmation that I'm Jayson Hamilton and I've been working at Gamble for five years. Then it asks for privacy, blah, blah." He held the paper out to me.

"You cool with what it says?" I asked.

He nodded. "It's pretty standard."

"I don't need to read it. Long as you're cool."

Hopper tossed the paper back on the desk and returned to his seat, picking up my hand once more. "Release it," he said.

"It's going out first thing in the morning," Gamble informed us.

"The press is going to be relentless." Joey worried.

Lorhaven made a sound of agreement. "They're already out."

"I've had a room prepared for you in the empty wing of the house. It's best if you stay here a few days behind the gates, with security. At least until the statement is released and some other details are worked out."

We were supposed to stay here? The idea of security was nice, as was the thought of Hopper not having to watch his back every time he moved in front of a window, but I liked our apartment.

We looked at each other. Hopper was conflicted.

"Thanks, we'll take you up on it," I said, surprising everyone. Hopper's icy eyes flared. I gave his hand a squeeze. "It'll give you some room to breathe."

"Smart decision," Gamble replied. Then he quickly shifted gears. "Now, about the tell-all."

"Whoa…" I cautioned. "What tell-all?"

Gamble looked at me like he was definitely trying to be patient while gesturing to the statement Hopp tossed down. "That statement is only going to buy some time. Hopper is going to have to give an interview."

Loud rumbling thundered in my chest and up the back of my throat. "Like hell. He doesn't owe anyone an explanation."

"If he wants the cameras and the sensationalism surrounding his abrupt, dramatic exit from Motocross, the death of his partner, and the fact he was essentially a ghost for the last six years to ever go away, then yes, he does."

"Fuck the press." My voice was gravely and impatient. Sitting in this chair made me feel confined, and I wanted to pace. The muscles in my legs tensed. I thought to push up out of the seat.

Hopper stopped me. The grip on my hand tightened; he pushed our clasped fingers down into his lap so they were almost trapped by his thighs. Glancing over, I noted the way his body sort of leaned toward me, though he was in his own chair.

Shuddering with a deep breath, I forced myself to relax. He needed me close by, and I understood. It was a need that far outweighed my own.

"Like it or not, you're in the public eye, Arrow," Gamble said, no ounce of coddling in his tone. "You were even before the season started, but now that it has and you've been driving so well, you're becoming a household name with NASCAR fans. That puts Hopper there as well, especially since you're in a gay relationship."

"If he were a woman, no one would fucking care," I spat. It was hard to sometimes not feel resentful toward society as a whole. I just wanted to love him. I just wanted to be happy and mind my own damn business.

Why couldn't everyone else do the same?

Gamble nodded. "True. But he's not a woman."

"Unfortunately, he's right," Joey put in.

Hopper made a sound. "I'm so relieved you realize I'm not a woman, Joey."

Jace guffawed, and I rolled my eyes.

"You're a moron, and I meant my father." Her voice sounded exasperated. "The press is going to be ruthless, and the longer you're silent, the longer you hide, the more mysterious and exclusive you'll become."

"Especially since you've never talked to the media since Matt's death." Lorhaven chimed in.

Turning in my seat, I gave him a look. "How deep did your damn PI dig?"

Lorhaven met my stare. "You're my brother. Obviously, I wanted all the dirt."

My body leaned over the arm of my chair toward Hopp. "That true?"

He nodded. "I've never spoken out. Everything that's been reported has been from other sources and leaked police documents."

"My office has been fielding offers for an exclusive since the second the story broke," Gamble informed Hopper. "The more we say no, the higher the price goes."

Hopper snarled. "I don't want their blood money."

"I can understand why you feel that way." Gamble spread his hands in front of him as he spoke. "But it's not blood money. It's been almost six years. This is your chance to tell your side of the story. Matt's side of the story. No one is going to see this as you profiting off of a loved one's death. You're being forced out. May as well get a little compensation."

"What's a little compensation?" Jace inquired.

"The bids are over seven figures now."

Shock rippled through me. Over a million dollars for an interview? That was insane.

Hopper made a strangled sound, and his hand jolted in mine. "Are you fucking serious?" He gasped.

"I'm always serious about money." Gamble assured everyone.

Lorhaven whistled low.

"I think maybe some time to think about this—" I began, but Hopper cut me off.

Calmly, he announced, "I'll do it."

"What!" I demanded, shooting out of the chair. "Why would you want to dredge all that up again?"

Hopper remained seated. "It's unavoidable. The sooner I get it over with, the sooner we can move on."

I frowned. Was he doing this because he thought it was what I wanted?

"*GearShark* called." Gamble moved right on, accepting Hopper's agreement.

I looked to Jace for help. He shrugged. My stare moved to Joey. Her head bobbed encouragingly while she offered a reassuring smile.

"They aren't the highest bid, but they're close. A couple talk shows have called—"

Hopper cut him off. "No TV. Let's do *GearShark*. They've done articles on everyone else. Their reporter Emily is tolerable."

"This isn't going to be an article, Hopp," I pointed out knowingly. "It's going to be the cover story."

"Good, then I won't have to do it again."

I wasn't so sure about that, but a guy could hope.

"So it's settled. I'll arrange it with *GearShark* and let you know when and where," Gamble concluded. "Take the rest of the day off. Maybe tomorrow, too. I'll have some extra security put in place at the speedway to keep the vultures out."

Hopper nodded. "Thanks."

"Don't talk to any of them," he emphasized. "This cover feature must be the exclusive, all-access no one else is getting. It will drive up the price."

"I don't care about the money."

"It's not the money. It's the negotiation," Lorhaven told Hopp.

Gamble chuckled. "Spoken like a true businessman."

"What can I do to help?" Joey asked.

Hopp shook his head. "Nothing, but thanks."

"How about Jace and I go to your place and get you a change of clothes and stuff?" Joey offered.

"Yeah." I smiled at her. "That would be awesome."

It wasn't much, but I could tell Joey really wanted to do something.

"We'll go now." Her dark curls bounced as she tugged on my brother. "Dad, are you going back to the office?"

"Of course."

"Will you be home in time for dinner?"

"Probably not. I have a feeling it's going to be a long night."

Hopper grimaced. "I'm sorry, Gamble. You wouldn't have to put out fires if it weren't for me."

Gamble made a scoffing sound. "I always knew this day would come, even from the first day I came looking for you. Besides, it's good for business."

I didn't care for the fact that my boyfriend's pain drove up stock prices and interest in the Gamble name.

Joey groaned. "C'mon, Jace. We have stuff to pack and pizzas to pick up."

"Tacos." I corrected.

Lorhaven barked a laugh.

"Tacos it is!" Joey announced. "We'll be back later."

"Oh, one more thing," Gamble said, effectively freezing everyone in place.

Collectively, we turned to wait for him to speak.

"Since there seems to be such confusion about this being a family around here, I'm implementing a weekly family dinner. Friday nights, six o'clock."

"Friday nights." Joey groaned.

Gamble cut a silencing look in her direction. "Yes, and I expect everyone to be here, except of course when we're travelling for business."

We all gazed around, staring at each other.

"Well!" Gamble demanded. "Have I made myself clear?"

Everyone in the room (including me) mumbled various versions of, "Yes, sir."

"Good." He sniffed. "I'll see you Friday. Hopper, I'll let you know when we have the interview details."

Joey and Lorhaven were the first to head out. Gamble's phone started ringing, and he began negotiating (frankly, he was scary when he was demanding shit), and the housekeeper came to lead Hopp and me to our room.

Moving through the palatial home and the wing that was basically designated ours while we were hiding out, I couldn't help but wonder what it was going to be like with Hopp when we were finally alone.

Chapter Five

Photographs weren't just images preserved on paper. They were more than a moment in time captured forever.

They were time machines. Genuine transportation into the past. Time was anything but stagnant. The passing of it changed everything from the way people looked and dressed to the places they went. Even in much smaller ways, you often didn't notice until you looked back and were reminded of what used to be.

When I walked out on my old life all those years ago, I left everything behind. My identity, my family, and everything that went with it. That meant photos.

Walking into the room tonight and seeing that giant image of Matt filling the screen was startling. I was instantly transported back into a ghost town, a ghost town that once was filled with breath and life.

It made me remember things—things I knew—but the pungency had faded. Like how carefree he was, how happy. How there was this light around him that drew in others.

I had flashes of laughter, teamwork, and family. Then I relived exactly how it all went away.

"If you would require anything else," the housekeeper said, sweeping open the double doors to the room we were staying in, "I'll be downstairs."

"Thank you," Arrow replied, and I nodded.

The second she turned the corner of the long hallway, our bodies rotated toward the other. Still standing in the hall, we stared for long moments. So many undercurrents flowed between us they blurred together like a giant tangled mess, sort of like the cords behind a TV.

But there was one emotion that seemed to swell out around all the other tangled ones.

Arrow held out his hand. Surrendering mine, I let him tow me into the room as if our solitude were an urgent matter.

"They're gonna be back soon with the food and shit," he said, shoving the doors closed with a loud thud.

"Tell me what you need the most, then," I rasped, tugging his hand.

Surprisingly enough, he replied. Not with words or even to turn the question around on me, as I suspected.

Instead, he all but attacked me.

My back rattled the doors when I collided with the wood. Arrow's large palms covered my chest, pushing me into place before instantly moving in to plaster against my front.

The hunger in his kiss incited my own. I growled ravenously and palmed the back of his neck. His head turned and angled in, sweeping his tongue deep into my mouth. I went slack against the door, reveling in the way his lips ground over mine.

Between us, the heavy pounding of a heart was almost a mystery. Was it his? Was it mine? Was it both beating in tandem?

Arrow pulled at the fabric of my shirt with impatience, dragging his hands down my sides and to my waist. Briefly, one hand left me, reaching between my back and the door to throw the lock.

The sound rang of complete privacy, complete freedom. Gripping his shoulders tight, I pulled him back, held him at arm's length. Our lips were slick, both chests heaving, and his eyes were dilated like an animal mid-hunt.

"You're mine, Hopp," he demanded.

Withdrawing my hands from his body, I pulled the T-shirt over my head and tossed it away. His brown eyes deepened to the color of fresh-brewed espresso, and his nostrils flared.

With a smirk, I surrendered, pressing the backs of my hands against the door above my head. Arrow's teeth sank into his pouty lower lip. Shooting forward with impeccable speed, his hands hooked into the waistband of my pants and pulled.

Dropping to his knees, Arrow took off my shoes, socks, boxers, and pants in record speed. Dragging up the front of my legs, across my thighs, and then teasingly across my rigid dick, he stood to his feet, latching onto my nipple. It hardened instantly when his tongue swirled around, drawing the bud into his mouth for a suck.

I was panting, trying not to call out his name. My arms began shaking as his tongue roamed my naked body. The second they began sliding down the wall, toward my sides, he made a sound, pinned them back up, and pressed along my body.

My dick ached. It ached so much it actually tinged with pain. There was something about the dominant way he was coming at me right then. The greedy hunger he made no attempt to hide. The small part of my brain that still worked whispered the reason behind his complete need to claim me, and the rest of me urged him on.

I didn't want to think just then. I only wanted to feel.

Arrow's lips closed around the side of my neck and began sucking. I moaned, my hips jutted out, and he rubbed along my center like a cat.

Of its own accord, my body started grinding against his. Regrettably his mouth ripped away, leaving a searing wet mark on my skin.

I glanced over, shook my head, then tilted it, giving him full access to the spot again. "Come back."

Instead of complying, he dropped to his knees, grabbed hold of my hips, and took my dick deep into his throat.

Collapsing against the door, I let my arms fall. Arrow grabbed my hands, knotted ours together, then brought them back to my hips. We both held my body while he fucked me with his mouth and tongue. The way he would pull back and lick over my swollen head made my knees quiver.

"Babe," I begged in a shouty whisper.

Chill brushed over my wet dick when he pulled back. I shivered, but his hand wrapped around it, blocking any of the air.

His tongue licked over my lips, and I whispered his name again.

With his hand still wrapped around my rod, we stepped farther into the room, through the sitting room, toward the giant bed.

My eyes latched onto it because I so desperately wanted to sink into the mattress with his weight on me.

But he didn't stop there. He kept walking. I trailed along like a puppy behind him. The shower in the attached bathroom was the size of our entire bathroom at home. It was custom tiled with what looked like travertine, had two giant showerheads on each end, and a giant rainfall showerhead hung from the ceiling in the center.

Releasing my dick, A moved in, opened the seamless glass door, and turned on all three heads. The sound of falling water reminded me of a heavy rainstorm. Arrow closed and locked the bathroom door, figuring out the remote to engage the room-darkening blinds over the giant window and somehow illuminating the interior of the shower with low, glowing light.

Even though he hadn't touched me for several minutes, I was still rock hard. My balls were drawn up against my body, and my hands trembled like an addict who needed a fix.

Arrow finally turned. Only an arm's length separated us, but neither of us moved to closed the distance. My eyes followed his hand as it reached into the back pocket of his jeans and pulled out several single-use packets of lube.

Placing them between his teeth, he began undressing. My stomach muscles clenched as all his smooth, tattoo-covered skin was slowly bared. He was teasing me. Making me want him just as much as he wanted me.

He didn't have to try. Not ever.

I physically longed for him.

Once his clothes were gone and the shadows of the bathroom hugged his body, I grabbed my dick, jerking it once.

Arrow took the packets out of his teeth and walked toward the shower stall. My eyes went directly to his ass. Just the thought of burying my dick there made my breathing erratic.

"Figured it might be less messy in here," he murmured, glancing over his bare shoulder. "And that way when you yell my name, I'll be the only one to hear."

We stepped beneath the spray; it hit from every angle. My body, already completely sensitized from the thorough assault from A, broke out into goose bumps.

He tossed the packets of lube on a nearby built-in shelf and drew me beneath the waterfall shower.

We made out for a while, stroking each other's dicks, fingering each other's asses. It was a complete free-for-all the way our hands roamed beneath the gentle fall of the water.

My head fell back, and drops rained over my face and cheeks. Arrow licked down my neck, sucking up the water as he went, reaching a hand around my body and dipping his fingers into my crack.

"We need this shower at home," I murmured, sounding completely drunk.

Steam rose around us, creating a vapory veil that enclosed us like we were the only two people left on the planet.

Arrow rubbed a hand over my dick, and I practically jumped away. He chuckled knowingly.

Next thing I knew, he pushed me up against the wall of the shower, both my palms planted on the tile, my bare back and ass on full display. Arrow dropped down, gently held my ass, and licked up my crack. I shuddered and planted my legs a little firmer and let my head fall between my arms.

His tongue circled my hole, and I asked him to take me.

"I need some," Arrow said between licks. Bracing myself with one arm, I held two packets down, and his hand snaked between my legs to grab them.

Using one packet, he coated my ass thoroughly until his fingers slipped around with ease. Because we were against the back wall, the water didn't fully hit us, which kept the lube exactly where we needed it.

Arrow moved into position behind me, and I tilted out, giving him better access. I felt rather than saw him coating himself with more lube, and I almost groaned because he was touching himself.

Balmy air brushed over my arms and legs. The tip of his head pushed against my giving hole. With a single push, he slid home, and noise rushed out between both our lips. Arrow raised his hand, covering mine, while the other clamped around my hip as he thrust in and out.

My body nearly melted down the tile. Arrow held me up, using not only his body, but the force of his thrusts to keep me on my feet.

"Fuck, Arrow." I moaned as he brushed over my prostate over and over again. "Goddamn, babe. You feel so fucking good."

His chin brushed over my shoulder. Words echoed along with the sound of rain in my ear. "I love you, Hopp."

I panted. His hand fell, and both grabbed my hips. I bent farther so he could go even deeper.

Reaching down, I grabbed my dick, using my wet hand to slide over the quivering flesh.

"No," Arrow intoned, reaching around and forcing my grip away. "You're not allowed to come yet," he demanded. "You aren't allowed to come until you're inside me."

I jerked up a little, but he seemed to realize I would and pushed deeper. Both of us moaned.

"In you?" I asked when I could talk again.

"Oh yeah," he murmured, pulling out and then driving back in. "We're pulling a double. Right now."

We hadn't done that before. Usually one of us putting his dick in the other was enough to send us both shooting. Hell, I was barely holding on now.

But I had to admit the thought of getting inside him, releasing all this pent-up desire, all this pent-up energy right into the man who made me this crazy made dark spots actually form in my vision.

I glanced back up; there was enough lube. We could do it. If I could hold out.

"You better fucking go, then, babe. 'Cause just feeling you move in me makes me want to burst."

His fingertips tightened on my hips. Water splashed over my toes. I felt him holding back, but it wasn't what I wanted, and I knew it wasn't what he wanted.

"Harder, A," I demanded.

With a sound, he pulled out and drove into me. Then again. And again. My mouth opened as pleasure bloomed inside me and my nerves sang with bliss. I felt the front of his thighs shaking when they came into contact with me.

My palms slid down the tile, and I shoved myself down over him.

Arrow made a sound, a rough sort of grunt. One arm caught around my waist and held as his hips pumped against me in small, insistent movements.

Suddenly, a moan filled the steamy shower, and I felt him pulse deep inside me.

On impulse, I reached around, delving my hands between his crack and caressing his ass.

He shivered and jerked inside me some more. His mouth slid over the back of my shoulder, kissing softly, licking over the water.

Arrow didn't languish inside me like usual. Instead, he pulled out and moved back. I turned from the tile and swooped in to kiss him. We stepped beneath the waterfall, both arms wound around the other as my hard dick pulsed with need between our stomachs.

After a long, hot kiss, A pulled back, gave me a hot stare, and pushed me toward the long marble bench on one side. The tile wasn't cold because everything in here was hot. The seat was wet from the showerhead on this side, water pouring down and falling over my shoulder and chest.

My dick sprang up away from me, but I did my best to ignore it. I was so close to coming I knew if I touched myself, I might.

Arrow handed me the packets of lube and put his hands against the tile. I went to work instantly, working his crack and teasing his hole. The fact that we were both already so hot and he was already completely relaxed from being inside me made it a little easier.

Once he was good and slick, and so was I, I tugged him around.

Arrow straddled my lap, and I positioned my dick so he could slide right down over it.

My eyes closed and I shuddered the second his body sheathed me. His hips rocked, and I moaned.

"I like being in your lap," he whispered, his forehead resting on my shoulder.

"No more than I do." I grunted and thrust inside him.

We moved against each other, fucking in the shower, as water slid over our skin and words of pure pleasure dropped from my lips against his ear.

I lasted maybe a minute. No more.

The second my fingertips dug into his back, he bore down, rocked into my lap with perfect pressure, and wrapped his arms around my back. "Give it to me, babe," Arrow demanded.

I exploded, the intensity of the orgasm momentarily robbing me of sight.

It was powerful the way it rocked over me, probably because he told me I wasn't allowed to come until just now. Holding it back only made it more desirable.

I collapsed against the wall. He followed, and I wrapped him in my arms. I stayed inside him until both of us were able to move. When we finally could, we washed each other with Jell-O-like limbs before shutting off the water and toweling each other dry.

The air out in the bedroom was downright chilly compared to the steamy heat in the bathroom. Neither of us bothering with clothes, I pulled back the covers on the bed and slid between the sheets. Arrow hesitated just slightly before slipping in alongside.

We both knew this conversation was coming. I was pretty much resolved to it. Maybe that's why it seemed strange he appeared more reluctant.

"You're feeling pretty fucking possessive today," I murmured, rubbing a hand up his bare back.

"I'm possessive of you every day," he rebutted gently.

"Protective, yes. Slightly possessive, yes. But growly, predatory, and double sex possessive? No way."

His eyes swung to mine. Doubt and something else swam in their depths, something that made my chest hurt. He was bruised. Something was causing him pain.

"Was it too much?" he asked, a little insecure about our totally fucking boiling sex session.

I grinned. "Are you kidding? Hell no. That was probably the hottest sex we've had to date."

Relief softened his eyes. "You ever done that before?"

Inching closer… We were inching closer to the real subject.

I lifted an eyebrow. "Double sex?"

He nodded, almost as if he were afraid.

My hand slid from his back down to his bare ass cheek. "Never. But you can bet your sweet ass it's not going to be the last."

He laughed, a genuine chuckle that warmed my heart. "Yeah, we need a shower like that."

I didn't say anything else. I just waited him out, letting my fingertips dance along his lower back, something I'd developed a habit of doing. I watched his face. His eyes grew heavy as I caressed him.

I thought maybe I was going to have to stop, pull back, and force whatever it was out of him. It was unusual. Normally, we were so open. So honest, almost painfully so, with each other. Just like I'd told him outside, I was see-through. And he'd agreed.

Just as nerves twisted my guts, he sighed. "I'm not really a jealous guy. Everything you've been through, the people who've been part of your life… they're part of you. And I love all of you, so I can't be jealous about what made you who you are."

"I know that, babe," I said gently. "But you know, it's okay to still get pissy when someone calls me Jay or when you're not too kindly reminded I was in a relationship with someone before I met you."

"I don't want to be pissy," he whispered. "I want to be happy."

My heart squeezed. I loved him so goddamn much. So much it felt like my skin was stretched with the emotion. "Ah, babe. I love you so much."

He pressed close to me and laid his cheek on my chest, allowing me to wrap an arm around him to hold him close. "I saw those pictures today. The way your eyes latched onto the screen and refused to look away. The way you looked at him, I realized something."

My mouth was dry. My chest hurt. My limbs weighed a million pounds. I forced my voice to be low and free of any kind of emotion. "What?"

"If he hadn't passed… if Matt were still alive today…" He hesitated, then rushed on. "You wouldn't be in love with me right now. We likely wouldn't be together."

Ah, fuck.

That explained it. The reason Arrow seemed more reluctant to have this talk was because he was. I knew something that I didn't realize until this second he didn't know. I knew the sooner we had this talk, the sooner my past was out in the open, and the sooner I dealt with shit I let drag on way too long, there was an entire life on the other side.

A life with Arrow.

A proposal. A marriage. A future.

Yes. I knew he was going to say yes. I would take no other answer.

I didn't know which was worse. Knowing how much my past was affecting him *or* realizing he wasn't as absolute about what happened next.

"There's something I need to tell you," I said, pulling back so he wasn't able to lie on my chest.

Arrow moved back, rested his head on a pillow, and gazed up at me, almost shy.

Holy fuckity fuck, his inhibition was always my ultimate undoing. He never expected anything from me. Every moment since I said the words, Arrow acted as if my love were a gift and something he would never take for granted.

Supporting my weight on my elbow, my head in my hand, I smiled down at him. I made a soft sound, brushing the damp hair out of his eye.

"I could wait and tell you this on a different day, maybe on a more… *pivotal* day between us." *Ahem, like our wedding day.* "But something tells me it wouldn't mean as much as it would right now. Right here. This feels like a pretty pivotal moment, doesn't it?"

"Good pivotal or bad?" he asked, still kind of reluctant.

I tugged his hair and scowled playfully. "Good, obviously."

That earned me a ghost of a smile. I sighed. The last thing I wanted was to make him wait, to make him teeter on the edge of not knowing and think the worst.

He nodded, one quick, decisive nod. "All right, Hopp. Tell me."

I chuckled even as the extreme weight of the words I was about to utter pressed down. God, this was fucking hard. *So fucking hard.*

All at once, Arrow pushed up, as if he suddenly knew about the boulder-sized lump in my throat. "It's okay, whatever it is. You don't have to tell me. It doesn't matter anyway."

I swallowed. The action scraped my throat. "It does matter. I want to tell you. It's how I feel; I just…"

He tucked his legs under him, scooted close, and tugged the blankets up. Grabbing my free hand, he lifted, kissing the backs of my fingers.

I drew so much strength from him. So much courage.

"Seeing him today, you know, on the screen, so big…" I began.

Arrow nodded encouragingly. "It was hard for you."

"Yeah. I hadn't allowed myself to look at a photograph, any kind of picture of him… us… for almost five years."

"Was it how you remembered him?"

I swallowed. "Yes and no."

Arrow tilted his head and gave my hand an encouraging squeeze. If he could tell me that dark fear I knew ripped right out of his deepest place, then I could tell him the one thing that haunted me, that made me feel like the shittiest human being to ever live.

Even shittier than being responsible for Matt's death.

It was just such a betrayal to say, even if it were true. It was almost like blasphemy. Something maybe Lorhaven had forced out, or at the very least forced open the metal gates that caged the words in deep.

I knew rationally… I knew voicing the feeling was really not that different from feeling it. But that was the thing about speaking vs feeling. Feelings could be kept secret. They could be held private. Speaking, though.

Putting voice to the feelings made them real, didn't it? It made them near impossible to hide.

It was like a high-functioning addict standing up in a crowded room and boldly admitting he had a problem.

"Matt, was, ah…" I began. Just tasting his name on my lips hurt. "My first love. He was my forever."

Arrow shifted. I felt him pull away from me.

I hurried on to say, "Seeing his picture was like a punch right in my gut… but not in the ways I expected."

"It's okay, Hopper. I understand."

"No," I said, taking his hand, forcing it against my chest beneath the heavy blankets. "You don't.

"My reaction to the TV earlier hurt you, and for that I am so intensely sorry. I did get dragged down into some kind of world, some kind of trance. It wasn't because I remembered how much I loved him, and it wasn't because if he were still here, I would run to his side."

Arrow's eyes lifted to mine.

I nodded. "I couldn't be at his side today; my infinity was never his. It always has and always will be yours."

Arrow's breath caught.

I plunged on, wanting to say it all before regret and betrayal clogged my throat. I was loyal to Matt; I would be always. But when it came down to loyalty to him or the pain of the man I loved more than life itself… Matt would lose.

"I realized it when I saw him today. I miss him. He was my best friend. And yes, I loved him… but, Arrow, I love you *more*."

Arrow's shoulders actually slumped as if he were so relieved he was physically going to collapse.

I shoved up off my side, mirroring his position. Our knees knocked together, and the blankets and pillows fell all around us.

My heart was beating so incredibly fast my chest actually hurt. But I'd said it. I spoke the words that were the heaviest I'd ever known.

And remarkably, I felt a little lighter. Like their weight just wasn't as foreboding.

"I love you more," I whispered, grabbing his hands, linking us together. "I will never love anyone as much as I love you."

"I feel how much those words cost you," he said, breaking one hand free of mine and brushing his fingers across my cheek. "I never would have asked you to say that."

"I know," I said, pushing against his hand a little farther. He would never ask for something that might cost me. He'd rather suffer forever. It was exactly the reason I had to say it.

Someone as fiercely loyal and protective as Arrow, someone who wholeheartedly only wanted the best for me deserved everything. Even my deepest secret.

"We would be together today, A. Right now. All the minutes after. We would, no matter what. Maybe Matt and I would still be friends. Or maybe we wouldn't. Maybe he'd be living in the burbs with another man and some kids. I don't know. I do know I would want him to be happy. It wouldn't have been with me. I can't love him the way I love you… I can only give my heart away like this once." I turned my wrist up, revealing the infinity tattoo with an arrow through it. "I can only give this kind of love to you."

Moving swiftly, Arrow lunged forward, wrapped both arms around me, and held tight. I returned the embrace, and we both rose onto our knees, kneeling in the center of the bed, clinging to each other as our hearts beat in sync.

"Thank you." Arrow's voice cracked, muffled against my body. "Thank you so much for that. You never have to say it again. Ever. Because just once is enough to carry me through all eternity."

I squeezed him tighter.

I thought admitting I loved him more made me a bad person. I thought it would somehow make me feel like the lowest scum on the earth. That giving a voice to that sentiment would break me in a way I hadn't broken before.

I was wrong.

Loving him this much didn't make me a bad person.

Giving him the words he needed so desperately didn't make me scum.

It was just the opposite.

I was better now. Stronger. And oddly… maybe even more deserving of Arrow's love.

Did the feeling of betraying Matt, of what we once had, still niggle at me?

Yeah. It might always. It was hard to be happy when someone else didn't get the chance.

But it wasn't going to crush me. And it wasn't going to crush Arrow.

I pulled back far enough so I could look into his eyes. He smiled at me, and my heart melted. "That's why I have to do this interview, A. The tell-all. It's why I'm finally opening up. It's time to move on. You and me. It's time for us to have the life we're meant to have. No more hiding."

He nodded, full understanding dawning over his features. "For a minute, I thought you were cracking under pressure, agreeing to all that shit," he admitted.

I laughed. It felt good. "Not cracking. Healing."

"Healing," he echoed.

I kissed him deeply, feeling him smile against my lips.

I licked the smile up, swallowing it down.

Now more than ever, even in the midst of all my past coming to light, I was convinced that proposing to Arrow was exactly what I wanted to do.

Chapter Six

"Do you trust me?"

Looking between Hopper and the blindfold dangling between his fingers, I laughed.

"I got on an airplane with you even though you refused to tell me where we were going or why, yet you still ask?"

Hopper's teeth flashed. I loved the contrast of his pearly whites against the dark stubble of his jaw. Lifting the blindfold a little higher and rocking back on his heels, he asked again. "Do you trust me?"

"Always," I replied. "No matter what. Even on a plane in the center of an unknown sky, even traveling toward an undisclosed location. Even blindfolded with impossibly dark fabric. As long as it's you beside me, I'll go anywhere."

His hand fell to his side. Our shoes bumped when he stepped close. "That answer is exactly why we're here right now." He murmured and brought his lips down.

Just as they were about to brush over mine the captain of Gamble's private plane came over the intercom. "We're beginning our decent. Take your seats."

Hopper smiled, pulling his lips away. I made a sound of impatience, wanting the kiss we almost had. "Soon," he vowed, stroking this thumb over my lower lips

We sat down beside each other, when I reached for my seatbelt Hopp pushed my hands away and pulled it around my hips. I gazed up as he buckled the ends and adjusted the strap. He was so beautiful to me.

Taking his seat beside mine, he took much less time to buckle his own belt. The plane started to descend, and I looked longingly toward the window, which was covered by the blind. All the windows were covered. It was the only reason I wasn't blindfolded right now.

A few nights after we went back to our place, he'd come home and said he wanted to take me somewhere. I got in the car without a second thought.

When we arrived at Gamble's private airstrip, I realized somewhere wasn't a movie or out for a pizza. He wouldn't say, though; he just grabbed my hand and asked me follow.

I wasn't sure how long we'd been on the plane, not too long, but it was still a place we needed a plane to get to. I glanced away from the closed windows to him with a question in my eyes.

He smiled and held up the blindfold.

Leaning forward, I surrendered as he tied it around my eyes and waited patiently as he knotted it at the back of my head. When it was on, I felt him sit back.

"How many fingers am I holding up?" His voice sounded amused.

"Two." I guessed. The black cloth was impenetrable. Everything in front of me was dark.

"Leave it on 'til I say," he instructed.

"What is all this, Hopp?" I wondered.

In response, two warm palms settled over my jaws, his fingers spreading to cup my face. Gently, he tilted my head to the side, covering my mouth with his.

All curiosity about our destination fled from my thoughts. I was already here, exactly where I belonged. The total darkness the blindfold provided seemed to enhance my sense of touch. His fingertips whispered over my cheeks, along the sides of my neck. Swaying forward, I fell into his lips a little deeper. His mouth parted, and my tongue swept inside, stroking over his.

The kiss was warm, his lips the perfect combination of malleable and firm. Fog wrapped around my entire body, muffling my brain. I reached around, pulling him as close as I could. My fingers dug into the muscles of his upper back as I sucked in a deep breath without breaking the kiss.

The roughness of his tongue stroked my lower lip, and a shiver actually quaked my body. Hopper's palm slid away from my cheek, melting down the side of my neck to my chest, then settled directly over my heart.

"I love you," I murmured, between attacking his mouth with mine. "So fucking much."

In response, he kissed me harder. Our teeth knocked together, but neither of us pulled away.

The jolt of the plane hitting the runway with a hard bounce finally broke us apart. My chest heaved, his palm still resting there as he pulled back into his seat.

"Leave that on, babe," he said, his breathing heavy.

I waited impatiently for the plane to come to a stop. The sound of Hopper's seatbelt clicking open made me reach for mine.

"Hang on," he insisted, pushing my hand from the buckle.

"You're not getting off this plane without me," I said, unable to hide the hint of worry in my tone.

I felt his heat, the way his large body hovered over mine. "Never," he vowed and kissed my forehead.

I listened to his movements and the murmur of his voice along with the pilot's.

Finally, he came back and undid my belt.

Before I could move, his hand brushed over my dick, and I groaned a little. "You must be getting a pretty good hard-on with all this secrecy tonight."

He laughed and folded my hand in his. With our fingers linked, Hopper led me through the plane. Cool spring air hit me, and then he grasped my other hand to quietly guide me down the plane steps.

Once we were outside, I felt a sort of familiarity in the air but wasn't sure why. There was a heavy breeze tonight, and it pulled at my T-shirt and made me wish I'd grabbed a hoodie before Hopp had stolen me off to unknown places.

I was pretty sure I heard him blow out what sounded like a nervous breath, but before I could ask, he started walking, pulling me along with him.

"Nothing like a walk at night, in the dark, with a blindfold," I cracked.

He chuckled. "How do you know it's dark?"

"I'm pretty sure we weren't in the air long enough to go to a different time zone, Hopp."

His response was to tell me to keep walking.

After a minute or so, I heard the plane start up again, the wind around us picked up, and goosebumps rose along my bare arms. "Don't we need that guy for a ride home?" I asked.

"We're not going home tonight."

Nothing like this had ever happened to me. I'd never had someone set up some kind of surprise. I'd never been taken on an impromptu trip. I'd never had someone think so much about anything that involved me at all.

For those reasons, and those alone, it didn't matter if there was a heap of garbage waiting for me when he finally pulled this fabric off my eyes. It didn't matter if it was all just to hand me a pack of gum.

I loved it, and it was the best gift anyone had ever given me.

"Thank you for tonight, Hopp," I whispered, turning my head in his direction.

His footsteps faltered. His body turned toward mine. "You don't even know what's going on, babe," he mused. "And you're thanking me?"

"It's from you. That's all that matters."

He made a sound. "You kill me, A. You really fucking slay me sometimes."

I cocked my head to the side. "Just sometimes? I can do better than that."

An amused groan cut through the night. "What if I'm leading you out into the woods to kill you and dump your body?"

"Morbid," I mocked. "And I have to say if that's the plan, then you're fucked because your getaway plane just took off without you."

He chuckled, and I sighed. "Guess it would be a good way to go, then, at the hand of a man I love more than life itself."

There was a beat of immeasurable silence. "Killing you would be like killing myself."

I squeezed his hand. "How about you show me why we're really here?"

We started walking again, only to stop a moment later. "Hang on."

A door creaked on its hinges when he pulled it open, and another note of familiarity came over me.

Hopper grasped my hands again. "Up some steps."

Some steps was more like several flights. But soon, we reached the top, and he positioned me in the center of a room, commanding me to stay.

After a low click of some kind of switch, there was another heartbeat of silence, only to be interrupted by Hopper. "Outdid themselves," he murmured.

"What?"

"Nothing." I felt him step close, his fingers tucked beneath the blindfold. "Ready?"

I smiled.

The second the fabric was gone, I blinked rapidly as light flooded my vision. Swiveling my stare, images and light became apparent and my mouth ran dry.

Swiftly, I glanced at Hopp. He was watching me, clearly nervous. I went back to gaping. We were in the control tower. My control tower, the one at our airstrip. The one I used to sit in, in the dark, and drown in thoughts and pain.

It wasn't a dark, painful place right now. Hell, right now I probably couldn't feel pain in here even if I tried.

Usually cold and dark, empty and sort of sterile, this round room was anything but. White lights were strung around the ceiling and around the control counter circling the room. A giant paper star hung from the center, and it too was lit up. The single rolling chair was pushed off to the side, out of the way. In the center of the floor was a giant air mattress covered in blankets and white pillows.

There were some candles placed around the mattress, all in various sizes. They weren't the kind with actual flames, but the flickering battery-powered variety. The lights reflected off the windows, which in this tower took up basically every wall. The whole space glowed around us, and outside, the dark night was the perfect black backdrop. Well, it wasn't totally blank; the sky was dotted with stars, as if they too wanted in on the sparkling action.

Slowly, I pivoted in a circle, taking in the tons of candles, the lights, and the bed.

"You did this?" I asked reverently.

He nodded.

"How?" I asked, still shocked, still unable to stop looking around.

"I had some help."

My eyes went back to him, an unspoken question in their depths.

"Drew and Trent," he replied.

"They sure know how to string some lights," I said, gazing around again.

He half smiled. "Drew said something about them having some experience with this kind of thing."

I had no idea what that meant. I didn't care enough to ask. I sank down on one end of the air mattress, which was supported by some kind of metal frame. "This is pretty awesome," I said, a little awestruck. "I can't believe you did this."

"You like it?"

I made a scoffing sound. "Are you fucking kidding?"

He smiled and reached for my hand. "It's not all."

Allowing him to pull me up, I tugged him close. "You look sexy in all this candlelight."

His mouth curved up. "You kinda look like an angel."

"It's the blond hair." I confirmed. Inside, my stomach flipped, my heart beat erratically, and I was pretty sure my palms were turning clammy as the seconds ticked by.

Of all the things I'd imagined tonight, this wasn't even on my radar. Romance was something I never, not ever, assumed was for me.

His smile flashed.

Quickly, I tugged him to me in a crushing hug. His arms went over my shoulders, around my upper back. My arms tucked around his waist, pressed in against his lower back, and held him hard. I wished we could fuse together in that moment. I wished I could slip beneath his skin, wanting so desperately to be as close to him as possible.

Eventually, he began to pull back. I made a sound, clutching him close again.

His chuckle vibrated my ear. "There's more."

Pulling back, I studied his eyes. "More?"

His Adam's apple bobbed.

"Why did you do all this?"

Taking my hand, he maneuvered me around the candles, pulling me toward the control panel flush against the expansive window. Hopper stepped in front of me, his back to the window, leaning against the counter. His thighs parted, and I stepped closer, between his legs. The string of lights lining the counter behind him glowed, and I noticed right beside where he sat was some kind of switch on the end of one of the cords.

"Do you remember that night up here?" he asked, glancing around.

I nodded. "I thought I'd lost you. I'd come up here to let that pain eat me alive… Then you walked through that door."

"I saw the open gate, and I felt sick. I thought something had happened. I couldn't get to you fast enough." He recalled.

"You told me about your past," I murmured, remembering how painful that night was but also how it had set me free.

"You told me about yours."

I shifted just a little closer. "You love me in spite of it."

"I'm going to love you forever, A," he vowed.

"I think I may love you longer."

One side of his mouth curled up. "You trying to outdo me, babe?"

I glanced around again, pointedly surveying everything he'd done. "I'm pretty sure there is no competition."

Hopper linked our fingers together, shifting a little farther against the control counter. "I didn't know I could love someone so much. We connect on a level I honestly didn't know existed," he told me, glancing down at our linked hands. Lifting his eyes to mine, he went on. "But it's not enough."

My body jolted as if he'd slapped me. All the warm and fuzzy I'd been feeling was blown away by a frigid wind. "What?"

"I want more, Arrow. I want you in every way possible."

"You have me," I swore. "In every way."

Hopp shook his head. "There's one way I don't."

"What's that?" I asked gruffly.

With a sound, he stood, but I didn't move back to make room. Instead, our bodies bumped together as he moved to stand beside me and pick up the small device with the switch. "Look out the window, A."

I gazed out into the dark night, not seeing whatever it was he wanted me to see.

"You looking?" he asked, glancing at me.

"I'm looking."

I heard the switch click. Light flickered outside, below the tower.

Shock rippled through me, and my gasp filled the room.

I stared down at the words below, scripted in white lights.

Marry Me

Hopper was asking me to marry him.

Shock rendered me immobile for a few heartbeats. Then I jerked upright to stare between him and the illuminated words.

"We're already bound in ways no one can ever touch." His voice was raspy, slightly shaky. "You already own me body and soul… but I'm selfish, babe. I want you in every way—on paper, in the eyes of the law, in the eyes of everyone who sees your left hand. I want to be irrevocably bound, not just in our hearts, but by name."

I swallowed, my tongue thick, then blew out a breath.

My body trembled.

"I want you to take my name. To be my husband. To have yet another piece of me no one has ever had or will ever have. Marry me, Arrow. Say you'll marry me."

I rubbed the back of my neck, staring down at my shoes. Tears made my vision blurry as I glanced back at the giant words, then at the man who'd just asked me to share his name.

"Almost my entire life, I thought I wasn't worthy of love," I told him. "Then later, I was completely broken, lonely in ways no one could fathom."

He spun, his chest pressed against my side.

I turned, staring into his eyes. "Until you."

"Until me."

I curled my palm around the back of his neck. "I belong with you."

"Fuck yes, you do, babe. Just like I belong with you."

I sniffled, trying to hold my shit together.

Hopper shifted, reached into the side pocket of his cargo pants, and produced a small black box. He sat on the control panel again, raised the lid on the box, and held it out. "Marry me."

"You got me a ring?" I choked out.

He made a face. "Is it too much? Do dudes give each other engagement rings?"

I laughed but immediately freaked. "I don't have a ring for you."

"I don't need a ring, babe. I just need to see this one on your hand."

I nodded.

"Is that a yes?" He made a sound. "Put me out of my misery here, A."

I hadn't answered.

A huge smile broke over my face. You know, the kind of smile I didn't think my mouth was possible of forming?

I did. Except it was far bigger than even I thought was achievable.

"Yes."

He made a triumphant sound, ripped the ring out of the box, and tossed it over his shoulder. The black velvet bounced off the window and fell against the string lights.

Lifting my hand between us, Hopper gave it a squeeze. I spread my fingers wide, and he poised the band at the fingertip.

"We aren't married yet, but I want this on you."

"I won't take it off, Hopp." I promised.

He slid it home. The wide band fit perfectly. I had no idea how. Maybe fate. Maybe he was really good at guessing ring sizes.

"I hope you like it," he murmured, brushing his fingertips over the metal.

"Actually, it's pretty fucking sweet," I told him, tilting my hand to look at it closer. I'd barely glanced at it before. It could have been a bread tie for all I cared. It was from him, and the words he'd spoken when he gave it to me made it priceless.

It was a wide band, dark, almost black. In the center was a row of diamonds that sparkled beneath the lights hung around the room. It was a little flashy, and it made me smile because I recalled what he'd just said about people looking at my hand and knowing I was taken.

But it wasn't so flashy it would look ridiculous.

"It's, ah, this metal is called black tungsten. It's supposed to be hella durable. I figured with all the work you do under a hood, it would be good."

I blinked furiously, feeling its weight around my finger.

I had a tattoo on my chest, a tattoo representing everything Hopper was to me. This was different, though. This was something that would always be on display.

"It has diamonds." He went on, the nervousness in his voice fucking cute. "I wasn't sure about them." He cleared his throat. "But the simple ones were too plain… I wanted you to have better. You deserve some diamonds."

I chuckled, rubbing over the metal with the fingers on my opposite hand. I was already getting used to seeing it there, even after mere minutes.

"If you prefer something else, we can take it back—"

My head shot up. "No way. It's perfect."

"You're cool with wearing a ring?" He shifted from foot to foot.

"I'm cool with wearing *your* ring." I still couldn't believe this was happening. I couldn't believe someone was so willing to tie themselves to me in every way humanly possible.

Hopper blew out a breath. "I was so fucking nervous."

I grinned. "Are you kidding? You had to know I'd say yes."

He shrugged, and I laughed again, pulling him in by the back of his neck until our foreheads touched. "Yes," I whispered. "Yes. Yes. Yes."

Between us, his hand found mine, and his fingers began twirling the metal around on my finger.

"I'm gonna get you a ring," I vowed. "Just seeing it on your finger is gonna give me a hard-on."

Hopper tugged my ring-decorated hand to his fly, pressing it close. He was sporting an impressive hard-on of his own.

"I love you," I told him, caressing his rod.

"I know it's a little unorthodox," he said, thrusting into my palm. "But you'll take my name?"

Pulling my head back, I locked eyes with him. "I'll change it tomorrow if that's what you want."

"What do *you* want?"

"I want you. Your name. Your ring. A lifetime with you."

His eyes closed as if he relished my words.

"I also want you inside me."

They sprang open at the same moment he lunged for me. As we locked around each other, our lips crashed. A definite urgency filled the tower. Even though we'd just basically promised each other a lifetime, it seemed as though in this moment, it wasn't enough.

I raised my leg, about to lock it around his hip, but he reached under my ass and lifted. Both my thighs locked around his waist, Hopper carried me as if I weren't almost as heavy as him a few steps away from the window toward the bed.

Instead of putting me down, he stood there holding me. With my lips a little above his, I took control of the kiss, working his mouth with all the passion inside me. There was a lot of it. I'd bottled it up for years and years before Hopper showed up at this airstrip many months ago.

Rubbing my palms over his stubble, I groaned and rocked against him. His hands gripped my ass, kneading the flesh through my jeans, and I moaned.

Yanking free of his mouth and dragging my teeth across his cheek, I latched onto his earlobe and sucked.

"I want you so fucking bad right now." Hopper groaned.

Sliding up the back of his neck, I grabbed a handful of his hair and yanked his head back to stare down into his face. "Take me."

His eyes flared. Suddenly I was on my back, staring up at the ceiling and all the lights draped there.

My legs were halfway off the bed, my feet on the floor. Hopper stood between my spread knees, gazing down at me with possession in his face.

It didn't make me nervous, I didn't even stop to think about it. I wanted him to want me. In fact, I wanted to possess him just as fiercely. Over the course of the last several months, his touch was something I grew very familiar with. When I told him I trusted him, I meant it wholeheartedly. Even physically.

The fact I was raped would always be there. I might always be weary of new people and being touched by anyone.

But not Hopper. His patience, gentleness, and the kind way he always treated me made it near impossible to not look at him with anything but love.

I had to say, though, something shifted tonight—something within me. Like a final lock being thrown into place. Or maybe the last shackle from that night behind the dumpster finally broke free.

All I knew for certain was without Hopper, none of this would have happened. I would still be stuck, hurting, in a suspension that was destined to last forever.

The intensity burst inside me, leaving it impossible for me to remain on my back. I pushed up into a sitting position, reaching for his pants. My face was in line with his crotch. Moving furiously, I undid his cargos and yanked them down. His snug, black boxers molded around his rock-hard dick, making my mouth water.

I covered the bulge with my mouth, too hurried to bother pulling down the boxers. He moaned and gripped my shoulders. Latching my lips onto his rod, I teased him through the cotton, grabbing his ass with my hands.

Hopp bunched my shirt beneath this fingers and pulled. I sat back long enough that he could pull it over my head and I could yank down his boxers. The smooth, silky cock called to me. I took him instantly into my mouth, sucking hard with persistent, deep strokes.

He whispered my name. I cupped his sack and sucked deeper.

I felt him take his shirt off as I pulled back a little, licking over his tip. His salty flavor hit my tongue and exploded.

Gently, Hopper pushed me back with a hand to my shoulder. I lay down and watched him kick off his shoes and slip the pants and boxers onto the floor. Completely naked, he reached for me, for the button and fly on my jeans.

In seconds, I was just as naked as he was, except I didn't stay that way. He covered me with his body. The warmth he radiated seeped into my skin, and I sighed. He felt like a hot shower on sore muscles. I stretched beneath him, wrapping my arms around his waist, and held his body against mine.

Touching from toe to chest, his weight was delicious. The way his back arched pushed his hips into mine, allowing him to lift his shoulders, and his light eyes stared down.

He looked at me like I was all he saw. Like I was some kind of painting that was so exquisite it didn't matter how many times he saw me; he'd still find something new and just as equally amazing.

Overwhelmed was an understatement. This was the last thing I expected. A ring. A proposal, a request to change my name.

I wasn't alone, and I wouldn't be ever again. There was a connection between us I knew would never fade. All the insecurities I might have felt about Matt, about Hopper's past… they were gone. He chose me.

And deep down, I knew even if Matt hadn't died, Hopp and I still might have found a way to each other. We had to, because there was nothing and no one that would be able to severe the connection we had.

Hell, if anything, I was grateful to Matt.

He paved the road that led here. To us.

As if he knew my thoughts, Hopper leaned down and picked up my left hand. I stared as he lifted it between us. Flexing my fingers so the ring was on full display, I watched him stare. The look on his face was just as awestruck as I felt.

"Hopp," I rasped.

Hopper kissed my hand, the ring, and the finger it was on. Releasing my hand, he came over me. When his skin lay upon mine, breath hissed between my lips.

I got lost in his kisses. In his touch and the feel of his heart beating so forcefully against mine. The lights illuminating the room and the flickering candles played over his skin and left a sort of roadmap for my lips to travel.

We teased each other so much with endless kisses. It peaked with the pair of us tangled together in nothing but a heap of limbs and our weeping cocks.

Hopper ripped his mouth away, his lips red and swollen. I felt the mild stinging of my skin from the constant rubbing of his beard. Hot, wet kisses trailed down my abs. I reached blindly for him, but he gently pushed my hand away and continued lower.

The second his lips wrapped around my swollen cock, my eyes shot open. I didn't see anything, though, but the shimmer of the lights overhead, rocking my hips as he gave me head. All the muscles in my body tightened with the insane urge to release.

As he sucked, his fingers delved below my sack to caress my entrance. I murmured something incoherent. Hopper released my dick, dragging his tongue down my taint to swirl around my sensitive hole.

I relaxed into the mattress and succumbed totally to his hands and mouth. When he pulled away completely and stood, my body followed.

A warm chuckle filled the room. He pushed me back onto the bed. "One sec."

There was a small duffle by the door. He reached inside and pulled out a bottle. As he carried it back over, I spread my legs and moved farther up on the mattress. Hopper went back to work, coating his fingers and my crack with the silky-smooth lube. The sight of him between my legs, on his knees, with his strong cock jutting out below his rippling abs took my breath.

Snatching the lube from beside us, I sat up and generously coated him. The feel of his fingers running through my hair as I worked was a reward. When he was nearly dripping with the stuff, I lay back, gazing up at him with passion-filled eyes.

Hopper didn't enter me right away. Instead, he leaned down to kiss me languidly. Between us, he stroked and pumped my cock until my toes curled.

His tip slid against me, and I moaned. His lips came back, and ours locked together as he filled me. The feel of his thick, hard dick sliding in and out of my body was bliss. As he pumped into me, I caressed his chest and hips, occasionally leaning up to nip at his shoulder and kiss his neck.

With a shudder, Hopper folded over me, our chests colliding. Brushing my lips along his cheek and hairline, I felt him smile.

"If you don't stop that, I won't be able to control myself."

"I don't want you to."

He drew back just enough to meet my eyes, and the hunger there was unmistakable.

I made a split-second decision and pushed lightly on his chest. "Up."

Even though he was fighting release, even though I knew he wanted nothing more than to pound into me until he spilled out every last drop of his intense desire, he pulled back instantly.

The hawk-like way he stared at me and the grimace twisting his lips made me love him more. If that were even possible.

"I hurt you," he half spat, angry at himself.

I held up a hand before he could torture himself further. "You didn't. You never have." Pushing up off the mattress, I tossed a smile over my shoulder. "I just can't see the lights outside from my back."

I knew he didn't understand what I was saying. When I stepped up to the control panel, I planted my palms on the counter and showed him my bare ass. Slowly, realization dawned.

He sucked in a breath. "Babe…"

He'd never entered me like this. From behind. We shied away from the position because of my past. It didn't matter anymore, though. With Hopper, nothing was off-limits.

"Come here," I beckoned.

His teeth sank into his lower lip while his fist closed around his dick.

"I want to feel you inside me while I look at the lights below."

"You kill me, babe," he whispered, moving up behind me.

"I hope not," I mused. "I need you."

Strong arms locked around my waist from behind; his lips latched on my neck. Arching into him, I rubbed my ass along his hard dick. His groan vibrated my throat.

"If—" He whispered, but I made a sound, cutting him off.

"No ifs, Hopp. I know what I want."

His hands moved to my hips. My palms flattened on the counter as I looked down at the words. His dick slid inside me with ease, and both of us groaned.

My head fell back. He gathered me close, and I lay against his shoulder. My stomach dipped and flipped with every stroke. This angle allowed him deep, and I shuddered against him.

His hand came around me, closing over my dick to stroke.

I leaned forward, slapped a hand against the glass of the window, and moaned.

Hopper surged deeper. His head brushed over my G-spot, and my knees threatened to buckle.

"Okay?" he murmured, voice strained.

"Don't stop," I pleaded.

He didn't. He fucked me so good. Sounds ripped out of my throat, and I didn't bother to hold them back. We were alone in this tower, alone and in love.

The candles flickered around us, and his hand… it was magic.

"I'm gonna fucking come," I rasped.

Hopp shoved deep, rotating his hips as he jacked me firmly. I started coming, the release pouring out of me, over his hand, and my body shook.

His free arm wrapped around my waist like a vise. He thrust in me twice more. His teeth sank into my shoulder, his arm tight at my waist. "Babe…"

"It's okay. Let go." I urged, still quaking from my own release.

I felt him pulse inside me. His lips latched onto the back of my shoulder as his orgasm ripped him apart.

I pushed down onto his dick and swiveled my ass. He made a sound, and I felt more seed spill within me.

When both of us were finally steady enough, still clinging together, we collapsed back on the bed, tangling our limbs.

"That was…" His voice was breathless, and his sentence trailed away.

I smiled up at the ceiling, stroking his back with my hand. "I know."

"How soon will you marry me, babe?" Hopper asked.

Another one of those really big smiles filled my face. "As fast as we can get to an altar."

Chapter Seven

Hopper

When a man gets married, he's got a lot to think about.

You know, stuff.

Not the kind of stuff like last-minute jitters or thinking to himself, *"Shit, this is the last dick I'm ever going to have in my lifetime."*

Well, maybe some men think that. Those men probably shouldn't be getting married. But that ain't my business.

Not me.

I was goddamn lucky to be getting married. Doing something like that seemed so far out of reach it wasn't even on my bucket list.

Fuck. Who was I kidding? I didn't have a bucket list.

I might have once. A lifetime ago.

Now I just resolved to grab happiness and hold tight.

Happiness = Arrow.

I wasn't much of a romantic guy; I was pretty simple. Still, the night I proposed to him was the best night of my life.

Seemed like I had everything, right? A second chance, a new family, absolute love.

I did have everything. More than maybe I deserved. More than I would ever think of giving back.

Everything included just what it implied. *Everything.*

Guilt.

An emotion that seemed to be the bane of my existence. My cross to bear. Everyone had one, didn't they?

Everyone probably hated theirs.

I did mine. 'Course, that made me feel guilty, too.

For the first time in a long time, sleep was hard to come by. I remembered this feeling, though tonight it seemed somehow worse. Probably because I wasn't used to it anymore. I'd been given a reprieve. How hard it was to go back to something that didn't seem all that difficult when it was the norm.

I was tired right now. Weary but wired. My body was done, but my mind was amused. As if it laughed in the face of my desire to rest. The energy gathering inside me threatened to spill out, presenting itself in fidgeting feet, tapping fingers, and an insane urge to get up and pace.

I didn't want to.

I wanted to lie here with A. The weight of him against my side and across my chest was the only thing holding me in place. Of course, wanting to lie here with him while the urge to move gnawed away at my insides left me frustrated and annoyed.

I wanted peace. And wanting peace made me feel guilty as well. Just when I thought I had a handle on it, there it came, rearing its ugly head. It was a vicious cycle to which I saw no end.

Matt's face appeared in the back of my mind. My eyes popped open, staring up at the darkened ceiling. It was like a sky without stars. Endless.

Even though my eyes were open, his image didn't go away. With it came memories and thoughts. More pictures, more feelings.

Carefully and gently, I wiggled out from beneath Arrow. Sliding out of the bed, my bare feet hit the floor. Wearing only my boxers, I stared down at my blond-haired love and longed to crawl back in bed.

Instead, my torso twisted. I shuffled out of our bedroom and into the living room.

Everything was dark out here, but all the shapes and shadows were familiar. The middle of the night looked exactly as I remembered it. Empty.

Yes, even with the familiar shapes. Even with Arrow in my bed. Even though I no longer lived alone.

If anything, those things made me feel worse. I didn't want to feel this way.

It was inescapable.

I wandered to the window, peeking through the blinds to stare down into the lot surrounding the apartment building. Golden, artificial glow spread out over the concrete, blasting everything with harsh light. There wasn't much green space here. This building wasn't far from the speedway; we could see it from the bedroom window.

Sometimes I missed the green. The rain. The way the leaves would get so wet they stuck to everything, the streets, the roads, my shoes. The tires of a Ducati.

I'm getting married.

Softly shuffling feet cajoled me out of my thoughts. Arrow moved out of the bedroom and into the dining room. His face widened in a strong yawn. Blond hair fell over one of his eyes and stuck out at the back of his head.

Just looking at him, my lips curved. He made me so happy.

"What's wrong?" he asked, rubbing the back of his neck, his words thick with sleep.

"I tried not to wake you."

Grunting, his bare feet padded across the tile toward me. "I don't know how to sleep alone anymore, Hopp."

Palming the side of his face, I felt my chest cave a little. Just when I thought he had all of me, he would go and claim another little piece. One I didn't even know I had.

I felt his eyes, the piercing way he always saw me. Avoiding the stare, I glanced down. Frowning, I asked, "Why are you wearing pants?"

"I'm hungry."

The incredulous sound I made floated between us in the dark. "It's three o'clock."

"My stomach doesn't have a clock, Hopp. You know this."

"Want me to make you some eggs?" I offered. Eggs was about as good as I got in the kitchen. At least for now. I was trying to get better. Someone had to feed my husband-to-be.

He shook his head, leaned around me, and snagged a set of car keys off the counter. "We're leaving."

The intimacy of the conversation changed. Even though technically we still spoke of food, we weren't really.

Arrow knew I was struggling. The urge to walk the sidewalk, find an almost empty diner with horrible coffee and blurry windows looking out onto the street, was so overwhelming for me he felt it, too.

Without another word, he walked off, passing by the sofa, snagging a T-shirt he'd thrown there, and shrugging into it as he went to the door. With his feet barely shoved into a pair of black high-tops, he gestured for me with his chin.

I dressed in silence, barely paying attention to the jeans and shirt I put on.

We said nothing at all in the elevator or parking garage as we walked to the "incognito" car we had there.

The press were rabid lately. They wanted a piece of Jayson Hamilton. Although Gamble wanted us to stay longer at his mansion, a few nights was all we could take. We liked the bubble we lived in, the world we'd created together.

We came home. I proposed almost immediately, and we started driving a car that wasn't recognizable. Eventually, the press would realize. Hopefully, by then, it wouldn't matter.

Arrow drove the red MINI Cooper a few blocks from the speedway.

Yes. A MINI Cooper.

We were all embarrassed. What kind of race car drivers drove a MINI? Hell, if the press saw us, they'd have a field day about us squeezing our gay asses into this thing.

God. But one did what he must. Unfortunately, riding around in a car no one would expect us to put even one toe in was it.

Once my exclusive interview was over, I hoped to never again ride in one of these *humiliations*.

"Pathetic," Arrow mumbled as he parked the car near the twenty-four-hour diner I knew well.

Smothering a smile, I moved onto the sidewalk. Even though it was summer, the evenings still cooled off. It wasn't cold or even chilly really, but without the sun, it wasn't hot either. Dragging in a deep breath of night air, I felt it slog through my airways and fill my chest.

The street was quiet except for a few cars in the distance. The sidewalk was lit up a few feet ahead with the neon sign in the diner window.

Remaining silent, Arrow stepped up on the concrete but hung back. He was giving me space, the space I needed but also didn't really want.

He fell into step when I did. I jammed my hands deep into the pockets of my jeans as I walked. The sounds of our footsteps echoed over the dry pavement. I noted there were several parking spots near the door of the brick building, but instead, Arrow parked a short way down the street.

He knew I liked to walk at night; I always had before he'd come into my life.

In some respects, it was cathartic.

He held the door open, motioning for me to go inside. I did, not going too far until I knew he was right behind me. Leaving him alone outside on the street was something I would never, ever do.

The mere fact he parked far enough away to give me even a short walk in the middle of the night proved (as if I needed proof) just how much he loved me.

The first night we met, he told me not to walk alone at night on the streets. I hadn't understood the weight of that until later, but it was a weight I still carried today.

A familiar waitress looked up from behind the counter. Surprise flashed in her tired eyes, along with recognition, before both gave way to the default appearance of a woman who worked the boring nightshift.

I didn't acknowledge her or the look. Instead, I shuffled to my usual seat over by the window, in a booth that wasn't very comfortable.

Arrow slid in across from me, still without a word.

I stared out the glass, which was always wet with some kind of condensation even when it was bone dry outside.

Seconds later, the woman appeared, slid a mug of coffee in front of me, dropped a handful of creamers in the center of the table, and then slid an identical cup at Arrow.

Usually at this moment, she would leave. This time she hesitated, not knowing if our usual ritual stood or if the fact I wasn't alone somehow altered everything.

It altered everything.

And at the same time nothing.

Slowly, she began pulling a menu from beneath her arm. Before it was out, Arrow waved her away. She retreated instantly, relieved.

I glanced across the crappy Formica tabletop. "I thought you were hungry," I whispered. It seemed wrong to speak.

"I said that 'cause it was the only way to get you out the door."

We fell silent. Wrapping my hands around the white mug, ignoring the cream, I looked out the blurry window.

A few seats down, the neon light hanging in the window flickered and made a static sound.

Arrow said nothing, did nothing. He was just there.

It was all I needed, for him to just be there.

He could have stayed in bed when he realized I wasn't there. He could have rolled over and let me deal with my demons as I had all the years before we met.

Alone.

Arrow never acted as if what I needed was somehow an insult. Or an imposition. He knew what it was to be broken. He knew how irrational all those little pieces inside us could be. There was no offense in his body language for the fact I couldn't stay in bed tonight or because I had to retreat to old ways to try and cope with what knocked around between my bones.

I knew he knew who I was thinking about. Someone that wasn't him. Someone who had my heart before he did.

Still, he sat here. Even if I hadn't told him my deepest thoughts, my deepest secret, he would sit here.

Again, another little unknown piece of me surrendered.

The mug wasn't as hot against my palms when I finally spoke. The words came out raspy, like the sound of Velcro being pulled apart. "Moving forward sometimes reminds me of all the stuff I'm leaving behind."

"Bring it."

The two words ripped my eyes off the street and across the table. Arrow had been resting back against the seat but pushed off to lean forward and wrap a hand around his mug.

The ring he wore on his finger was a dark stripe against the light ceramic. Every time I saw it there, a flutter of something quivered my stomach.

I liked the symbol of that ring. The possession in it. The promise.

My eyes still on the ring, I asked, "What?"

"You don't have to leave anything behind with me. Bring it all. I love all of you."

Wasn't that what marriage was all about? The good, bad, the ugly?

All our cards were on the table, had been from the moment I showed up at his airstrip. Instead of pulling us apart like it might some, it seemed to bond us closer.

We were gonna be a good fucking married couple.

"I think about them sometimes. A lot more lately," I whispered, leaning closer over the table.

"Who?"

"My family."

"You haven't told me much about them."

"I'm sure they've seen the news. They probably know where I am. What I've been doing all these years."

"You want to see them." Arrow observed.

I nodded slowly. "I think I might."

"They've been waiting for you."

I looked up from the band on his finger at his dark eyes. He seemed so sure about people he'd never met. "How do you know?"

"Because it's what I'd do. You're worth the wait. No matter how long."

My chest swelled with love for him but also with hope he might be right. Sliding my arm across the slightly sticky, cold tabletop, my fingers extended. Arrow released the mug instantly, meeting me halfway. The warmth in his fingers melted into mine as I clung to him a little more desperately than I wished I would have.

"I feel guilty."

"Guilty for being happy?"

I shook my head in swift denial. "Guilty for having all the stuff he never will."

Arrow was silent a moment, digesting. I knew he understood. Oddly enough, I never felt I had to hold back what I felt from him in fear of hurting him. I knew he could take it. I knew he knew it wasn't personal.

Just as we both understood whatever was in our past wouldn't stop us from being together, he knew with whom my heart lay.

I felt a slight shift in the air. Glancing up, I saw a small smile play on his thoroughly pouty and kissable lips. "I wouldn't be so sure. I hear heaven isn't such a bad place."

I hadn't thought of it like that before, not really. I'd only focused on what I lost. What Matt lost. I never thought maybe he had indeed gone to a better place.

Cocking my head to the side, I pondered the thought. "You believe in heaven?"

"Why wouldn't I?" he responded instantly. "I know for a fact hell exists."

And so he did.

I could argue I did as well.

I smiled. Kind of an odd reaction, I know, when someone is so sure hell exists. But it was that surety that gave me hope. That gave me something else to battle the guilt with.

Matt wasn't suffering where he was. He was in a far better place than this old, musty diner with really bad windows and coffee.

He might have lost a life here on Earth, but something told me he lived on. Not just in my memories either.

Abandoning the mug to the crappy napkin dispenser at the end of the table, I stretched my free hand across the space between us. Once again, Arrow met me partway.

"You're a brave man, touching this sticky table."

"You're doing the same," I smiled.

"Anything for you."

Our hands clasped and held. We sat across from each other in the crappiest place on the block and smiled.

Maybe this place wasn't so bad after all.

"There he is," Arrow mused, his stare bouncing between my eyes.

I arched a brow, silently asking what the hell he was talking about.

"I was waiting for you to come back."

"Thanks for coming here tonight."

He glanced around, taking in all the empty tables and old décor. "I kinda like the place."

I made a rude sound.

"Actually, I think it might be kinda perfect."

I glanced at his mug. "What the fuck she put in your tar?"

He chuckled, and my stomach dipped with the sound. "Seriously, I think it may be actual tar."

After a couple minutes of guffawing like a pair of idiots, Arrow sat up a little. "I have something for you.

Been carrying it around a few days, waiting for the right time to give it to you." He glanced around again, over to the counter where the waitress usually was but wasn't just then. The place was empty.

Except for our booth beside the condensation-filled glass and mugs filled with tar.

"I think now is good."

Begrudgingly, I surrendered one of his hands when he tugged it back. My throat grew tight as he reached into his pocket and brought out a small black velvet box.

"I told you I was gonna get you one of these," he said, setting it beside our clasped hands in the center of the table.

Looking between him and the box, my heart beat erratically. "You got me a ring."

"The day after you asked me to marry you."

"I had no idea," I murmured, surprised.

He flashed a smile. "I fought the urge to give it to you every minute since. It's been burning a hole in every pocket of all my clothes."

"Why now?" I asked, clearing my throat because my voice had gone hoarse.

"Because sitting in the crappiest diner in this entire town, in the middle of the night, with some bleary-eyed waitress lurking is still the most beautiful place I've ever been." He squeezed my fingers. "Anywhere with you, with any conversation, even the darkest kind, is exactly where I will always want to be."

My teeth sank into my lower lip. I felt their sharp edges press against the soft flesh as he untangled our hands, reached for the box, and opened the lid.

The band was black, matte black just like my Audi. The entire circumference of both edges was lined with small black diamonds set down in the metal.

I fucking loved it.

"If you think I'm worth diamonds, then you definitely are, too," he said, a little sheepish.

I was overcome with gratitude, overwhelmed with love, and mildly in awe he could somehow find the most perfect moment to give me exactly what I needed.

"So what do you think, Hopp?" A began self-consciously, pushing the ring box closer to me. "I'll take your name if you wear my ring."

I was a lucky bastard. "I honestly don't want anything more."

Smiling fast and yanking the ring out of the box, he held it out. I offered my hand to him. The ring slid right over my knuckle and settled against my skin as if it knew exactly where it belonged.

"Pretty sexy," A murmured, brushing his thumb over it.

I couldn't stop looking at it. I knew it was removable, but it felt like a brand upon my body. "It's perfect, babe."

"Think you're ready to get out of here? Go home?"

Turning my hand over so I could wrap it around his, I asked. "Back to bed?"

"I could definitely be convinced."

Without releasing hands, we slid out of the booth simultaneously while I tossed some cash onto the table. It was way more than enough to cover the sludge in our mugs.

A generous tip as a thank you for making herself scarce so we could have this moment in a place that, up until tonight, represented a lot of pain, self-loathing, and loneliness.

It wasn't that place anymore. This crappy building with the annoying, buzzing sign was hopeful to me now. Pretty, even. Too bad it had taken this long to grow fond of the place, for I knew I wouldn't be back here.

We pushed out onto the sidewalk. The summer night air ruffled my hair, and the weight of the band on my finger grounded me in ways I never thought possible.

No, I wouldn't be back to this diner. Not ever again.

I didn't need to come here anymore.

Everything I needed, even on restless nights, was at home.

Gamble wasn't kidding when he instituted family dinner night.

We all got matching texts the morning of our first dinner, demanding our presence at the mansion. It was kinda funny really, or maybe kinda odd, to see such a powerful, rich man as Ron Gamble yelling into the phone and making stone-cold business deals with ease one moment while acting kinda like a father the other.

What was even stranger was he viewed me as part of his family.

Strange can be good, though, because while most people probably groaned and did everything imaginable to get the hell out of obligatory family dinners, I looked forward to it.

To being part of something.

For so long, it was just me and Lor. Then Hopper stepped into my life, and now suddenly there was a ring on my hand and texts about family dinner.

I wasn't sure how to dress. Family dinners back in the day were only ever for client meetings when my father had someone to impress. He pulled out the family like we were show horses. We polished ourselves up and paraded around in front of the clients until my father was satisfied enough to send us on our way.

I was pretty sure tonight's dinner wasn't going to be like that. Still, Gamble was, well, Gamble. I wasn't sure he'd want me showing up to his table in my regular T-shirt and ripped-up jeans.

"Babe!" Hopper's voice bellowed through the apartment.

Leaving the dresser drawer open, I went out into the main room, smiling. On his way toward me, his keys hit the counter, his red hat hit the floor, and his eyes roamed my naked chest.

We collided, lips latching instantly, fingers entwining. As we kissed, we took turns spinning the rings around on each other's finger.

"I'm tired of waiting," Hopper growled, then attacked my lips again.

When the kiss finally ended, I smiled. "It's only been a week."

"A week too long."

I chuckled. "You said you wanted to do the interview first. That way the press might be off our asses and not snapping pics as we say I do."

I'd been skeptical about the exclusive tell-all with *GearShark*. Of any interview, really. I didn't want him put into that position, forced to replay events that broke him just for the entertainment of people intent on knowing shit that wasn't theirs to know in the first place.

I'd been pacified, even somewhat convinced, after our session in the giant shower and the talk that followed right after. Hopper needed to do this; he wanted to move on once and for all. I saw now how not doing it would hold him back. He was haunted, and it wouldn't ever end until basically he exorcised the ghosts inside.

But now that it was basically standing between me and taking this guy's name, well, I wanted to do it like yesterday.

"I'm tired of waiting," he said again, pulling me closer, about to kiss me more. I wanted to, even dipped my head to surrender, but at the last second, I pulled back.

Hopper groaned. "You being a cock tease right now?"

I grabbed his package through his cargo pants. "Maybe. If I kiss you right now, we'll never get out this door on time."

"Fucking family dinner," he muttered and pushed his hips into my hand. I gave him a gentle squeeze, and he groaned.

"Later." I promised.

Hopper put his hand on the tattoo over my heart. "Gamble has all the interview details. He's giving them to us tonight."

I was about to reply when his lips brushed over where his palm had just been. All the words fled my mind.

"You ready to tell everyone about getting married?" he murmured.

"Of course." I sighed, grabbing his hand. "Help me find a shirt."

Hopper allowed me to lead him into the bedroom, where he barely glanced into my drawer, plucked out a red T-shirt, and tossed it to me.

"This is kinda casual." I frowned.

"It's family dinner, not the White House."

I shrugged and pulled on the shirt. Hopp was wearing pretty much the same thing.

"C'mon, babe, we better go before I tackle you onto the bed and tell everyone we ain't coming."

We drove the red MINI Cooper to the estate. Every time I got into it, my Camaro cried. I couldn't wait to take this car back where it came from and never see it again.

The white Lotus was already in the driveway when we pulled up. I didn't park beside it, 'cause you know, putting a MINI Coop beside a Lotus was sort of like putting a carrot next to a donut.

Everyone was in Gamble's study. The second I walked in, I glanced at what my brother was wearing—

jeans and a T-shirt. A sigh of relief left my lungs. Gamble was behind his desk, but he wasn't wearing a suit. Instead, he had on some nice-looking T-shirt that looked like it was made of silk. I guess even his casual was fancy.

There was a crystal glass at his elbow and a relaxed vibe around his head.

Joey got up from her chair before we even crossed the room and came to hug me. Then she shifted and hugged Hopp, who was right behind me.

"What the fuck!" Jace exploded, catching everyone off guard. Joey spun around, her eyes wide as Jace stomped across the room and grabbed my left hand.

"What the shit is this?" he demanded.

"Hopp asked me to marry him, Jace," I said, not even hesitating.

Jace wasn't looking at me, though. In fact, he didn't even seem that surprised. Instead, he was staring at Hopper. More specifically, Hopper's left hand. Dropping my wrist, he pivoted to Hopp, grabbed his wrist, and stabbed a finger at the ring on his hand.

"I gave you permission to ask him, not to do it without me!" Lorhaven growled.

"We aren't married," Hopper said, mildly amused.

I wasn't amused. Not at all. Inserting myself between my brother and my guy, I pushed his hand off Hopper. "Hands to yourself," I intoned.

Joey made a sound of excitement and bounced forward, pushing Jace back farther. "You guys got married!"

"No," we both said at once.

"Then why are you both wearing rings?" Jace demanded.

I glanced over at him. "You knew Hopper was going to ask me to marry him?"

Lorhaven crossed his arms over his chest. "He asked for my permission."

Hopper made a rude sound. "I asked for your blessing. Not your permission. *Big* difference."

Totally ignoring their pissing contest, I turned toward Hopp. "You asked Jace for his blessing?"

His eyes softened when they swung to mine. "I thought it would make you happy."

My name might be Arrow, but it was Hopp who'd pierced my heart like one.

I grabbed his hand, held on tight, and turned toward Gamble, who was watching all of us with an amused expression. "When's the interview?"

"Next week. *GearShark* is meeting you in Vegas, right after your next NASCAR race."

Like the pull of a magnet, mine and Hopp's eyes connected.

Vegas.

"I like it," Hopper told me.

I smiled. "Me, too."

"Now just a damn minute." Lorhaven cut in on our mental planning. He pointed to my ring. "So you aren't married yet?"

I shook my head. "They're engagement rings."

That seemed take some of the fight out of him. For one second. Then it was back. "You can't just get married in Vegas."

"You really gave Hopp your blessing?" I asked.

He rolled his eyes. "Duh."

"You wanna come to Vegas next week?" I asked. "I need a best man."

"We're invited?" Jace asked with a sniff.

Like I'd really get married without you there. I smiled. "Duh."

"Well, ah, yeah. I guess a Vegas wedding would be pretty cool."

Joey grinned wide and lurched forward to hug both Hopper and me at the same time. "This is the best news ever! Congratulations!"

Gamble got up from his desk and came around. "You better not let any reporter see those things 'til after the interview."

"We've been careful." Hopper agreed, shifting from one foot to the other. I could tell he was a little worried about what Gamble might say.

Maybe I shouldn't have just announced it all like that without talking to him first.

"Let me know the plans," he said, gruff. "So I can be there."

Hopper's eyes widened. "You want to come to our wedding?"

"Clearly, my daughter is never going to have one. May be the only chance I'll have." He gave a pointed stare to Jace.

My brother didn't shrink at all beneath the glare. It was like he barely even noticed it.

"Dad," Joey admonished.

Hopper lunged forward and hugged Gamble. Threw his arms around the man and hugged hard. Surprise rippled through me. Hell, it rippled through the entire room. Even Gamble's eyes widened over Hopp's shoulder before he closed his arms around him in return.

Hopper wasn't much of a toucher. Except for me, of course. Beyond that, I'd never actually seen him touch anyone. So for him to launch at Gamble so uncharacteristically said a lot.

"Thank you," I heard him whisper before pulling away.

"C'mon, then," Gamble said, clearing his throat. "Dinner's gonna be cold."

"I'm starving." I complained.

Everyone groaned.

On the way to the dining room, Joey started naming off venues and places to get married in Vegas. I'd never actually been there. And it was suddenly very overwhelming.

As if he knew, Hopp materialized at my side, taking my hand.

"I don't think we really planned on something big and, uh… planned," Hopper announced. "I figured we'd just pick a twenty-four-hour chapel and walk in."

He glanced at me, and I nodded eagerly. Sounded perfect to me. I didn't need anything fancy. Just a marriage license, a justice of the peace, and him.

Oh, and my family.

Joey halted abruptly, and we all damn near fell over trying not to mow her down. She gasped, the curls on her head bouncing when she bolted around, planting her hands on her hips.

"You will not get married at a drive-thru chapel!" She was horrified.

"They have those?" I asked.

Lorhaven barked a laugh. "Complete with guys who look just like Elvis."

"No!" Joey gasped.

Her eyes pleaded with me and Hopp. "You cannot do that."

I shrugged. "You pick the place."

Everyone groaned, and Gamble laughed from inside the dining room.

"What?" I asked dubiously.

"You have no idea what you've done," Lorhaven vowed.

I wrinkled my nose. "Joey's not an over-the-top kind of woman."

"Simple," Hopper intoned at Joey as if I were the only one who thought she wasn't about to plan something lavish. "I know you love us. I know you want to do something to show it, but please…" Hopper's voice faded.

"Simple." She nodded. "Got it." Her eyes sparkled with excitement. I glanced over at Jace, but he was watching her, the softest look I'd ever seen him wear plastered all over his face.

He was so totally in love with her. Maybe I'd convince him to hit up a drive-thru chapel. I glanced down at her ring finger, wondering how big of a rock he'd put there.

"Seriously, Joey." Hopper pressed. "They last thing we want or need is media attention."

Her sigh was heavy. "I get it. Secret and simple."

"Just family," I told her.

"Secret, simple, *and* small." She amended. "You guys are so bossy."

Jace wound an arm around her waist, pulling her into his side, and kissed the top of her head.

"I'm eating without you!" Gamble yelled. "I'm eating your plate first, Arrow!"

My eyes whipped to my sister. "He wouldn't."

She laughed. "He might."

I left them all in my dust as I rushed into the dining room.

Their laughter followed, wrapping around me as I sat down to a giant steak. Grinning, I picked up my knife and fork while Gamble ordered everyone to eat and Joey rambled on about our wedding.

Underneath the table, Hopper's hand settled over my thigh. Butterflies took off in my belly.

This was the best family dinner I'd ever been to.

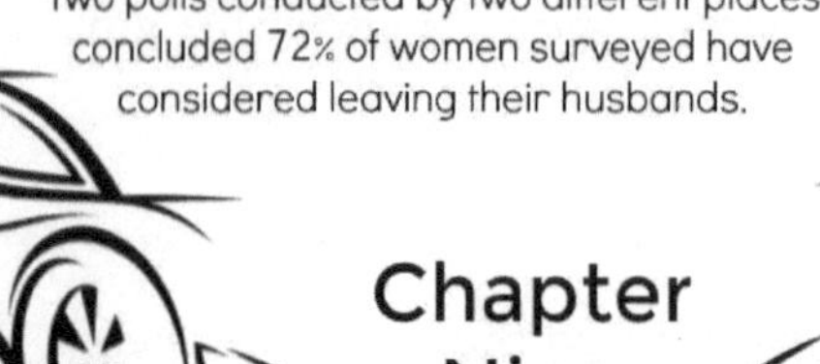

Chapter Nine

What happens in Vegas stays in Vegas.

Unless of course you get married. That shit will follow you anywhere.

Thank God.

My inner thoughts aside, if anyone dared call my marriage to Arrow shit, I'd deck 'em.

Neither of us was the flashy type. Flash kinda went out the window when you lived like you might rather be dead, then came back to life, only to be hounded incessantly by the press.

Oh, they were still clamoring for a piece of me. Or rather Jayson. Frankly, it was driving me mad. If I'd been protective before over what I found with Arrow, I was even more so now. There was no other way to be.

I would protect what we had until my very dying breath.

The build-up to the *GearShark* interview was kinda intense. Or maybe it just felt that way because right now it seemed like a deep, divisive line between where I was now and where I wanted to be.

Again, guilt trailed me. Guilt that I was basically trying to hurry up the tell-all so I could move on. It felt a little like I was trying to shove away everything with Matt.

Rationally, I knew that wasn't true. Still, sometimes the thoughts taunted me.

When they did, I looked at A. Remembered the talk we had at Gamble's that night, then the one at the empty diner.

He calmed me down. Gently. His mere presence was like a massive dose of epinephrine to my body when I was collapsing inward, suffocating myself.

Well, shit.

I was allergic to myself. Even my own damn body tried to get away from my head.

Good thing I found the cure. Arrow was my walking lifeline.

I couldn't wait to marry him. To see his signature with my last name on every piece of paper. Maybe it was archaic. Maybe some gay rights activists would buck the fact he was taking my name, as it was part of a traditional system that shunned people in same-sex relationships since nearly the dawn of time.

No, I supposed being gay wasn't traditional. Not in the least.

But being in love was.

Love was the oldest institution in existence. It was basic human nature to seek and be sought, to connect to someone in a way you didn't connect with anyone else.

Screw tradition. Screw contemporary. Screw everything and everyone who ever tried to pigeonhole love or the way humans showed it.

I was going to do what the fuck I wanted.

Having Arrow Ambrose become Arrow Hamilton was exactly what I wanted. More astonishing? He wanted it, too.

The day of A's race seemed to drag on, though it was filled with speed. Vegas was hot, especially compared to Maryland. The stands were packed, the competition was fierce, and my ring was burning a hole in the pocket of my shorts.

Yep. We took off the rings.

Let me tell you how much I didn't want to do that. I almost didn't. I almost walked out of the hotel room with it wrapped around my finger. God knew I wanted to.

There was too much press, too many cameras, and way too many watchful eyes scrutinizing everything I did. This was the first race since my real identity broke. The first time I was out in the open for a lengthy amount of time.

Same for Arrow.

Watching him take off his ring? It felt like someone was gouging out my eye with a hot poker.

He didn't want to do it any more than me, but that didn't make it any easier.

Gamble called right before, though, like he knew we were seriously considering letting everyone have an eyeful. "Don't blow this, Hopper. Tomorrow is the interview. After that, you can tattoo his name across your forehead for all I care. Until then, keep it contained. My entire staff worked hard on this. You're being paid so well even I'm impressed. Understand?"

Fuck. "I understand." I agreed, contrite. "I won't let you down."

"I know you won't," he returned, gruff. "You need anything, you call. If not, I'll see you after the race."

"Hey, Gamble?" I asked before he could hang up. He didn't say anything, but I knew he was still there, listening. "Thank you. For everything. I'm not sure where I'd be right now if you hadn't found me all those years ago."

"You'd have been just fine, son. Of that much, I'm sure. You're a survivor."

His reply made me oddly homesick for people I hadn't seen in so long I wondered if I even had the right to feel homesick for them anymore. We disconnected the call, and I tucked the ring into my shorts before pulling my fire safe suit over my street clothes.

Arrow wore his on a chain around his neck, secured beneath his clothes. I'd offered to hold it while he raced, but he refused to give it up.

I forced myself to stay focused during the race. The interview, our pending wedding, and everything else going on was definitely more enticing, but none of it would matter if A got hurt because my head wasn't on the track with him.

He drove better than he ever had. It was something spectacular to witness. He drove with the fierceness of a tiger, but the grace of a butterfly. And the speed… he went for it. All the way.

He drove like he'd somehow ended up in Jurassic Park and the not-so-much-extinct, man-eating dinosaurs were really hungry and decided he was the meal.

He placed in the top five. Top fucking five, baby.

I wasn't even the one behind the wheel, but the rush? It was the same. He was goddamned incredible.

And he was mine.

Once again, the press were vultures. When we finally walked off the track, they swarmed around us like flies on fresh horse shit. Frankly, it turned my stomach. It brought back memories of when I was first released from the hospital after Matt died.

I hadn't been prepared for the onslaught of the wicked storm that met me in the parking lot that day. The questions. The rumors. The blame. Then there was the police. The Motocross division… It went on. And on.

I dealt with as little as humanly possible, then ran like hell.

I disappeared like smoke.

Became a ghost.

Even though I expected the onslaught today, I still felt ill-prepared. Per Gamble's instructions, Arrow did barely any press after the race, other than a pre-vetted short interview that was strictly about his performance on the track today.

Throughout the entire interview, I saw the woman giving me the side-eye. I saw the desire, the unspoken questions on her tongue just dying to come out. Clearly, she'd been warned to not ask, but oh, she wanted to.

It put my back up. I was defensive just standing there, waiting for her to blurt something at A he wasn't going to be ready for.

I'd lose my shit. That's what I'd do. No one was going to hound him the way they did me back then, the way they wanted to now.

His short interview went well. He smiled and talked driving, gave credit to his entire pit for how well he did. I got caught up in watching him, in the sound of his voice while he finished up.

That's probably why I hadn't seen it coming.

"Thank you, Arrow, for taking the time to talk with us," the reporter said.

"Anytime." He smiled.

"Now that the official interview is over…" she cooed, lowering her mic as if that lent itself to some kind of privacy. "I was wondering if you had a comment on the fact that people are saying you're in a relationship someone who some consider to be partly responsible for another man's death. Another man he *claimed* to love."

My jaw dropped, like full on hung open, exposing all my back teeth. Just when I thought the bitch was going to abide by the rules, just when I was all taken in by his bad-boy driver smile, she dropped a grenade.

My mouth made a snapping sound when it lashed closed. Tension radiated, and my body was stiff when I leapt forward. My chest met Arrow's palm. Gently, he pushed me back, and I stared at him with incredulous anger.

His eyes met mine; he shook his head once, like one swift swipe of a blade freezing me mid-flip-out.

"What people?" Arrow asked, his voice icy quiet.

My eyes widened. This was a new tone.

He moved predatorily, putting his body between mine and the reporter and her henchman, who was still aiming his camera at us all.

The reporter gave a nervous laugh. "It's being reported—"

"So *you* just made it up." Arrow cut her off, his voice sharp and deep. He didn't yell. He didn't even sound angry.

But oh my, he was deadly. Protective. Not at all caught off guard the way I thought he would be. It was as if he was prepared—*no*—expecting this to happen.

"Of course not. It's no secret."

"It's no secret you were told not to speak to me about anything that didn't involve today's race," Arrow said coldly. He reached out, yanking off the press pass that was clipped to her blouse. "You won't be needing this ever again. Pissing off Ron Gamble is career suicide."

"I beg your pardon," she said, haughty.

He rose, his back muscles tensed, and he motioned to someone in the distance. I followed his lead and watched as two security officers came striding over.

"These people need to be shown the door," Arrow said when they were within earshot.

"How dare you?" The reporter fumed. "You can't just tell me to leave."

Without a word, Arrow made a show of slyly tucking her press pass in his back pocket.

She lunged at him. Another thing I didn't see coming.

With a growl, I surged forward, but his back blocked me. Instead of reaching out to protect himself, he reached behind him and palmed my sides, taking care of me first.

The woman didn't make contact. She was hauled off by the guards, her cameraman left to follow.

Arrow stood and watched in stony silence, which, quite frankly, was as unnerving as it was hot, because damn, he was a lot more like Lorhaven than I gave him credit for.

When she was completely gone, his hands dropped away and he turned. "We should work on your interview skills before tomorrow."

I gaped at him. Then with a growl, I crossed my arms over my chest. "She asked you how you felt about dating a killer."

His face darkened. "You're *not* a killer. And she was a total cunt."

I blinked. Blinked again. "Did you just say…?"

"Yeah, and I hate that word, but that's exactly what she was."

I laughed. A laugh that rumbled up from my guts.

Arrow's lips twitched. Before it could turn into a full-on smile, his eyes sharpened on something over my shoulder. His mouth flattened, and that Lorhaven-like look came over his face again.

"No," he half yelled, half roared.

I glanced around in time to see another reporter turn and scurry away.

"I thought I needed to protect you from all of this," I murmured.

Arrow laughed. "I got this, Hopp. I got you."

Yes. Yes, he did.

Clearing my throat, I changed the subject. If I didn't, I might jump him right here and give all the photogs hanging around a nice payday. "You drove like a fucking beast today."

His pearly whites flashed. "You like that?"

"Seriously, the heat was on. What gave you that extra push?"

Pinning me with dark eyes, he said low, "I pictured you standing at the finish line with a marriage certificate in your hand."

My mouth ran dry, and a groan rumbled my throat.

"The faster this race was over, the faster we could get to getting married."

Glancing down at his empty finger and then back up to his eyes, I said, "About that. This no ring shit? I fucking hate it."

He half smiled. "How 'bout we get the hell out of here so we can put 'em back on?"

I shook my head. "I'm gonna need something a little more permanent."

"Marriage is pretty permanent, Hopp." Arrow chuckled.

"More."

He lifted his eyebrows. "You can have it all, babe. Just tell me."

My stomach did a little dip. Reaching for his hand, I opened my mouth to tell him what it was I wanted. But, of course, people interrupted.

Damn fucking people.

Sensing my anger, Arrow squeezed my hand and pulled me a little closer to his side. His hair was damp from all the sweat he'd shed while in his car. I knew the clothes beneath his suit must be soaked. He was probably exhausted. Hell, I was, too.

Lorhaven and Joey came forward, Gamble right beside them. "That was the best driving I've seen you do, bro!" Lorhaven said, his voice excited.

"Thanks, Jace." Arrow smiled. Then he handed the confiscated press pass to Gamble. "She needs to be fired."

Gamble frowned at it. "Didn't listen to the stipulations, did she?"

"No."

"I'll call her office."

"That's not good enough." Arrow held his ground. "Fired."

"I can't have her fired for being nosy," Gamble rebutted.

"I'm sure she has a list of shit a mile long she's done wrong. Just have someone dig around."

I glanced at Lorhaven. "You teach him this?"

Lorhaven smiled as if it were the greatest compliment he'd ever gotten.

"Don't encourage him." Joey shushed me.

"Baby, you know I don't need any encouragement," Lorhaven drawled.

I rolled my eyes.

Gamble tucked the press pass into the inside of his suit pocket. "Dinner tonight at the hotel. I rented a private area of the dining room so this doesn't happen again," he told us, patting the place he'd just put the pass.

"We have details to go over," Joey said slyly.

"Just tell us where and when, Joey. Nothing else matters," Arrow replied.

My chest swelled. I fucking loved him.

Joey nodded, and Arrow gave my arm a tug so I would follow as he began moving away from the group. "What time for dinner?" he asked no one in particular.

"Eight," Gamble answered.

"See you then," he called as we walked off alone. "Longest day ever," he muttered. "I just want to be alone with you."

Back in the hotel room, the first thing we did was put the rings back on.

And everything else we were wearing? It all came off.

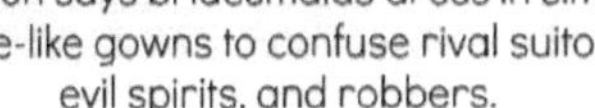
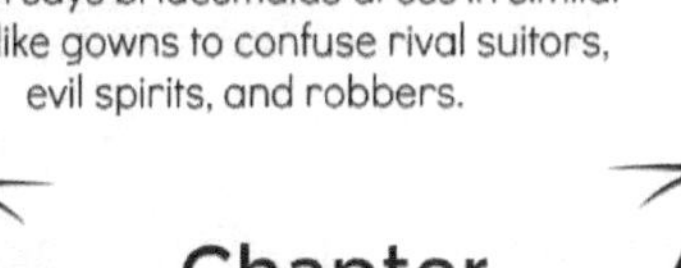

Chapter Ten

An exclusive tell-all with GearShark in Vegas equated to them renting out a huge private suite in a luxury hotel on the strip.

Add that to the fat paycheck Hopper was getting for this little sit-down, and I might wager this was one of their most expensive cover stories yet.

Hopper was worth it, though. Every single bit of it.

It was a big day for him. For both of us really. Not only was it his interview, but after this, we had last-minute wedding shit to do because we were getting married tomorrow.

Tomorrow. Fucking hell yes!

I didn't think I'd *ever* looked forward to anything more in my entire life.

Funny, isn't it? How a man can spend so much time bucking all the shit that tried to tie him down, bucking so hard it actually caused scars that would never go away, only to then willingly tie himself in every way possible to another human being.

Life, people. Life at its finest.

I also had a sort of wedding present for Hopp. Something he was going to get tonight instead of tomorrow.

It was a gift I'd put a lot of thought into. And a lot of stress.

I really hoped it didn't blow up in my face.

Between my gift and the interview, both of us were a bundle of nerves. I tried to hide mine, shoved it deep. He didn't need it right now. He needed nothing but my support.

We got up early because the interview was scheduled that way. Maybe they figured it would be more incognito at the crack of dawn. Who the hell knew? Hopp was more of a morning person than me, but I seemed to be instantly awake the second he was.

I sensed his restlessness, knew he would be turning inward a lot today. How could he not? It would be weird if he didn't, really. Which again made me nervous about my timing.

Since we were up, we didn't have to rush around to meet the car they were sending. I ushered him into the shower, where I paid extra attention to his tense back and shoulder muscles and made sure he was extra clean for the photoshoot.

By the time we were dressed, both of us in shorts and T-shirts and a baseball hat covering my head, he was a lot more relaxed.

I had magic hands. Or maybe a magic mouth.

We headed down to the car that was waiting outside and held hands the short distance to the luxury hotel where *GearShark* waited. There were a lot of luxury hotels here in Vegas. This entire town was crammed full of shit to see and do. We didn't get to do much because of the press following us around, but I didn't care.

The car pulled into some exclusive parking garage beneath the building, drove down into a dark concrete section, and stopped at a set of glass doors where a pair of elevators sat.

"Thanks, man," Hopper said, leaning up to speak to the driver. As he spoke, he pulled out some cash from his shorts.

The man shook his head. "That's been taken care of."

We slid out. My eyes swept the entire space for lurking paparazzi as Hopp went inside. In the elevator on the way up to the suite, I turned to my guy.

"If you don't like the shit they ask, we'll leave. Screw this."

He smiled. "Screw it?"

I grabbed his other hand so I was gripping them both and stared hard into his pale-blue eyes. "Hell yes. This is *your* life. Your past and *your* decision."

"You're wrong." He shook his head. "This is *our* life."

"Yes, but this interview isn't for me, Hopp. I know you're ready to move on, and I support that. I support anything you say and do. But this is for you. No one else."

"Babe." He sighed, wrapping an arm around my waist and pulling me into his body. "I love you."

I kissed the side of his neck, squeezing him. "For infinity."

The elevator doors opened, but we stayed like that until I heard them start to close. Moving fast, I stuck my foot out and stopped it. "Ready?" I whispered.

His eyes met mine. "I really am."

We walked in wearing our rings. When I started to take mine off this morning, his whole face darkened; his voice got all growly and sexy. I liked it, but I didn't tell him that. However, I suspect he knew I was silently amused, because suddenly, he began sliding his off as well.

I turned growly, too.

Needless to say, they were still on our hands. We were going to *GearShark* to spill anyway.

The entire staff noticed the rings the second we walked into the all-white suite. The place was pristine. Glossy white tile floors, large windows that overlooked a view of a just-rising sun. The only color came from the people rushing around (who were also dressed in a lot of muted tones), the food setup in the full kitchen, and a giant display of red roses in a crystal vase in the center of the main room.

A low buzz traveled around, everyone in a tizzy because, clearly, the rings meant a bigger story than even they'd hoped for. They thought we were already married, just like our family originally did.

Hopper leaned close, so close his lips brushed my ear. "Don't tell them we aren't."

I turned my head. Our noses bumped because he didn't move back. "Wasn't going to," I whispered.

Seconds later, we were surrounded by people, and I knew we wouldn't get another moment alone for several hours.

I glanced at Hopp, making sure he was ready for this.

His smile was all the answer I needed.

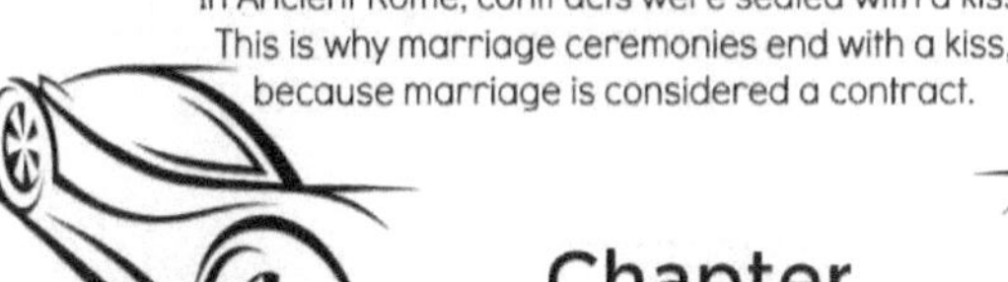

To the extreme, right?

I once was an extreme Motocross racer.

An extreme accident shattered my life.

Most people consider the way I reacted extreme. I shut down. Became a ghost, a mere shell of a man, and moved permanently into misery, which was actually my comfort zone.

The more things change, the more they stay the same.

So it made perfect sense that the only way for me to step out of my comfort zone and fully embrace the new life I wanted so badly was also to the extreme.

I took a breath, grabbed Arrow's hand, and went from saying nothing to admitting all to anyone who listened.

It was cathartic. Uncomfortable. Scary.

Sometimes the best things in life are all of those things.

I was changed. Still shattered yet somehow whole again.

Oh, and PS: I was also thoroughly amused. Because sweatpants.

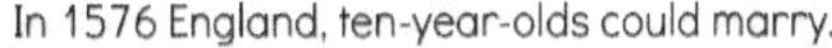

Chapter Twelve

Fucking sweatpants.

They were harmless, comfortable pieces of fabric lots of people liked to wear. Including me.

I was betrayed. Deceived by the very pants I thought of as great casual attire.

Now sweatpants were nothing but traitors. I probably would never look at a pair the same way again—as would anyone else who dared view the cover of *GearShark*.

I didn't really think much about the photoshoot that went along with the exclusive interview, until of course we were in the suite, the photographer was all set up, and they pulled Hopp into another room for wardrobe.

Only there was no wardrobe.

He stepped out of the room in nothing but a pair of light-colored sweatpants. And nothing else.

I'd been leaning against the wall, waiting patiently and wondering if they were going to try and fix his hair the way they did mine. I hoped not. I liked his hair. I liked the dark curls that sprang up around the back of his neck and the way it sometimes fell onto his forehead.

The door swung open mere minutes after he'd stepped in. Glancing up, I expected to see one of the wardrobe girls coming out.

I did a double take. And then another.

It wasn't a wardrobe girl.

It was Hopp, and he was naked.

My eyes nearly fell out of my head. My mouth ran dry. The most immediate response inside me was complete heat. God, he was fucking sexy as hell. All wide shoulders, smooth chest, and muscle. The way his waist narrowed into a V made my palms tingle with need. The pads of my fingers craved the feel of him beneath them.

All that chest just waiting for my tongue.

Someone dropped something out in the other room, startling me back to reality.

Jerking away from the wall, I balled my fists at my sides. "Why are you fucking naked?" I demanded, shoving forward to plant my hands on his chest, trying to cover up all that stark sexiness.

"I'm wearing pants, babe. Not naked."

I barked a laugh. "Those are not pants."

"No?" Hopper asked, lifting an eyebrow. The bastard thought this was funny. "What are they?"

"This is a joke," I deadpanned. "Ha-ha. You got me."

All amusement faded. "It's not a joke. This is what they had me put on."

"And you just agreed?" I snapped.

He drew back. He was surprised I was this incensed over the fact he was wearing nothing but low-riding sweatpants.

You're damn right I'm pissed. My God, everyone wants a piece of him. He's mine. Mine. *And I'm tired of sharing.*

The inner rant shocked me. Surprised me so much I actually drew back, away from my own thoughts.

Hopp said nothing, wrapping his hand around mine and tugging me into the room he stopped in front of the two wardrobe girls. "I need a shirt."

The girls blinked. Their eyes slid to me, then back to Hopp. "The photographer was pretty specific. Very relaxed attire, no shirt." She glanced at me again. "It's to represent the nakedness of the interview. You know, a side of Jayson no one has ever seen before. A stripped down, tell-all version of the story everyone has been waiting for."

My chest heaved as I sucked in a deep breath. Even though my own thoughts shocked me, the possessive almost territorial feelings still clamored for control.

I was being stupid, but even the realization made it hard to stop.

"I'm still gonna need a shirt." Hopper replied.

The girl nodded once, went to a rack of clothes, and pulled out a white wife-beater-style tank top. She looked at me. "You wore a tank for your shoot, so this is good, right?"

Clearly, she knew I was the one having a fit over the lack of clothes on his body.

"It's fine," I answered.

She tossed the shirt across the space to Hopp, who snagged it midair. After clearing her throat once, she motioned to the other girl. "We'll give you a minute. Come out when you're dressed. The photographer is ready."

"Thanks," Hopper said.

On the way past, the other wardrobe girl stopped beside me. She was the one who'd fixed my hair for my interview. "I get it," she whispered. "When your husband is that hot, you probably get sick of people checking him out."

I made a sound that could have been an agreement, and they left the room, closing the door behind them.

"Babe," Hopper intoned, stepping forward.

I let out a breath, feeling like a balloon being deflated. "Jesus. Sorry, Hopp. I, uh—"

He laughed. A genuine laugh that brought my head up. "I love you."

I blinked. "I love you, too. But yeah, I think maybe I have a problem with jealousy."

The smile that bestowed his face was so beautiful I wanted to rub my palm over his scruffy cheek and press my face into his neck.

As if he knew, Hopper reached out, tugging me close, wrapping me in a hug. Against my hair, he whispered. "If you have a problem with jealousy, so do I. Two guys who have lost as much as we have, then found even more… It would be weird if we weren't overprotective."

His skin was warm. Warm and soft. His body was scented with the fancy soap from our hotel shower, and I could feel the heavy beating of his heart against me.

My eyes slipped closed.

"I think I owe you an apology," he said as his hand reached beneath my shirt and began caressing my back. "I was too caught up in how this interview made me feel. I didn't stop to think how it affected you."

"This isn't about me," I replied, feeling like an ass for making it that way.

"Yeah, it is. You're part of my story now. The biggest part there is."

I pulled away, even though I didn't want to. Grabbing the shirt in his grip, I threw it on the floor.

"We're here for you. Forget the shirt. Forget my Lorhaven-like asshole outburst. I gotta admit the photographer is on to something. Your chest is gonna sell a lot of magazines."

"I think your asshole-like outbursts are sexy." His smile was lopsided.

I groaned, locking my lips against his. When finally I pulled back, my palm rubbed over his beard. "Don't let anyone touch you."

Hopper laughed. "I don't want anyone touching me but you."

The shoot went by quickly, half the time it took for mine. Hopp was a lot more photogenic than me. I think maybe the wardrobe girls warned the photographer, because he didn't touch Hopp; he didn't even go within arm's length of him.

Or maybe it was because I stood there with hawk-like eyes and watched the entire thing.

After it was done, Hopp put on the clothes he came in, and both of us sat down for the interview. It took a lot longer than the shoot, but the time went quickly. Everyone on set, even the people who normally packed up and left when their part was done, stayed. Everyone was enthralled by Hopper and his story.

You could have heard a pin drop as he spoke and answered questions. Even I learned some shit I hadn't known before. Stuff I wondered about but never asked because it seemed too painful to bother bringing up.

I hadn't planned on being part of the interview at all. I was there for moral support, but I ended up answering some questions, mostly about our relationship and our marriage.

Overall, I thought it was going to be a good piece. The piece everyone was waiting for. Some of it had been recorded, something about them running a portion of it on TV for even more promotion and audience.

It was past lunch when we finally walked into our hotel room.

The second the door closed behind us, I turned to Hopp. "How do you feel?"

He looked a little drained, a little wrung out from all the reliving he'd just done. My stomach cramped a little thinking of the "gift" I still had to give him. *What if it's too much?*

"It was hard," he admitted. "But it was good. I feel lighter."

Moving forward, sliding both hands up the back of his neck, I ruffled out his hair, allowing all the curls and strands the wardrobe people combed down to spring back up. It had been driving me crazy. "Tell me what you need right now."

To my surprise, he fished into his shorts, pulling out his cell. "I need to make a phone call."

Chuckling as he hit the screen, he winked at me.

Oh, winks were sexy.

"Hey, it's Hopper. … Yeah, we're ready. … Sounds good, thanks." He disconnected the call and tossed the phone onto the nearby couch.

Stepping close, Hopper grabbed me around the hips, pulling me into his body. "Remember yesterday at the track when you told me I could have whatever I want?"

We'd been talking about our rings. I nodded.

"You meant that, right, babe?"

"I meant it, Hopp." I vowed. "Anything."

"I got us a wedding present. Not sure how you'll feel about it, though."

I made an impatient sound. "Tell me."

"That was my tattoo guy. He cleared his afternoon. He's on his way over."

"You want to get another tattoo?" I asked, smiling.

"I want us both to get one." He held up his left hand between us, pointing to his ring finger, right above the ring I put there. "Wedding bands."

"Wedding band tattoos," I echoed. It was fucking brilliant.

"I'm getting your name, babe. I'm having your name tattooed around my finger, right above the engagement ring. So if I ever, for some unfathomable reason, have to take this ring off, your name will still be there."

"Now I feel even worse for being such an ass over a shirt," I quipped.

Hopper threw back his head and laughed. His laughter faded, but I didn't say anything more. I just stared at his ring finger, imaging my name there.

It was incredible. *He* was incredible. This life was incredible. Hopper was more than I could ever have hoped for. And now not only was he marrying me, but my name was going to be permanently part of his body.

"I can call him back, cancel the appointment," Hopper said, clearing his throat.

"No!" I burst out, rushing forward. "I want this. I want your name on my finger, too."

"Yeah?" He seemed relieved.

"Oh yeah. More than anything." Lifting his hand, I brushed a kiss over his finger. "Tattoos here aren't exactly painless." I warned him, kissing the spot again.

His eyes sparkled with warmth. "You gonna hold my hand, then?"

"Always."

Chapter Thirteen

Hopper

The tattoos were small, but what they represented was so large.

Little fuckers hurt, too.

I didn't complain, though; I didn't even wince. There was far worse pain in life than getting the name of your infinity etched on your finger.

We got matching art—same font, same black ink. The only difference was what the letters spelled.

The artist wanted me to take off my ring so he could work. I was an ass and refused. I wanted to make sure everyone would be able to see the name when I had the ring on. The best way to do that was to have it done with the ring in place.

It probably made his job harder. I didn't fucking care. I paid him well. Better than well. Not only did he get extra for being basically on call that afternoon, but he got paid more because he came to our hotel rather than us going to him. It was just another precaution because of the press.

A left his ring on, too.

We sat beside each other the entire time he worked, our free hands clasped together. And though we made small talk with the artist, I felt the pull between us.

I honestly thought getting married was just one more way to make him mine… like, on paper. In the eyes of the law. I already thought he was totally mine in all other ways.

I was wrong.

A marriage was more than rings and signatures on a paper. It bound us in a way I likely would never have known without doing this.

I felt as if the energy always surrounding him stretched out, changed shape, and entangled with mine. Like we were two trees planted beside each other in the forest, but when we started to grow, when our roots started to spread out, they were together.

Inseparable. There was no beginning or end to either of us as individuals because I was no longer made up of just me. Arrow was no longer made up of just him.

My stomach quivered; my entire body was buzzed and jittery, as if I'd had too much caffeine.

We were knotted together, tied in ways that would never be undone.

Our fingers were wrapped in identical white bandages as the tattoo artist tucked away the stack of crisp cash I handed him and picked up the case of his equipment.

We followed him to the door. I shook his hand. Then he shook Arrow's.

"Thanks for coming here," I said.

Nodding, he grabbed the door handle, then paused and turned back. His stare moved between Arrow and me for a moment before he spoke. "I've done a lot of tats on couples." He gestured between us with his finger. "But you two? You two got some serious vibes. You're the real deal. It's been a long time since I did tattoos like this and didn't know, without a doubt, the couple would be back in a couple years to have them covered up with something else."

"That's not gonna happen," Arrow said. "These are here to stay."

I nodded.

"I actually believe it," he replied, then let himself out without another word.

We grinned at each other like a couple of fools the second we were alone.

"You keep inspiring me to get tats, babe, and I'm gonna have a full sleeve like you in no time."

"I love you just the way you are," Arrow shot back instantly. "But you want tats? I'll hold your hand for all of them."

I backed him against the door, covering his body with mine. His lips parted, allowing my tongue to slide deep. Arrow growled, grabbed a fistful of my shirt, and increased the pressure of his mouth against mine.

Dragging my fingers through his hair, I tipped his head back, forcing our lips apart to kiss down his chin and neck. The arrow on the side of his neck called to me, and I answered. I sucked into the hollow just behind his collarbone, and he moaned.

Arrow started fidgeting as if even though I was plastered against him, even though his flesh filled my mouth, it just wasn't close enough.

Releasing his skin, I pulled back, grabbed his waist, and lifted. Knowing what I was going to do, Arrow pushed up off the floor, wrapping his legs around my waist.

Backing away from the door, I carried him into the room to sink down on the couch. Arrow rocked, our hips ground together, and his teeth scraped over my earlobe. A few deep sounds vibrated in the back of my throat. I reached around, filling my palms with his ass as he rode me.

A pulled back, grabbed the neckline of my T-shirt, and yanked, revealing some of my chest. His lips moved over the bare skin, kissing as much of it as he could.

"I like the way you taste, Hopp." He spoke against my skin.

I took his face, lifting it so I could surge upright and attack his mouth once more. Our mouths collided like a ten-car pileup. Kissing and licking, biting and stroking each other until the furious way we were going at each other dissolved into something smoother. Our lips stopped coming back with fervor. Instead, everything changed into one long, languid kiss. We stayed locked together, lips rubbing in a continuous motion, tongues caressing endlessly.

Between us, our cocks were rock hard. The feel of his against my abs was deliciously sweet, but I didn't make a move to get more of it. Kissing him was enough just then. It was speaking without words; it was like reciting our wedding vows before we even got to the wedding.

My brain grew heavy, all thoughts weighed down with passion.

A low buzzing sound began in my ears. I gave myself up to the heaviness. To the deafness. I gave myself up completely and got lost in him.

Eventually, Arrow pulled away. Before sitting back completely, he licked my lower lip, then kissed the end of my nose.

No one had ever kissed the tip of my nose like that.

It made me smile.

As if he knew, he kissed me there again.

Between us, Arrow picked up my left hand, gently peeling back the white bandage. I watched him stare down at his name, which was now inked into my left ring finger.

I loved the rings; hell, they were my idea. But his face as he gazed at them? The barely-there caress of his thumb rubbing just above where his name now resided?

It was the thing about all of this I loved most.

"With this ring, I thee wed…" Arrow murmured quietly, still looking down.

Goose bumps traveled down my spine. The good kind.

"It's me and you, babe." Curling my fingers around his hand, I leaned down, kissing his fingers. "Love you."

"I love you, too." I watched him wrap the tattoo back up, taking care to do it just so. As I watched him, I noted a slight change.

"You hungry?" I half teased. "It's been a long day. We missed lunch."

"I'm good." He surprised me further by leaning in, lying against my chest, fitting his face into my neck.

Rubbing up and down his back, I frowned. "What's wrong?"

Reluctantly, he replied, "I got you a wedding present, too."

"Yeah? Why don't you seem too excited?"

"I'm not so sure you're gonna like it." He sat up, his deep-brown eyes wary.

Sitting forward, I cupped his cheek. Tenderness surged through my fingertips and brushed across his smooth skin. "I don't like that look, babe," I murmured. "You gotta know I'm gonna love anything you give me."

He half grimaced. "This is different, though… maybe not something I should have given you the night before our wedding."

I flashed a smile, my heart still squeezing with love. "You worried whatever it is might make me change my mind?"

His gaze skirted away.

My feet dropped off the coffee table. I sat all the way up, taking him with me. "Look at me."

His eyes obeyed.

I tried to look fierce. I tried to make sure the words I said translated not only through speech, but through my eyes. It was hard to look at him fiercely, though. It was hard to look at him with anything other than serious love.

"Nothing. And I mean absolutely *nothing* will ever make me change my mind." I lifted his left hand, giving it a slight squeeze. "With this ring, I thee wed."

His pouty lips curved upward. Interestingly enough, Arrow pulled out his cell and made a call of his own.

"Hi," he spoke quietly into the line. "We're here. Come on up." His stare met mine as he listened to whoever was on the other end. "I am, right now."

After ending he call, he climbed off my lap. I was kinda sorry to see him go.

I followed him over to the window overlooking the strip, wrapping my arms around him from behind.

"I keep going back and forth with the decision I made. Sometimes I think it's going to be good, and other times I wonder if I've just stuck my nose where I shouldn't."

My chin hit his shoulder. "Just tell me, babe."

"I called your mom. I invited her here… to our wedding."

I sucked in a breath. My hold around A's waist went stiff. His hand covered mine, pressing it against his chest like he was truly afraid I would shove away from him.

I was shocked. This was the last thing I ever would have expected.

Even so, I would never shove him away. Something like that would cut him deep, a cut I would never intentionally make.

"You miss your family. I know you think about them, think about calling, and I know you worry if they would even answer. Thing is…" His voice faded away.

Squeezing him a little tighter, I said, "Thing is?"

His head turned toward the sound of my voice. Without thought, I kissed his cheek. Arrow's hands gripped mine a little tighter.

"Thing is I know what it's like to not have many people. To feel alone, without family. To think I wouldn't have one ever again. I want better for you, Hopp. You have an entire family who loves the shit out of you. They accept you, and for that, you're lucky." He turned his head toward me again.

In his ear, I promised, "I'm listening, babe."

He nodded once. "I thought you might someday regret it if we got married and she wasn't here."

I blew out a shaky breath. "You called my mom."

"You still had her number in your phone."

I laughed lightly. I did still have her number. Even after all this time, I couldn't bring myself to get rid of it. "I'm surprised it still worked."

Arrow turned, placing his back to the window, and looked at me. I saw the knowledge in his eyes. He knew what I was afraid to say. What I was afraid to know.

"She cried," he told me. "As soon as I said your name and who I was… she started to cry. She's been waiting for you. Your whole family has. They've missed you."

My eyelids fell. Relief and something more pooled in my feet and began to rise, like the slow rise of a building flooding with water. Except I wasn't filling with water; I was flooding with emotion.

"She booked a flight while we were still on the phone." He grabbed my forearm. Just the feel of him soaked into my skin. He grounded my body, kept hold of all the feelings that tried to float away. "She couldn't get to you fast enough, Hopp. She wanted to come to our place, but I was afraid that would be too much. At least here in Vegas it's neutral territory."

Just knowing after all these years my mother still claimed me, still cared enough, even after I shunned her and all of them, made moisture gather in my eyes. The center of my chest was so tight and heavy, and even though I was apprehensive, I was also so fucking grateful.

My worst fear, the thing that kept me from picking up a phone these past few months, was the dread of rejection. Even though I was the one who ran, I was responsible for pushing them away, for isolating myself completely, if they turned me away, it would feel like losing them for a second time.

I wasn't good with loss… not at all. So I told myself it was for the best. Better for all of us if I just lay in the bed I made and didn't attempt to call. I had Arrow now; he was enough. He would always be enough.

Arrow didn't accept that. *He wanted better for me.*

Bless him. Every single thing about him.

Without a word, I shot forward, grabbing him hard, yanking him against me. Our bodies crashed together, and my arms tightened around him until they trembled with effort. Or maybe they quivered because my body was trying to say what my tongue could not.

Embracing me, Arrow didn't shy away from the strength with which I held him. After a few moments, he asked, "So does this mean you aren't pissed? We still getting married tomorrow?"

I made a gruff sound, pulling back from him. I grasped his jaw, holding it so I could stare into his face. "In my heart, we're already married, babe. Tomorrow is just details. I'll be there. There's nowhere else on this planet I would rather be."

Relief flooded his face.

There was a tentative knock on the hotel room door. I felt my eyes widen, looking to him for help. "Is that her?"

Arrow grasped the front of my T-shirt. "Breathe," he instructed. I sucked in a loud, sloppy breath. His lips twitched. "That's her. You still haven't told me if you want this."

Glancing around at the door, then back, I felt my fingers shake. "I'm nervous."

"I know."

With more bravado than I felt, I made a choice. "I want to see her."

Like a lover who truly cared, Arrow smoothed out my shirt, pushed the hair off my forehead, and ruffled the hair at the back of my neck. Before leaving me and stepping to the door, his gaze latched on mine. "I love you."

"I love you," I echoed.

The sticky feeling of my palms was gross, and I was rubbing them up and down on the fabric of my shorts when Arrow yanked open the door.

Because of where I was in the room and the way the door opened into the suite, I couldn't see her. Just the fact that Arrow could affected me.

Even though my eyes didn't touch over her features just yet, I still saw her through the lines of Arrow's shoulders, the tilt of his head. He was smiling at her.

Maybe not the kind of full-on smile he gave me, but it was a smile. I sensed it. I felt it.

"Is he here?" A voice so familiar reached into the room. The tone was like a punch to the gut. Quick memories flashed over me. Her calling up the stairs for me to come down to dinner. Yelling off the front porch when it was time to come inside.

It hurt. God, it fucking hurt.

But even with the pain, my eyes sought her out, waited to see if she looked the same. If the fact that I'd been gone all these years would echo in her eyes, if it would create some sort of chasm between us that I never knew before.

Arrow nodded, saying something so softly I couldn't make out the words.

Charged silence filled the room, but no one moved. Then sluggishly, as if everything was forced into slow motion, Arrow stepped back. The hand holding the door pushed so he could invite her inside.

She burst in the room like a prisoner who had finally been unchained. I stood physically frozen, but everything inside me was like a storm. Wildly, she gazed around, seeking me, until finally I was found.

"*Jayson.*" She said it as if I were revered. Like her longstanding prayer had finally been answered.

Just like the storm inside me, she blew across the room as fast as her still freakishly small feet would go.

Just before wrapping me in a hug, her body halted. Sweeping her eyes over me with one long glance, she hesitated for a moment, as if she wasn't sure what she should do. The sound of the door clicking closed jarred her. My mom swept forward again and wrapped her arms around me.

She smells exactly the same. A rush of familiarity enveloped me. With it came even more flashes of memories. Of feelings.

It was the feelings that were the hardest to recall.

All the things I ran from. All the reasons I hid came flooding back.

In a strange way, it was like recalling a movie, a film about someone who wasn't me. About another man who was so different from me.

Yet somehow eerily the same.

Her hug reminded me of that most of all.

Still standing stock still, my arms at my sides, my mother hugged me tight. Sniffling against my shirt, then rubbing her likely running nose against the fabric.

Fondness—no, *love* choked me.

I swallowed, desperately seeking Arrow, who was standing near the door. Just seeing him there calmed me. Reminded me who I'd been was okay because it led me to where I was now.

He smiled slightly, more of an encouraging expression.

I was able to move again. Lifting my arms, I hugged my mom. She started crying just a little harder, wiping her nose on my shirt again.

"It's all right, Mom." I promised, still gazing at A. "Everything is fine now."

In that moment, the guy I was just remembering and the man I was right then somehow merged together. We didn't fit exactly, but it was close enough.

And the promise I'd just made her hadn't been empty, comforting words. The words were genuine. I meant them.

Now everything *was* fine.

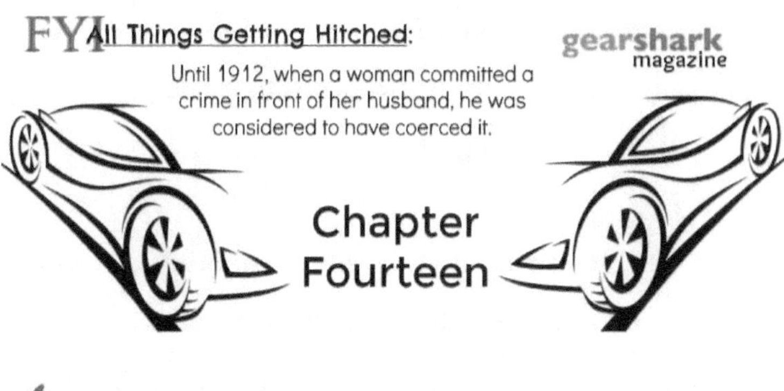

You know how sometimes those talk shows on TV played reunions of long-lost twins or of a child with their birth parent they'd never met?

People got choked up about that stuff all the time.

I admit one time I got choked up, too. It was some story with a puppy. I'd rather not go into detail about. You know, 'cause my emotions were already fucking all over the place.

Anyway, my point is usually that shit didn't hit me with the feels like most people. I was too jaded, you know? I knew after the cameras shut down, real life began. The people who were reunited were left staring at a stranger they were supposed to have some deep, knowing connection with. The questions would start, and a lot of times, the answers created friction.

But this? Seeing Hopper with his mother right now?

Let me just say it was probably good there wasn't a puppy in here also, because my man card would be incinerated and I'd be excusing myself to the bathroom for a wad of tissues.

Thank all the lights on the strip tonight Hopp wasn't beyond pissed at my meddling. My stomach was still in knots over it, over how bad it could have gone.

'Course, they'd barely said two words. They were still hugging. His mom looked small against him. She didn't even come to his shoulders. How a woman that small gave birth to a man as big as Hopp I would never quite understand.

She was thin, but not the kind of thin that made her seem fragile. By no means was she underweight. She was just small. Probably around five feet tall with a soft build. She was wearing a dress in a fabric with flowers on it, and it floated around her. Her hair was dark like Hopp's, cut short to just about her chin. And it had some curl to it. Oddly, it was that curl that made me like her the second I saw her.

Maybe because it reminded me of him, and anything that reminded me of Hopper would always be okay in my book.

Finally, she pulled back but didn't pull her hands away. I understood that. She was afraid if she let go, he might disappear.

"Oh, look at you," she crooned, cupping the side of his face. "You have a beard and your hair is longer. But you're just as handsome as ever."

He smiled down at her, fondness in his gaze. "You got snot all over my shirt, Mom."

She laughed and hugged him again.

"And where did all your hair go?" He wondered.

She pulled back and fussed with the short strands. "I cut it off. Life's too short to try and brush out this mess every day."

The mention of a short life brought a slight change over Hopp. I fought the urge to go to him. Curling my fingers into my palms, I forced my body in place. He needed to do this, no matter how much I wanted to rush over there and insert myself in front of him like a shield.

His mom pulled back. "I didn't mean—"

"It's fine, Mom." Hopper cut her off. Gesturing toward the couch, he said, "Have a seat."

"I'll, uh, give you two some space." I offered, preparing to leave.

"No," Hopper rushed out. "Stay."

I hesitated, unsure what to do. His mother probably wanted time alone with him. She likely didn't want a stranger in the room while she was seeing her son for the first time in almost six years.

Hopper held out his arm, fingers outstretched for mine. I couldn't deny that. I wouldn't. His mom would have to get over me being here.

When I made it to his side, he linked our fingers together. I had to admit I was surprised. I guess I expected the affection we showed each other all the time might not be so forthcoming in front of parents.

I certainly didn't have the best of luck in that department.

"Mom, this is Arrow. He's my husband."

Warmth suffused my skin, crawled up the back of my neck, and wrapped around my chest. Sure, we let everyone think we were already married this morning. But this was the first time Hopp ever introduced me to anyone as his husband.

I liked it. I liked it so much.

"Yes, we spoke on the phone a few times." She nodded. To my surprise, she came forward, wrapping her arms around me in a tight hug. I hugged her back with one arm, as my other hand was still being held by my *husband*.

"I've seen your picture in the magazines and on the sports channel of course," she said, pulling back. "But you are even handsomer in person."

"Thank you," I said. Because what else was I supposed to say?

Unexpectedly, she hugged me again. "Thank you for bringing my son home," she said against me.

I glanced at Hopper. He smiled.

"Sit, sit!" She fussed at us, waving her hand. "I want to know all about you both. Where you met. How long you've been together. Where's the wedding?"

Now it was my turn to be overwhelmed. I mean, just like that? Just like that, she accepted me. She accepted I was marrying her son… another man?

There wasn't an ounce of anger, disgust, or even disappointment around her. It was as if she truly didn't care. Her eyes clung to Hopper as if he were a priceless piece of art that had just been uncovered. Her eyes were blue, just like his, but hers glistened with tears.

"That's really what you want to know most?" Hopper asked, his voice dropping.

She sighed and moved from the chair over to the couch, perching right beside Hopp so he was in the middle. "All I need to know is that you're happy. That you're doing well. It's all we've ever wanted. We just want you to be happy, Jayson."

She was a saint. This woman was a bona-fide saint.

Hopper's voice was apprehensive, a little low. "How is Dad?"

Her eyes slid to me, as if she were guilty of something.

I frowned.

"He's here," she admitted.

Her eyes were pleading when she looked back at me. "I know you just wanted me to come, and I totally understand that. The last thing I want to do is overwhelm Jayson, but my husband…" She looked at Hopp. "Your father, he refused to stay home. You know how stubborn he can be." She brushed at the newly falling tears. "He's missed you so much."

"It's okay, ma'am," I said, trying to make her feel better.

"Linda," Hopper corrected. "She's not a ma'am."

"I beg your pardon!" She gasped, smacking Hopper on the leg. Then she turned to me and winked. "He's right. I'm not. Linda is my name, but you can't call me that."

"Mom," Hopper said, his voice hard.

I wasn't really offended. I expected as much. Besides, I wasn't here for her acceptance. I was here for Hopper.

She shushed him, which, frankly, was pretty amusing. Turning to me, she said, "Just call me Mom."

My breath caught for a moment, as if my own brain forgot how to breathe. "Just like that?" I rasped after a second.

Reaching forward, she gave my hand a squeeze. "Of course, we're family now. You're my son."

I was rendered speechless. My mind was blank. I had no idea what to think or feel.

Hopper knew. Bringing my hand into his lap, he covered our clasped ones with his free hand.

"Dad's here, too?" he asked, bringing the conversation back to him.

"He's in the hall."

Hopper tensed slightly. "Let him in."

Linda (I still had to get used to the idea of calling her mom) rushed across the room and flung open the door. A man as big as Hopper filled the doorway.

He had gray hair, blue eyes, and basically looked like an older version of his son.

"Dad." Hopp got to his feet. I did the same 'cause it was rude to just sit there. Tension radiated off him, and it put me on the defensive. I knew firsthand what fathers could be like. Just because his mom seemed to readily accept me didn't mean this man would.

His father's footfalls were heavy across the carpet. He kept his eyes locked on his son as he moved. Without any hesitation, he grabbed Hopper by the shoulder and jerked him against his body, folding him in a hug.

"So proud of you, son. So glad to have you back."

Oddly, this father's obvious love was hard for me to swallow. It was a cold, hard reminder of something I would never, ever have.

Unabashedly, Hopper hugged his father back. They embraced longer than I expected…

Hell. Everything about all of this was unexpected.

These were good people. Possibly better than any I'd ever met. It made all the second thoughts I had about calling them disappear.

Finally, he released Hopper… and reached for me. Before I knew what was happening, I was being hugged by this man.

When he pulled back, he slapped me on the shoulder. "Call me John for now. When you're ready, you can call me Dad."

I jerked as if he'd smacked me. I didn't mean it. In fact, the reaction made guilt slam me hard. "I'm sorry," I rushed out, not even sure what I was sorry for.

Hopper's arm came around my waist, tugging me against his side. "It's okay, A." Then to his father, he said, "Arrow isn't used to family who likes each other."

John made a sound. "You'll get used to us, son," he said, like it wasn't a big deal. Then he sat down in the nearby chair. "You ain't seen nothing yet."

Linda laughed. "Don't scare him, John!"

"He drives a race car for a living, Lin! He ain't scared."

I was kinda scared.

Hopper chuckled. The tip of his nose brushed against my cheek, and then his lips pressed against my skin.

My eyes closed briefly. Then I remembered we weren't alone. I shot a look at both his parents, but they were just arguing over how scared I really was.

Everything inside me relaxed.

It was going to be okay.

"Better have a seat, son," John told Hopper. "You have six years of catching up to do."

Tugging me with him, Hopp sat down on the couch.

Linda squished right up against him, sniffling.

"How's everyone… at home?" he asked.

"Excited as hell to see you," John replied. Linda made a sound and nodded. "Your sisters have nearly an entire notebook of questions they want to ask you."

Hopper groaned. "I'm glad you left them home."

"They're gonna love you," Linda told me. "All that blond hair."

"It's just like I never left," Hopper mused suddenly, his voice faraway.

I turned toward him, wondering if I was going to need to bring him back. Make sure he stayed right here with me.

"No," Linda said quietly, drawing both mine and Hopp's stares. "Things are very different now. But there is one thing that stayed the same. One thing that will never change."

"Now you listen to your mother," John chimed in.

Linda nodded sagely. "You're our son and we love you."

Hopper reached for her hand, and she gave it. "Thank you for coming," he whispered.

"Nowhere we'd rather be." Her voice was sincere. After clearing her throat, she spoke again. "Now tell us all about your new life."

And so we did.

Chapter Fifteen

Sometimes life surprises you.

In bad ways, but also in good.

Most people would likely say the good and the bad balance each other out, but not me. I don't really know what the balance would be for death—except, of course, life.

But life and death are so intertwined it's hard to keep them separate.

Hell, it's easy to pick a word compliment: Life: Death. Happiness: Sorrow. Small: Large.

But picking words that are opposite each other is a whole lot easier than drawing a line between feelings.

All I really knew was kind of cliché.

I once was lost, but now I was found.

Found by love. By death. By life. Being found is profoundly better than being lost.

My family was back in my life, and though we were different, my mom was right. Our love was still the same. I wasn't scared of love anymore.

Yeah, I was scared of losing it. I always would be. However, I was more afraid of not loving at all.

We had dinner in the room, me, Arrow, and my parents. Sometimes the silence was a little awkward, but that was to be expected. We talked a little about Matt, about what happened and how I ran. How they wished I hadn't.

I didn't apologize, because the truth was I wasn't sorry. I did what I had to do. If I hadn't run, I might never have found Arrow. If I hadn't gotten lost, he never would have found me.

Mostly, though, we talked about my job, Gamble, and racing. We talked about our wedding, and Arrow sat there secretly enthralled that my parents loved him from the second they stepped in our room.

Well, it wasn't a secret to me. Obviously. But I for sure didn't call him out on it.

As we were finishing dinner, Joey and Lorhaven knocked on the door. Turns out they knew my parents were in town. They'd already met. Joey said she was anxious to see how things were going, but I knew just by one look it was Lorhaven who really wanted to do some checking.

He needed to see for himself my parents were treating Arrow the way he deserved. I respected that.

Mom cried when dad pulled her out of the room. They bickered all the way to the elevator about how I needed sleep since I was getting married tomorrow.

They hadn't changed a bit. Except for some wrinkles and some gray hairs. It was a little unsettling because I felt so different.

"C'mon, Arrow. Let's go," Joey said the second I let myself back in the room.

I was instantly alert. "Go where?"

She made a rude sound. "You can't stay in the same room tonight," she announced. "You can't see each other until the wedding."

"No," Arrow and I both declared at the same time.

Lorhaven barked a laugh. "Told ya," he ribbed Joey.

She gave him a sly look, then turned to us. "It's tradition."

"Look at us," Arrow quipped. "Is anything about us traditional?"

Joey's chin jutted out. "It's bad luck."

"It's stupid," I argued.

She crossed her arms over her chest, turning sad eyes on Arrow. "You would deny your *only* sister this?"

I guffawed. That shit wasn't gonna work.

Arrow sighed.

"Hey!" I protested. That shit wasn't supposed to work! "No way."

Glancing at me, Arrow's eyes were torn.

Well, hairy goat balls. I wasn't about to put him in this position. Caught between me and Joey. She was important to him. Family who took him in when he didn't have any.

"Fine." I sighed.

Joey grinned triumphantly, turning to Arrow. "You can stay in our suite tonight. The couch is big."

Arrow moved toward me, but Joey intercepted him. "Save it for tomorrow."

As she led him from the room, I watched him go with equal parts horror and resignation. It was going to be a long fucking night.

"See ya in the a.m.," Lorhaven drawled.

It sounded stupid, but as A got on the elevator, an empty feeling cramped up my stomach.

I took a shower, put the room service outside in the hall, flipped through the channels on TV, and then finally gave up and went into the bedroom.

Thoughts set in.

To say today had been overloaded was an understatement. The interview, photoshoot, tattoos, and my parents… It felt like an entire year crammed into several hours.

Now that I was alone, the room was dark and quiet, and everything kinda hit me all at once.

Shoving off the blankets, I catapulted out of bed and wandered to the window. The strip was all lit up, people milling about.

There was a rock in my stomach, an unsettled feeling knocking around beneath my skin. My hand slapped against the window, a flash of white catching my eye.

Looking over, I saw the bandage still wrapped around my new tattoo.

A wedding band. A name.

My entire life.

Spinning away from the window, I practically marched to the door. It banged against the wall when I flung it open, surging out of the room. Intent on my mission, it took a second to register someone moving down the hall toward me.

We both stopped. Stared.

Arrow was barefoot, without a shirt. His hair was rumpled as if he'd been running his hands through it, a gesture he did when he was restless.

I was reminded of the first night we spent in our apartment, back when it was just his. I tried to stay at my place that night… and we both ended up in the hall, searching out the other.

I held out my hand. Arrow slid his home.

Saying nothing, we went back into our room, closing the door behind us.

"You doing okay?" he asked. He was worried about me.

"I'm much better now."

With an ornery grin, he confessed, "I snuck out."

"I was about to burst in the room and kidnap you," I said, returning his smile.

"I'll have to sneak back in the morning."

"You're here now." Lifting his arm, I kissed the back of his hand.

"Let's go to bed, Hopp," he murmured, pulling me with him as he walked.

"I'll go anywhere with you, babe."

"Oh, c'mon!" A familiar but highly annoyed voice intruded on my sleep.

Cracking one eye open, I glanced toward the exclamation. Joey was standing over me, glowering down.

"Ahh!" I yelled, jerking upright. Grappling for the covers, which were grossly tangled around my and Hopper's legs, only made me more alarmed. The outburst got an immediate reaction from Hopp. It was as if he hadn't heard Joey at all, just me freaking out.

His body jerked up, his arm automatically whipping out in front of me like a shield. "What the fuck?" he bellowed, his voice still thick with sleep.

"Down, boy," Joey muttered. "It's me."

Hopper blinked at her, glanced at me to make sure I was fine, then dropped back onto the mattress like nothing even happened.

"Holy shit, Joey! How did you get in here?" I exclaimed, not feeling the same lax attitude toward this situation as my lover.

Muffled laughter from the other room floated through the door.

Oh my God! My brother was there, too.

She didn't seem to think there was anything wrong with breaking into our hotel room, storming into the bedroom, and staring down at us while we were in bed.

Jesus Criminy, we were practically naked.

I shot forward. This time it was me who flung an arm out over Hopper. He *was* naked! Forgetting about covering myself, I piled the thick, white comforter on top of him so only the top of his dark head was visible.

Joey didn't seem to care I was freaking the fuck out at her creepy lurking. Her hands were planted on her hips, her dark curls wild around her shoulders. The green of her eyes fired flames at me. "You snuck out of our room last night! You aren't supposed to be in here."

"I'm pretty sure it's you who isn't supposed to be in here," I pointed out, gesturing to the fact I was in bed—in my drawers and nothing else.

With a very dry, matter-of-fact tone, she retorted, "Oh, please. You don't have anything I haven't seen before."

"You better not have," Hopper rumbled, a mere voice beneath a cloud.

I grinned. Well, it was about time something about this got some sort of grumble out of him.

Joey rolled her eyes.

"Sorry, Joey. I meant to sneak back into the room, but I didn't wake up." I apologized, squishing closer to Hopp, trying to cover some of my skin. I mean, really, it wasn't a big deal, but she was my sister and I was in bed with my husband.

My husband. I was getting married today.

"Actually…" I corrected. "I'm not really sorry."

The edge of the white blankets popped up, and Hopper's arm snaked out, wrapping around my waist and pulling me close. When I was right up against him, he snatched the edge of the covers, yanking them over us like we were in a tent. Now she couldn't see us at all.

"Go away!" he growled.

"You have five minutes!" she swore. "If you aren't out, I'll be forced to come in after you!"

"Jace!" I yelled. Surely he wouldn't let his woman just climb into bed with two other dudes.

"Whatever," she muttered, her voice retreating. "Five minutes!" she yelled again. The sound of the bedroom door closing was kind of like an angel singing.

Hopp and I looked at each other beneath the blankets; neither of us bothered to push them back down. We liked it under there. I liked being anywhere alone with him.

"She will seriously try and get in this bed with us." Hopper warned.

I kissed him. Under the covers like this, the air was hot and thick, almost suffocating. Stroking my tongue over his, our mouths folded together, our limbs intertwined, and the blankets over our bodies felt heavy.

His thick, hard cock pressed against my stomach, rubbing against it as we kissed. Horniness buzzed beneath my skin.

Groaning, Hopper pulled back. "It's a good day to get married."

"A good fucking day." I agreed.

"You're going to be late for your own wedding!" Joey yelled through the door.

"We're coming!" Hopper called back. His head hit the pillow with a grunt. "Tomboy my ass. She's loving being in charge of this."

"Girls do like weddings." I agreed.

His fingers dragged through my hair, pushing against the back of my head to bring me closer. "How about you, babe? You like weddings?"

"Just ours," I whispered.

Hopper pressed his forehead to mine and groaned. "We have to get up."

"I'll find you some pants."

The feel of our joyous moments in our "homemade tent" that morning carried me through the rest of the morning and afternoon.

The ceremony wasn't until later that evening, but holy shit balls, did Joey keep us busy.

And separate.

Frankly, it made me surly. The only thing that made it better was when I snuck off to text him. Until she took my damn phone.

I loved my sister, but I was about to go ape shit.

The whole time I showered—in Jace's suite—I wondered if Hopp was a floor up doing the same. I thought of how the soap coasted over his hard body, making his skin slippery and slick. I remembered the night at Gamble's in that giant-ass shower.

I was making a bucket list. Right here. Right now.

The first thing was getting a giant-ass shower like that, because shower sex with Hopper was mind blowing.

I thought about it a few more minutes. When I came out of the practical fantasy playing in my mind, my hand was wrapped around my own dick. It felt good, but it wasn't my hand I wanted. No one—not even me—was a match for Hopper. With a heavy and annoyed sigh, I released myself and promised my cock it would see Hopp later.

Once I was out of the shower and my cock was no longer searching for my guy, I stepped out of the bathroom to find Jace in the bedroom.

"Took your sweet ass time in there," he quipped, taking in the towel wrapped around my waist.

"I was hiding from Joey."

He laughed. "Why do you think I'm in here waiting for you?"

"She bossing you around, too?" I asked.

He chuckled like he thought she was cute. "She tries."

"Where is she?" I whispered and looked at the door.

Around a toothy smile, he said, "She's upstairs bugging Hopper."

Grabbing the duffle I took from our room earlier, when Joey informed me I wasn't allowed back there, I rummaged around for a pair of boxers.

"I brought your suit," Jace said, gesturing toward a garment bag hanging nearby.

"Sweet, thanks." I barely glanced at the bag. I'd seen the outfit several times, including this morning when Joey insisted I try on the jacket one last time to make sure the tailor did it perfectly. I already knew he did. She'd dragged me to the shop to be fitted, then again when it was done.

I didn't bother reminding her of that this morning, though. I just put it on and made her happy.

"So…" I began, abandoning all the shit I'd just pulled out of my bag and turning toward my brother. "She seems in her element planning this wedding,"

Jace made a sound. "Thanks for letting her be so involved. It means a lot to her, to have a bigger family now."

I nodded. I totally understood. "Me, too."

Lorhaven sat on the giant bed he and Joey shared. "Speaking of. Were Hopper's parents good to you?"

I tilted my head to the side. "You came up and saw them. You know they're good people."

He nodded. "But were they good to *you*."

That was my brother. He couldn't care less if Hopper's parents were saints. He only cared if they were nice to me.

"They were great," I said. "It was strange." I hesitated. "You know, to have people accept me instantly."

"Donna and I accepted you instantly, A." He glowered.

I rolled my eyes. "You know what I mean."

He rubbed a hand over his jaw. "Yeah. I do."

"I think they're going to be around a lot. Hopper seemed really glad to have them back in his life. He wasn't pissed I invited his mom here."

Lorhaven smiled ruefully. "He was probably too shocked to be pissed."

He'd been shocked all right. But even so, his loyalty to me came before that. He was so good to me, so much better than I honestly thought I'd ever have.

"I still didn't tell him about Seattle," I murmured, more or less thinking out loud. "I was going to today, but your girlfriend is being a Nazi."

Jace barked a laugh. "Who knew she would be such a bridezilla? And not even with her own wedding."

"Speaking of… What about you, bro? Why haven't you put a ring on it?"

"What is this, a rap song?" he quipped.

"You like rap," I pointed out.

He sighed. "I'm working on it."

A smile split my face. "Yeah? About time!"

"Shit, everyone acts like we've been together ten years. It's only been one. Joey and I might like speed, but this ain't something I'm rushing. I'm keeping her, and I'm not going to let anything ruin it."

I pondered that a second. Somehow his words hit something inside me, as if he were no longer speaking about his own relationship, but mine. "You think Hopp and I are moving too fast?"

Lorhaven shoved off the bed and came forward, his eyes serious. "If I thought you and Hopper were moving too fast, I never would have given him my blessing."

I smiled, thinking of that and how it must have gone down. "I can't believe he asked you," I mused.

"Fucker better have." Jace glowered. Then he relented. "It earned my respect."

"Thank you, Jace," I said sincerely.

His mouth drew up, puzzled.

"For accepting me for who I am. For accepting Hopper and not making it weird. You've always had my back. You've been the most important person in my life for a long time. I know it can't be easy to, umm…"

"Get shoved out of the way for a piece of ass?" he joked.

I punched him in the stomach, but only hard enough to make him wheeze a little. "I'm not shoving you aside, fucker," I insisted. "And Hopp isn't a piece of ass."

"I know." He hackled, rubbing at his midsection.

"I was going to say to make room for someone else. I know it was hard with our age difference, my past… what went down with Joey."

"It's all water under the bridge."

I nodded. "Point is I made it here because of you. Without you…" My voice fell away. It was hard to open up so much, hard to articulate to him just how much he meant to me. Especially when that someone was my brother who liked everyone to believe he didn't have feelings.

His hand fell onto my shoulder, squeezing. "I know."

I glanced up. "There's no one else I'd rather have standing next to me today."

"Nowhere else I'd rather be, little brother."

I let the *little* brother thing slide just this once. I gave him a quick hug but then pulled back because, well, I was only wearing a towel.

I glanced away, back at my clothes, trying to shove back all the emotion rising inside me.

Jace cleared his throat. I looked up, my eyes widening.

He was holding a square, black velvet box between us. "Think she'll like this?"

I snatched it out of his grip and popped it open. Glancing between him and what was inside, I blew out a whistle. "Well, if she doesn't like it, you can always take it back and buy a *small country* instead."

He crossed his arms over his chest. "I'm not giving my girl a puny diamond."

"Well, it definitely ain't puny." I agreed and shut the lid before I breathed on it or something. God, that rock had to be worth a fortune.

After tucking it back into his pants, he asked, "Is it too much?"

I laughed. "Is that actual self-doubt coming from the all-powerful Lorhaven?"

"Fuck you."

I laughed some more. He turned surlier by the second. I rather enjoyed it. When I was done making fun of him, I put him out of his misery. "It's awesome. She's gonna love it, Jace."

He swallowed like there was a canary in his throat and it was fighting against him, trying to get out.

"Something tells me we aren't going to get away with an elopement like you and Hopper."

I snorted. "Ron Gamble wouldn't allow his only daughter to elope, and we both know it."

"Who cares? Long as Joey is happy."

"That's the thing." He worried. "This whole time she's been planning your wedding, she's gone on and on about how sweet it is. How intimate. How romantic. A giant, high-society wedding isn't her thing."

I saw his point. "And you think Joey will sacrifice what she wants to make her father happy."

"She has a history of doing just that," Lorhaven pointed out.

I thought it over a minute. "Yeah, but she has you now. And we both know you won't bow down to Ron Gamble."

"You have a point." He smiled.

"I'm happy for you, Lor. You picked a good one, and I'll be thrilled when you make her officially my sister."

"Look at us," he mused. "Making a family and shit."

"Think that ring will be on her finger by the time we get back from our honeymoon?"

"We'll see," he said, sly.

Out in the other room, the door to the suite open and closed. "C'mon, it's about time." Joey stopped and gasped when we came into sight. "Oh my God! Neither of you is dressed!"

"Sorry, baby. Lost track of time," Jace replied, sheepish.

"How's Hopp?" I asked, glancing around for signs of my phone.

"Hopper is fine. He's dressed and ready. Unlike *some* people."

"You're not dressed either," I pointed out.

She threw her hands up in the air. Her curls were already pulled up in some kind of style on top of her head, with a few loose tendrils coiling against her neck.

"Well, maybe I would have time to get dressed if my family didn't consist of a bunch of boneheaded men!"

Jace stepped past me, giving me a shove. "Don't sass your sister or I'll kick your ass."

"You're not dressed either, Jace," Joey growled.

My brother was hardly intimidated. Either he knew she was just talk, or he actually liked it when she bit. I was guessing the former. Grasping her face in his hands, he ducked down and kissed her. "I need help getting dressed."

She made a sound but went in for another kiss. "You need help putting on pants?"

"Hey." He drew back. "You're the one making me wear a monkey suit. Not even Arrow has to wear one."

She shrugged. "I wanted to see you in a tux. You'll look hot."

"I'd tell you to get a room," I grumbled, "but since we're standing in it, I guess I can't."

Joey laughed lightly, then sighed, peeked around my brother.

"Bring your clothes out here. There's a big mirror. Jace and I will change in the bedroom and be out in a few."

"Fine, but if you two start getting it on in here, I'm leaving and finding Hopp."

She made a sound of impatience. "I'm not going to do anything to mess up this face! Do you know how long makeup takes to put on?"

"Yes." We both groaned.

"We were here while you were putting it on earlier," I added.

Hours. Like seriously. She held me hostage away from my guy for hours while she put this weird contraption on her eyelashes and use about fifty different wands and brushes to do God knew what.

Scowling, Joey marched into the room, grabbing the garment bag and a box of shoes, carrying them out into the suite. "Get dressed," she ordered. Then she held up her hand. "Don't drop that towel yet."

I stifled a laugh when she disappeared and came back with a hairdryer and a brush. "Dry your hair and try to tame it, would you? You can't get married looking like a Muppet."

I gasped. "That you would think so low of me!"

Jace laughed.

She started marching away, toward the bedroom.

"Can I drop my towel yet?" I yelled after her.

"I'm going to kick you in the balls!" she yelled back.

Jace and I grinned at each other before he followed her in the bedroom and slid the door shut.

Chuckling, I swung back around to my stuff, but my eyes strayed to the hotel landline. I was just picking up the receiver when the door slid open again.

Joey stood there with her hands over her eyes like she was afraid I really had dropped the towel. "Do not even think about using that phone!" she ordered.

"How did you know?" I whined.

"We're due at the hotel in like forty minutes. Just get dressed."

"I feel bad for my future nieces and nephews," I complained. "They're not going to get away with anything."

Beneath her hands, she smiled sort of wistfully, then slid the door closed, leaving me alone once more.

The first thing I did was blast my hair with the hairdryer and try to make it look the least "Muppet" I could. That meant I used a brush when drying it.

After that, I unzipped the garment bag so I could get dressed.

I wasn't wearing a tux or even a traditional suit. I wasn't really a traditional guy. We didn't want something too fancy or stuffy. This was Vegas after all. We cared more about just getting married than what we looked like while doing it.

'Course, Joey cared. But her ideas for what I should wear were pretty cool, so I went with it.

The dress pants weren't really my usual style, meaning they weren't jeans, they weren't ripped, and they weren't baggy.

These pants were what the tailor called modern. Made out of a dark-gray material, they were fitted… like practically skinny jeans. They were also kinda short in length, so part of my ankle would be exposed once I had on my shoes. I wasn't sold on them, but Joey loved them, said I had a good body for the style, and she'd never met any other guy who could rock pants like these except dudes in fashion magazines.

After I had those on, I pulled on a fitted white dress shirt and thanked God she wasn't making me wear a tie. Leaving the top two buttons undone, I tucked it into my pants, belted them, and reached for the shoebox.

The shoes were my favorite part of my wedding attire.

Everyone knew I loved a good pair of sneakers, specifically high-tops. Joey knew she was pushing me with the pants, so when she mentioned this style would look good with sneakers, I agreed.

Grabbing the brand-new pair of Adidas, I slid my feet inside and laced them up. The shoes were stark white, almost blinding white, with a rounded toe. The tongue was a little big and it stuck out above the laces once they were tied.

They weren't high-tops, but they were sweet. I was definitely going to have to get some more of these.

Next, I reached for the jacket. It was royal blue, fitted, and made of velvet. I liked the color; it was vibrant, but not over the top. I felt like me when I stood back and gazed in the mirror at everything all together.

It was modern, but it was pulled together and nice enough for a casual wedding.

Running my hand through the blond strands of my hair, I adjusted the jacket once more as butterflies began fluttering around in my stomach.

I anticipated seeing Hopper. I knew I'd just seen him this morning, but it was hours ago. I missed his face. I missed his presence. I wanted to hold his hand and look at my rings on his finger. I couldn't wait to marry him.

Lorhaven knocked on the door before sliding it open. I spun from the mirror, and my face split into a huge grin.

"Shut up," he muttered, pulling at the tie.

He was wearing a traditional black and white tux.

"You look like a penguin," I cracked.

Joey appeared seconds later, attaching an earring in her ear. "Leave him alone, Arrow. He looks sexy."

I snickered, but she gasped and rushed over. "It's perfect!" She turned to Jace. "Doesn't he look perfect?"

"How come he doesn't have to wear a tie and gets sneakers?" Jace complained.

She ignored him, turning back to me. Grabbing the lapels on the velvet jacket, she gave them a tug, then smoothed them out. Sniffling, her made-up green eyes connected with mine. "You look so amazing. I'm so happy for you."

I tugged her against me for a hug, wrapping both arms around her back. "Thanks for everything," I whispered.

She jerked back, swatting me. "Don't make me cry." I tried not to laugh as she fanned her eyes, trying to dry the forming tears.

"You look pretty amazing yourself," I told her.

"Sexy as hell," Jace half growled.

She smiled and did a little turn. "It's not every day your brother gets married."

Joey was dressed in a silver dress that hugged her curvy body like an ace bandage. It was short, ending at mid-thigh, and did this crisscross thing around her neck, leaving her shoulders bare. Her legs looked even longer than usual because the black stilettos on her feet had to be at least five inches.

Her hair was still pulled up, her makeup still on, with what looked like a new coat of something on her lips because they were shinier than before.

"One thing," she said, walking over to a small bag and pulling out something square. On her way back to me, she folded it, then tucked it into the pocket on my jacket. "There," she said, standing back to admire her work. "Perfect."

Glancing around in the mirror, I looked at the handkerchief just poking out of the pocket. It looked like a checkered flag.

The hotel landline rang, and I stepped toward it. Joey practically hissed me back as she picked it up. "Hello?" She listened a moment. "Okay, thank you."

After hanging up, she turned to us. "Cars are downstairs. Time to go!"

"What about Hopp?" I asked.

"I'm going up to get him. I'll ride to the hotel with him. You ride with Jace."

I blew out a breath. It was silly to feel nervous, especially when I was about to get everything I ever wanted.

"See you there!" Joey exclaimed, then breezed out of the room. How anyone could breeze around in shoes that looked like hers I would never understand.

Lorhaven went to the door and pulled it open. "You ready for this?"

A wash of calm came over me. "I'm ready."

"All right then, little brother, let's go get you married."

The entire way through the hotel and to the limo waiting outside, I craned my neck for Hopp. He was nowhere to be seen. After settling back into the leather of the car, it glided away from the curb, toward the Aria Hotel, where we were getting married.

The next time I would see Hopper, we'd be standing at the altar.

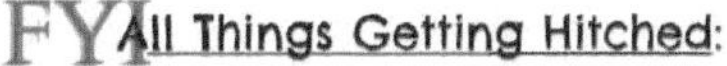

Chapter Seventeen

Hopper

I wasn't really sure what to expect when we basically gave Joey free rein to plan our elopement in Vegas. Hell, I wasn't even sure what I wanted in terms of a wedding. In all truth, I'd have been happy with one of those drive-thru chapels she forbade the second we announced a wedding.

I didn't care about the details. I only wanted him to be mine.

We knew the location of the wedding of course, the size, the casual feel… but when the limo pulled up to the Aria, I realized something. As I stared through the tinted windows, I realized it did matter where we said our vows, only because something that was so beautiful to me should take place in a beautiful place.

And man, this place was amazing. And this was just the outside.

Joey was sitting against the leather seat beside me, her long, tan legs crossed over the other, with a wicked-looking pair of shoes strapped to her feet.

"This place look as impressive on the inside?" I asked.

"It's better," she mused. "But you aren't getting married inside."

My brow wrinkled. I glanced around. "Okay, maybe I should have asked for more details."

She grinned, the wicked curve to her mouth matching her shoes. "Too late now."

The driver opened the door for us. Gamble, who was sitting opposite me, went first. "I'll meet you inside."

He was gone before I could even nod. Joey and I looked at each other, neither of us making a move to exit the limo.

I cleared my throat. I was bad at this stuff. Instead of speaking, I reached between us and linked our hands. "Thanks for everything, Joey. For not giving up on me even when I gave you every reason to."

"Family doesn't give up on each other."

"Thank you for considering me family."

She smiled, squeezing my hand. "Always, Jay."

"You're my best friend. My only friend until recent months," I admitted.

Her eyes glistened. "You're my best friend, too."

"I know I've let you down." I began. Why I chose this moment to bring up all the shit with the hazing, what happened to her under my management, and how we ended up not speaking for a while I wasn't sure. I just knew I needed to get it out before I got married. Suddenly, she felt like the final loose end in my life. I couldn't have any loose ends anymore. I was tying a bow.

"We haven't talked about that because we don't need to," she said gently, turning a little more toward me. "I was too stubborn and proud to tell anyone, and you were too lost in your own head to see."

"I should have been there."

"You were there. I just pushed everyone away. You know about that."

I made a sound. "I do."

"Everything turned out the way it should have. I'm happy. You're happy. And we get to be family forever."

Wrapping my arms around her, I pulled her close for a hug. "If you ever need anything, anything at all, come to me. I'm here for you."

Pulling back, she sniffled. "Don't make me ruin my makeup, Jay!"

I chuckled. "Thanks for being my best lady today."

That got me a smile. "Nothing else is traditional about this wedding, so why shouldn't your best man be a woman?"

"You're way better looking than any best man I've ever seen."

"C'mon." She pushed on my shoulder. "We have a wedding to attend."

"Wait," I said, pulling out a square white box with a black bow. "I have something for you."

Surprise lit her green eyes. Her hands hovered between us when I held it out. "This is for me?"

I nodded. "A thank you for everything you've done. For putting up with me. For being you."

"Oh, so it's a million dollars, because that's how much I deserve for dealing with you." She teased.

I felt my eyes crinkle at the corners. "It definitely isn't a gift that equals your worth, but I hope you like it anyway."

Taking the box, she pulled it close, untied the ribbon, and opened the lid. Her small intake of breath was sort of like my sigh of relief.

Do you know how hard girls are to shop for? Especially when it's your best friend, she's totally rich, and is kinda a tomboy. But hell, you wouldn't know that by looking at her tonight. Tonight, Joey was all woman.

"Oh my God," she breathed out, dropping the lid of the box into the seat.

"It's from me and Arrow," I clarified, wanting to make sure she knew it was from both of us.

Her fingertips caressed the white gold, crystals, and diamonds. "This is absolutely stunning." Her eyes came up to mine. "I was totally kidding about the million dollars, Jay. This is too much."

I was quick to smile. "Relax, it wasn't anywhere near a mil."

"But the diamonds alone…"

It was a wide cuff bracelet made of white gold with a cut-out design. The cuts were all framed out with Swarovski crystals, which seriously sparkled better than a lot of diamonds I'd seen. As an added bonus, there were larger yellow crystals throughout the design nestled between some of the cutouts.

"They aren't actually diamonds." I cleared my throat. "Swarovski crystals. I looked at all-diamond bracelets, but this one reminded me of your skyline, you know, 'cause of the yellow."

Her fingers dropped down to the bracelet, carefully lifting it out of the box. "You picked this out for me?"

"Me and Arrow both. I'm pretty sure the lady who helped us went in the back and drank when we left the jewelry store."

Joey laughed. "It's the most beautiful piece of jewelry anyone has ever given me."

"You really like it?"

I watched her slip it onto her wrist. It glittered and caught the light brilliantly.

"I love it." She hugged me again. "Thank you."

"You're welcome," I whispered.

Jolting back, she fished a giant wad of tissues out of her tiny purse she was carrying. Hurriedly, she began dabbing the corners of her eyes.

"Seriously, though," I drawled, dubiously. "How did you fit all those tissues in that bag?"

She kicked me.

"Ow!" I howled. "You don't kick the groom on his wedding day!"

"Get out of the limo," she ordered.

I slid out because I didn't want her to kick me again. Before she could follow, though, I turned, braced my arms on the doorframe, and leaned back in. "Oh, one more thing."

She arched a dark brow at me.

"Maybe don't call me Jay anymore. It kinda makes A jealous."

I thought she might kick me again. I was prepared to shield my boys. But she didn't. Instead, she nodded swiftly. "I totally get that. Names are important. Hopper it is."

Moving back, I helped her out of the limo, and we went inside.

We were greeted by a woman I assumed was an event planner or some shit. She led us for what felt like a mile-long hike through part of the indoor area until we made it outside again.

"Where are we going?" I complained, my eyes searching every inch for just a hint of Arrow.

Joey pointed ahead.

"Seriously?" I asked, impressed. "There?"

She nodded. "Told you it was impressive."

The woman escorting us overheard and chimed in like a tour guide. "The focus waterfall here at Aria is one of our best elopement attractions. It's a two hundred and seventy-foot-long by twenty-four-foot-high water wall—basically a living piece of art. You will say your vows with the synchronized rhythm of the water falling."

We were getting married in front of a waterfall. How freaking cool was that?

"And even though this is outside, you will find the sound of the cars from the road"—she motioned off behind her— "are barely noticeable."

She glanced at Joey, then at me. "As for privacy, we promised Miss Gamble as much secrecy as we can provide. We've been on the watch all afternoon and haven't seen anyone out of the ordinary lurking with a camera."

I leaned over to Joey, speaking out of the side of my mouth. "Can press just walk right up to us out there?"

She shook her head. "Standing room for ten only."

I nodded. "Well, we only have, what, five?"

Joey cleared her throat. "Ten."

I jerked back. "Ten?!"

"Here we are," the woman said, directing us.

The rhythmic sound of water falling eclipsed almost all the other sounds. I stepped toward the wall, which was lit with white lights and had some landscaping of rocks and various plants around it, gazing around in awe. The justice of the peace was already standing near the water, dressed in a suit with some kind of small book in his hands.

Butterflies kicked up just seeing the man there. I glanced down at the ring on my hand and Arrow's name above it.

Arrow was going to love this place.

"The guests are here," the woman said. "All we need to do is have you sign the marriage license. Then the ceremony will be performed."

"Oh, no," Joey said. "They'll sign it directly after the ceremony. Before we head into the private dining room we booked."

I glanced at her. "Private dining room?"

She waved her hand. "It's here at Aria. We rented a private room, you know, for privacy."

When I only stared, she made a sound. "You can't really think we'd just let you get married and that's it. We're having dinner and cake."

"You had a cake made?"

"You are such a man," she muttered.

"Where's Arrow?" I grumbled. This was awesome, but I wanted him. I was done waiting.

"Oh, here comes everyone now," Joey said.

I spun, thinking it was Arrow I was going to see. It was everyone *but* Arrow. My parents, Ron Gamble, Arrow's mom, and Trent and Drew.

"I had no idea you were coming." I grinned, holding out my hand to Trent and then Drew.

"Are you kidding?" Drew said, shaking my hand. "We'd never miss this."

"Congratulations, man," Trent told me, smiling.

They were both dressed in suits. Drew's was black on black, and Trent's was gray. Neither of them was wearing a tie.

"Thanks for being here. It's going to mean a lot to Arrow."

"We saw him," Drew said.

Trent nodded. "Dude looks sharp. Like the new tats."

"You saw him?" I asked, craning my neck around.

Trent laughed knowingly. "Joey keeping you apart I see. He's in there with Lorhaven. They're on their way out."

"If we could begin," the justice of the peace called.

"See you after." Trent promised. He and Drew moved toward the wall where Gamble and Donna were standing together, smiling at each other.

Well, wasn't that interesting?

My mom and dad stopped beside me on their way to their places. Mom was crying. Dad actually looked like he might, too.

"I'm sorry we didn't get to see each other much today. I know we have a lot of catching up to do."

Mom shushed me. "This isn't about us. This is your wedding. We're so proud of you, Jayson. I know we just met Arrow, but we can see how much he loves you and how happy you are. It's all we want for you."

It meant so much to me, more than I think they would ever understand. I grabbed my mom's hand. "We'll come to Seattle, visit. Catch up there."

"I would love that."

"Just might happen sooner than you think!" Dad quipped.

Mom elbowed him in the stomach. Before I could ask what he meant, she hurried him off toward their places.

Joey grabbed my arm, trying to pull me toward the justice of the peace. I dug the white Adidas sneakers into the ground. It was my ode to my husband. He loved a pair of sneakers, and I happened to think they looked pretty bomb with the blue chambray suit I wore. It looked perfectly summery (according to the tailor) with the pant legs rolled just once to give way to my white footwear. The white dress shirt I wore beneath was unbuttoned at the collar, and there was a white square of fabric in the pocket.

I wasn't wearing my leather bracelet today. No, today I was letting my infinity tattoo with the arrow and the coordinates marking Matt's death show. They were part of me. Of this day. Part of the journey I took to get here.

"Where is he?" I demanded.

"I'm going to get him right now," Joey said. "Go stand over there and wait."

Giving up, I went to the wall, but my eyes stayed glued to the corner where everyone else had appeared.

Just a moment later, Joey hurried to my side, taking up her place as "best lady."

There was no music.

No aisle with flower petals and no parade of a wedding party.

What we had was a night sky, a lit waterfall, and the gentle sounds of it cascading behind us. The people we cared about most in the world stood close by, giving silent support.

It was more than I thought it would be, yet it was nothing compared to the moment Arrow finally stepped around the curve of the water wall.

My heart physically stopped. Blood drained from my head and pooled in my feet. I saw nothing but him. He was the complete center of my universe for one long, blissful moment.

And then he smiled.

My heart restarted, blood rushed through my limbs, and a flush filled my cheeks. He was still all I saw, and amazed, I watched as he walked directly toward me.

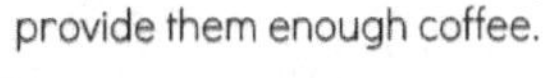

Chapter Eighteen

People who claimed to have seen the future—I understood them now.

Because I was looking upon my future right that very second.

For so many years, I thought I wasn't good enough, that happiness was for people who lived by the rules society dictated.

I was wrong. Happiness was attainable for anyone who had enough courage to reach for it. Just because I had to reach further than some only made it that much more appreciated. Today, in this moment, I was wrapping both hands around my happiness, grabbing it tight.

Hopper's hair was doing that curling thing it did at the back of his neck. Standing there by a giant waterfall, he looked like a model out of a catalogue with his perfectly tailored blue suit, crisp white shirt, and sneakers so white they almost looked fake.

The picture of perfection, a priceless work of art. My heart beat so fast, as if it were trying to tell my feet to hurry the hell up and get to his side. I listened to the heartfelt demand. Why wouldn't I? It seemed like days upon days since I'd seen him last.

I sped up. A few chuckles floated with the sound of the rushing water. I paid no attention to anyone, not even the freaking bomb scenery.

Hopper's lips curved, flashing his white teeth. He stretched out his hand.

This was why a guy needed to wear sneakers. He needed to have the appropriate footwear ready to go when it was time to rush toward the rest of his life. I couldn't get to him fast enough.

Thank you, Adidas.

The second my skin slid over his, excitement crackled in the air around us, reminding me so much of the night he showed up on the other side of my fence. We were electrified even then.

Maybe more so now.

Forgetting all of Joey's rules and wedding ceremony etiquette, I launched myself at him, refusing to give up his hand.

Deep laughter rumbled in his chest as his body moved. He knew I was coming; he'd been ready. Folding me against his chest, I rested my chin on his shoulder and, for the first time, took in the massive size and sheer cool factor of the giant curved wall.

"This jacket makes me want to pet you." His whispered words were proved by the way his free hand stroked over my back.

My eyes slid closed, forgetting all about the location and just feeling him. "Later." I promised.

The justice of the peace cleared his throat. Lorhaven grabbed me by the back of my neck, pulling me back. "Dude, you look desperate," he muttered.

Keeping my eyes on Hopp, I answered, "I am."

Someone sighed. I have no idea who. It was a girl. So it must have been one of the moms. Or maybe Joey, though I didn't peg her as the sighing type.

"I take it you are the one giving his hand in marriage?" the man officiating asked my brother.

"That'd be me." He agreed, then fell back at my side.

I glanced at Joey. She smiled, giving me a little wink.

"And who gives this man?" he asked the crowd, gesturing to Hopper.

"We do." Several voices rang out at once. I glanced around at Hopper's parents, Gamble, and Joey, who all spoke up for him.

Hopper's eyes softened. My heart swelled for these people who put that look of love in his eyes.

"Shall we begin?"

"Just get to the end," Hopper told the officiator.

Drew snickered, and I glanced around, behind me and Jace. They gave me a thumbs-up, and I grinned.

Everyone was here. I had a family now. A big one, filled with people who knew exactly who I was. And they loved me anyway.

My chest nearly burst with gratefulness.

Taking my other hand, Hopper commanded all my attention, and then the ceremony began. It was short because we were both impatient, and the officiator seemed to understand.

Or hell, maybe all Vegas weddings were some form of a quickie. We just got the hella nice version.

It didn't even matter.

We didn't write our own vows; we didn't need to. I already knew what was in Hopp's heart, and he knew what was in mine.

Even the ring part went fast because we were already wearing them. Not even my overbearing sister could get us to pry them off for the ceremony. Fuck that. I would live and die with this ring on my hand. It was now a permanent part of me, no less important than the air in my lungs.

Instead of slipping the rings onto our fingers, we kissed them. Finally, we got to the end. By that time, I was nearly bouncing out of my shoes.

"…by the state of Nevada, it is my joy and privilege to pronounce you partners in life… You may now kiss—"

He didn't wait. He didn't care we had an audience. Or maybe he was like me and forgot we had one at all.

Hopper palmed the back of my neck, pulling me close as his other arm anchored around my waist. The kiss was soft, gentle. Our lips brushed together like a summer breeze over the petals of a flower. Needing more, my tongue slipped over his. The tips of his fingers tightened on the back of my neck.

Just when it was starting to get good, Hopp pulled back, smiling.

Everyone began clapping, and I remembered where we were.

Our family converged on us, moving in like a single unit. Congratulations and jokes went around, until I glanced up and saw the officiator standing nearby with a piece of paper and a pen in his hand.

"We have something to do," I told Hopp, gesturing toward the man with my chin.

Breaking free of the group, we went and signed the marriage license. It was the last time I would have to sign Ambrose. From then on, I was Arrow Hamilton.

After posing for a few pictures, Joey led us into one of the restaurants at Aria. It was called Lemongrass. Gamble apparently rented a private dining room just big enough for our party of ten.

We ate Thai food that was really fucking good. I ate all of mine and half of Hopp's. Drew complained there were no fries, and Trent promised to order him some later at their hotel. I remembered being sort of jealous of them when I realized they were together and watching them interact. I didn't think I'd ever have what they did. Yet here I was.

I watched them for a few minutes, until Trent cast a knowing glance in my direction.

"I always thought it would be your wedding I'd be sitting at someday," I told him.

Drew groaned. "Dude, we hear this lecture from our sisters like on a weekly basis."

"No lecture." I laughed. "Just saying."

Trent nodded. "Forrester and I have it pretty good right now. Sometimes it's hard to mess with something that's already perfect."

Since I was already watching them both so close, I noted how Drew's hand slid beneath the table toward Trent. I knew what they were doing under there because Hopp and I were doing the same.

"Unless it's to make it even better," Hopper quipped. His hand slid a little farther up my thigh, brushing against my balls.

"You guys definitely are an example of that. We're happy for you." Trent agreed. Then a sly look crossed his face. "And I'm happy you won't be hitting on my person anymore."

"What!" Hopper's fork hit his plate.

I groaned. "Jesus. It was one time."

Hopper's nails dug into my thigh. I gave him a look. "It was barely anything. More like me trying to figure out if he was gay."

"When was this?"

I leaned close to him. "Before you. *Long* before."

The back of his hand brushed lightly over my dick. "I figured as much." His attention on only me was too short, though. He glanced up at Trent and Drew.

"I think you can stop giving me shit now, Trent. It's pretty clear I'm not gonna hurt him."

Trent chuckled. "Couldn't resist."

I gazed at Hopp, wondering what he meant. Hopper shrugged one shoulder. "He offered to break my neck if I hurt you."

"Keep doing shit like that, Trent, and I just might end up liking you after all," Lorhaven drawled. Clearly, he'd been silently eavesdropping on our conversation.

I wasn't sure if I should be flattered or pissed at the threat. Pissed was sort of more the way my mood was swinging. "You threatened him?" I jabbed my fork in Trent's direction.

Drew sat forward, looping his arm across Trent's shoulders. "Hey now," he warned. His voice was friendly, but there was an underlying steel note. "This guy is off-limits."

"So is mine," I growled.

"Truce!" Trent announced, holding up his champagne glass. "Here's to a future full of family." He toasted.

Everyone made sounds of agreement and sipped the alcohol. I glanced at him one last time before letting it go.

He winked at me.

I smiled. It was impossible to stay mad at someone like Trent.

My mom and Gamble were looking kind of cozy across the table, but I didn't think much of it. How could I when my husband's hand kept rubbing over my inner thigh?

Dinner lasted a few hours; no one was in a huge hurry to leave. The champagne was flowing, the food was fantastic, and the company was world class.

Toward the end of the night, the servers brought in a cake. It wasn't huge, but it was three tiers. The entire thing was covered with white icing so smooth I swear I could probably see my reflection if I really tried. The bottom layer had a giant silver arrow wrapping around the layer. The middle layer had a black infinity sign in the center. And on the very top layer, the two symbols were combined to look like a 3D image of our tattoos that came right off the top of the cake.

The best part was the inside. It was chocolate with some kind of gooey chocolate frosting between each layer. I ate three pieces. And half of Hopp's.

With the plates cleared, my stomach jam-packed with champagne and chocolate, and my hand in my husband's, all was right with the world.

Gamble appeared beside me, clearing his throat. I stood from the table and offered my hand. "Thank you for coming. And thank you for dinner tonight. I didn't expect anything like this," I said instantly.

"Get used to it," he said, releasing my hand. "We're family."

I wondered if I would ever get used to hearing that. In a way, I hoped I would, but in a way, I hoped I wouldn't. The familiarity that came with accepting and even believing we were real family was desirable, yet so was the feeling of awe I got when I realized I was no longer alone.

"I hope you and Hopper will be very happy." He continued, reaching into his suit, pulling out a white envelope.

"That's really not necessary." I shook my head adamantly when he extended it. "You being here is more than enough."

"Take it," he ordered.

I did what he said 'cause he wasn't a man you defied.

"Thank you."

He chuckled. "You don't even know what it is."

"It doesn't matter what it is. I'm grateful for it."

His eyes flickered with real emotion, almost as if my words pierced his usually unruffled façade. "It's a keycard to a room here in the Sky Suites." His voice was gruff.

"We have a room," I pointed out.

"This one is nicer."

I opened my mouth, but he held up his hand. "If you thank me one more time, I'm going to make you pay the dinner bill."

I grinned.

Even though we were anxious as fuck to leave, it took about twenty-five years to say our good-byes to everyone and make it out the door.

When we were *finally* alone and the doors to the dining room closed behind us, I held up the envelope with the keycard inside.

"Now that's a beautiful sight," Hopper quipped, snatching it out of my hand.

I laughed.

"Today was a good fucking day." His feet bumped against mine when he stepped ultra close.

"Husband," I murmured, fixing the collar on his shirt.

"You know what's even better than the wedding day?" His lips brushed the corner of my mouth.

I made a sound.

"The wedding night."

Deep down in my new wedding sneakers, anticipation curled my toes.

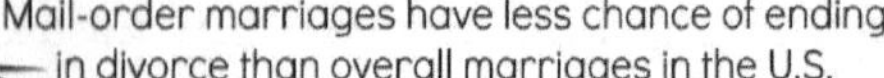

Chapter Nineteen

Our wedding gift from Ron Gamble came in a nearly fifteen-hundred-square-foot package. When he told A this room was better than the one we had currently, he wasn't lying.

This place was pure luxury.

We walked in, glanced around, then looked back at each other. Arrow whistled low. "Think the toilet is made of gold?"

I laughed, circling my arms around his middle and pulling him into me. "We could be in a cardboard box for all I care. It doesn't matter."

He nuzzled my cheek, then made a rude sound. "We both know you'd never let me hang out inside a cardboard box."

I cocked my head to the side. "You're right."

Holding hands, we took a tour of the place, starting in the living room area with an entire wall of windows overlooking the strip. The night was lit up like the world's largest carnival. There was something every place our eyes dared to wander. Tall buildings, wide buildings, attractions, and even huge fountains with light shows.

There was a suede sectional, a lounge chair, and a huge flat-screen on the wall. The mini bar was stocked, and on top was a huge gift basket with a white bow, our names scrawled across the card.

A nearby table had some sort of touchscreen system to control everything in the entire suite. The lights, curtains, TV, even the heating and cooling system. There was even a button to dial down to the kitchen and front desk.

"C'mon," I cajoled, tugging Arrow away from the electronics toward the wide-open door that led through a short hall and into the luxe bedroom.

There were double the amount of floor-to-ceiling windows in here. I don't even think I'd call them windows; they were the actual walls. The view of the strip was even more stunning in here.

"Who needs a helicopter tour of Vegas when you can sleep in here?" Arrow muttered, glancing out across it all.

"True that." I agreed. My mouth curled up. Turning from the view, I moved closer to him.

"You look like a cover model in your suit," he murmured, rubbing his palm over my chest.

"I am a cover model." I wagged my eyebrows, teasing him.

"Too bad *GearShark* didn't put you in a suit," Arrow muttered darkly.

I laughed. He looked amazing standing there in the fitted velvet jacket. The color was bold, but not loud. It kept my eyes the entire night.

"Is this jacket yours?" I asked, rubbing over the velvet for the hundredth time. "Or is it a rental?"

Arrow made a rude sound. "You know Joey wouldn't let us rent shit."

I nodded, approval lacing my tone. "Good. I like it. I want you to wear it again."

"Anything for you." He promised.

I whispered, "We just got married."

He whispered back, "And now we're at the top of the world."

Taking a moment, my eyes swept around the view once more, then fastened back on Arrow. "I never thought something like a wedding would mean so much to me."

"Me either."

"I'm glad we did this, babe." I folded his hand into mine.

He replied with a kiss with his thick, capable tongue. His moan carried down the back of my throat, making my sack tingle.

Nimbly, his fingers found the buttons on my dress shirt and slowly went to work, undoing them one by one. His hands felt like heaven when they glided beneath the fabric, over the warmth of my skin. He dragged his teeth down my chin and over my neck. Tilting my head back, I granted Arrow all the access he could want.

It was sweet torture the way he played with my hardening nipples, sucking and kissing my neck as if it were his favorite game. Arrow would pinch and tease, I would groan, and then he would suck deeper.

"My turn," I demanded roughly, pulling him back.

Instead of attacking him as the skin covering my body demanded, I backed up, my hands falling away.

Arrow followed, but I shook my head.

Stopping where he was, I continued on to drop on the end of the luxurious bed. The headboard was white leather, tufted, and reached all the way to the ceiling. Later, I was going to let him push me up against that leather and enter me from behind.

The bedding was cream colored, the pillows decorative, but I didn't care about them. My ass was sitting on top of a fur blanket, and all I could think about was stretching Arrow's naked body over the softness while I entered him.

Everything was visible because of the massive amount of lights brightening up the strip outside. I liked the way it hit certain points around the room, kind of making everything glow.

"Strip," I ordered.

Arrow lifted an eyebrow. "Bossy."

A note of wariness crept over me, and I worried I was going too far. "Is it okay?"

A brilliant smile took over his features. "Everything you do is fine, Hopp. Whatever you want tonight, you will get it."

"I want you to be happy." I confessed. Nothing else mattered.

"We're already there."

It moved me in ways I would never be able to understand. It also made me fucking horny. Tilting my head, I felt a needy glint come into my eyes. "Strip."

Inclining his chin, a wave of blond hair fell over one eye. Glancing up through it with molten heat in his gaze, he replied, "Your wish is my command."

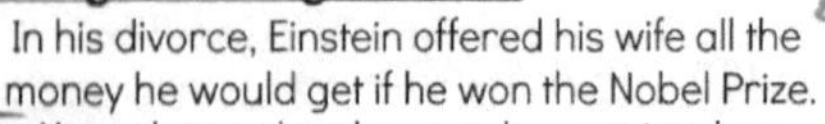

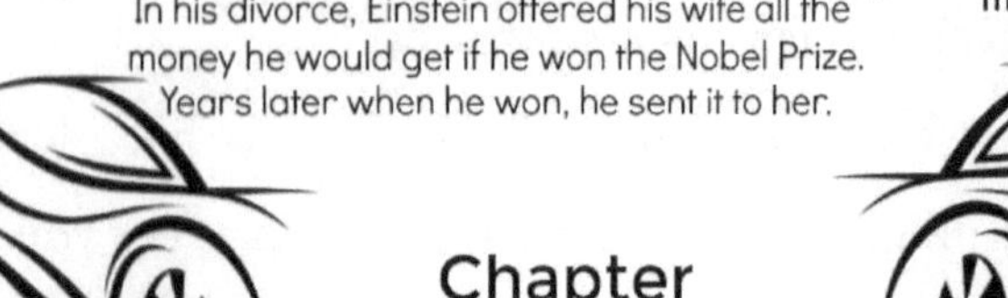

My feet were soundless over the thick rug as I stepped away from the bed. Kicking off my Adidas, I turned my back to him, staring out at the glittering nightlife.

We were high, so high up it seemed it was just us and the lights. Like an urban treehouse, but one that would exist in the future, with all the sleek, modern comforts you could imagine.

Even though we were sort of in a fishbowl, with glass almost on all sides, I still felt completely alone with him. Completely secluded in our own little world.

Starting with the royal-blue jacket he seemed to love so much, slowly I slid it down over my arms, revealing my back and shoulders as I moved. When it met my fingertips, I tossed it aside to a nearby chair. I could see his reflection in the glass, watching me as I moved.

I felt the pulsing desire coming off him in waves. The predatory way he studied my every move made me feel bold. Made me feel desired.

Pushing the hair back off my face, I undid the buttons on my shirt one at a time, just as I had his only moments ago. Peeling it off my body just like the jacket, it slipped off my limbs to pool at my bare feet.

There was a new tattoo on my back, one I'd only had for a few months. It stretched over the back of one shoulder, a racing flag with my car number in the corner.

I knew he liked it. Dude had a fetish with all my ink. So I rotated my shoulder in its socket, making it ripple.

His intake of breath made my sack tighten and spurred me on.

I moved to the rest of my clothes, leisurely taking them off, making sure to give a full show of my ass as the pants and boxers left my body.

My dick was at complete attention by the time I was naked, and he hadn't laid a single finger on me.

But his eyes… *oh his eyes* were everywhere.

Those icy orbs had the ability to freeze out just about everyone we met, but not me. To me, his eyes were so cold they were hot. Just like dry ice—so subzero it had the ultimate power to burn.

"Turn around." His voice was gruff.

I obliged, grabbing my rod to massage it and jack it slowly. Hopper watched, sinking his teeth into his lower lip. I stuck mine out just a little because I knew my "pouty" mouth drove him insane with desire.

"People can probably see you," he said. I couldn't tell how he felt about that.

"Probably." I allowed. "But you're the only one who can touch me."

He moaned.

Feeling bolder and surer than I ever had before, I spun back to the window, stepped up to it, and planted my palms on the glass, offering my entire body up for full view.

In the glass, I watched Hopper shoot to his feet and step toward me.

"Don't come over here unless you're naked," I intoned. If he could be bossy, so could I.

The rustle of clothes was too great a draw. Turning back, I surveyed him while he stripped. He gave me a show, just as I'd hoped. The guy was built, his entire body rippled with muscle. I loved the breadth of his shoulders, the power of his arms. I liked the flashes of the tattoo on the inside of his wrist as he threw various pieces of clothes around the room.

"Touch yourself," I demanded when he was completely bare.

I watched him cup his sack, gently squeezing it, stroking up his thick length.

The bottom fell out of my stomach, and suddenly I was so buzzed, almost as if the all the champagne suddenly decided to go to my head.

But it wasn't the alcohol; it was want. Need. Desire.

Crooking a finger at him, I beckoned. The heat in his eyes scalded me, but I stayed the course. Hopper reached out, pushing me against the glass of the window. I hissed out a breath because the smooth, hard surface was cold beneath my flushed body.

His body covered mine, pressing me farther into the glass. Rotating his hips, he virtually fucked me right there for all the world to see.

We made out while we humped each other. Eventually, my hand reached between us, seeking out his stick.

"No," he murmured, avoiding my grab.

An impatient sound ripped from my lips. Hopper grabbed my waist, spun me around, and used his chest to plaster my front against the glass.

I squeezed against it harder because the pressure against my swollen dick was heaven. I even rocked into it, my body searching for some kind of relief.

"You're only gonna get that kind of release from me, babe," Hopper vowed right before his teeth sank into my shoulder.

I hissed a sound. He pinned my hands against the glass, holding them there with his.

The way his dick nestled between my ass cheeks, just teasing, made my hot breath steam up the glass right beside my mouth. He didn't stay there long, though. Hopper worked downward, licking over the small of my back and kissing across my ass cheeks. I murmured something incoherent when he dropped to his knees behind me.

"Stay there," he told me. "Don't even think about moving."

I nodded. His hands grabbed my ass and parted my cheeks.

Goose bumps raced along the base of my spine, reaching as far as the top of my head. I leaned into the window, letting the glass support my weight. Hopper licked the most secret area on my entire body, making me shudder.

"It's a double sex kind of night, babe," he rasped. I barely recognized his voice.

"Yes," I answered, sticking my ass out a little farther.

Hopper licked and sucked, his hand reaching between my legs to wrap around my cock.

His mouth and hand worked me simultaneously as I moaned into the glass.

"If anyone is watching right now," he intoned, with one long, seductive lick, "they're gonna see you're completely mine."

"I can't stand any more, Hopp," I said, my knees shaking so fucking bad it was a wonder I hadn't fallen on my ass.

Pushing me to my absolute limit, his tongue pierced my hole.

My legs gave out. The sound of my hands sliding down the glass was earsplitting. Hopper grabbed me around the waist, supporting us both.

Turning in his hold, my tongue dove into his mouth as I kissed him like I never had before. I swear if kisses could deliver orgasms, this one surely would have.

Hopper wasn't completely steady himself, something I took great pride in. Beside the bed, I reached for the fur blanket, spreading it out over the giant luxury mattress.

With a gentle shove, Hopper fell back over it, and I covered his body with mine.

The tip of his cock was already slick, the tang of the silky-smooth liquid he wept salty across my tongue. Wrapping my arms around his thighs, I held his legs open wide and kissed every inch between them.

"I fucking love you," he growled when I came back from grabbing the lube from the other room. Before I could settle over him again, he rolled, pinning me beneath him, slithering down my body and sucking my dick deep in one epic motion.

My shoulders came up off the bed, my head rotated, and the blinding lights from outside blinked in my vision.

Before I knew it, the slip of lube swept over my ass. He used it to coat my own throbbing dick and even my balls.

"I want inside you so goddamn bad, babe," he partly begged.

I caressed his dick and helped him add the slippery liquid until he was dripping. The fur against my back was erotic, and the sensation of him coming over me made my pulse quicken.

His head rested against my throbbing hole, but he didn't push in. I rocked against him, half begging, but he held still. One large hand wrapped around my dick, and he stroked.

"You're not allowed to come, babe. Not until you're deep inside me."

I shuddered. I wasn't even sure I could keep that promise if I made it.

Releasing my cock, his hands fell on either side of my head, his lips brushed my hairline, and the pressure against my ass increased.

I moaned. "Please, Hopp."

He shoved deep. I stretched around him, welcoming him as part of me. Both of us began panting. He pushed up, supporting himself on his arms, and gazed down.

"Never in my life," he murmured, the veins in the side of his neck straining as he pulsed inside me. "Never have I ever wanted anyone as much as I want you."

I grabbed his face, held it strong. "You're my first and my only, Hopp. You're it for me. No one has ever been where you've been."

With a guttural sound, he began to move, pounding into me with greater freedom than he ever allowed himself before. It was utterly amazing to watch him let go, to fully trust that I trusted him with not only my heart, but my body.

He was good. So good my vision went dim, my body hummed, and my brain stopped working. I moved against him, fucking him as hard as he was fucking me.

The pressure against my sweet spot inside made my dick pulse anxiously, and a few times, I had to stop moving because I was seconds away from pouring out all over my abs.

Hopper collapsed against me, his lips fastening on that favorite spot of his where the arrow on my neck pointed. He sucked deep and cried out. Tilting my head, I urged him to suck even harder.

I felt his body's release, the way he pulsed and emptied inside me. His entire body shuddered and jerked as the orgasm went on and on. Small sounds of satisfaction filled the room. He released the spot on my neck and sighed. Both his arms slid beneath my body, tucking me along him so close it was as if we were the same person.

Eventually, my vision came back. I glanced up at the ceiling, blinking back the watery sheen. I wasn't crying… Men didn't cry during sex. Fuck no. But damn, he was everything.

To distract myself from the emotional rollercoaster sex with my husband turned out to be, I thrust my still stiff cock against his rock-hard abs.

He made a sound and rolled off me, onto his back. His fist wrapped around my rod, making me shudder and moan. I couldn't let him touch me. I'd blow right there in his palm. Crawling down his body, I shoved his Jell-O-like legs wide and dove in, preparing his body for mine.

He cursed, which sort of sounded like a prayer, as I played with his ass. The total putty his limbs had turned to grew tense the more I slid my fingers in and out of his body. I was bringing him back to life. So soon after he emptied, new desire stirred within. What a heady fucking feeling to know I had that much power over someone.

Once he was good and ready and my dick glistened with a fresh coat of liquid, I jumped off the bed.

He looked at me like I was insane, and I grinned back as if maybe I was. Holding out my hand, I asked him a silent question.

He answered by surrendering his. I led him across the room to a suede chair right in front of the wide window. I moved it sideways and then sat down, putting my feet flat on the floor.

My cock stood up from my center, and I patted my lap.

Hopper glanced at the window, then back at me.

"You wanted everyone to see you owned me… Now it's my turn to show them I own you," I explained.

Hopper smiled, straddled my body, and without any kind of waiting, sheathed my cock with his body.

My head fell back against the cushion, and I thrust up into him impatiently. His palms spread out across my chest, held me down in the seat, and he began to move.

My eyes slid closed. He took me in all the way, rotating his ass against my legs, rubbing my cock on all his inner walls.

Damn.

"I don't want to go yet." I panted, so close to release but wanting the bliss to last forever.

Hopper continued to move. I surged forward, wrapping my arms around him, and buried my tongue in his mouth. We kissed endlessly as our bodies moved in sync. I loved him so goddamn much it almost seemed impossible.

When I fell back against the chair again, he came with me. Our mouths stayed latched together.

The orgasm came hard and fast. It burst out of me with force like no other. I shouted into his mouth. He grabbed my head and pushed it into his neck while I shouted and moaned some more.

I emptied completely into his body, and when the bliss finally released me from its clutches, I fell back, completely spent.

Hopper draped himself across my chest, leaving my dick cradled inside him.

I sighed contentedly and stared out over the beautiful city lights.

Reaching up, I fingered the ring on his hand and the slightly raised, scabby new tattoo of my name.

How could a mere man possibly vocalize the depth of his feelings when they went beyond anything a mere man could even understand?

I could say it over and over how much I loved him. How profoundly he changed my life. I could cover all my skin with tattoos representing something about him I truly loved, but there still wouldn't be enough room.

I couldn't possibly explain to Hopper just how much my entire universe revolved around him because there wasn't an equation that existed big enough to compute the sum.

"You just did," he said. The emotion in those three words broke through my internal debate.

I lifted my head slightly to glance down at where he lay against my chest. "What?"

"You just told me, babe."

My head fell back against the chair, shocked and slightly confused.

"You said it all out loud," Hopper whispered, tucking his arm around me, pinning his hand between my back and the chair. "Those were the most beautiful words I've ever heard."

I wasn't sorry I said those things out loud. I wasn't embarrassed or even shy. Not anymore.

Pushing a hand through the curls at the back of his neck, I sighed. "Someday I'll figure out a way to show you, baby," I vowed.

I felt him snuggle into me. I wrapped him up in both my arms. I loved having him in my lap this way. I loved him every single way possible.

"I've already seen," he echoed. "I see it every single day when I look in your eyes."

"I hope you aren't too spent after that double, Hopp," I asserted, caressing the base of his spine like he always did for me. "'Cause I'm not done with you yet."

Deep sound rumbled out of his chest. I felt his smile against my skin. "Oh, babe," he drawled, "I'm just getting started."

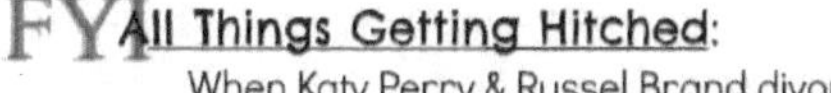
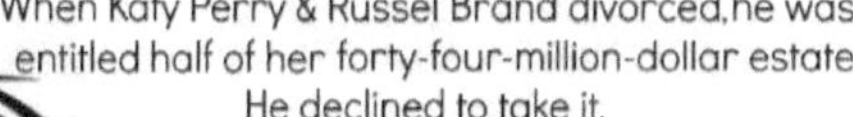

Chapter Twenty-One

Hopper

The bad part about sleeping in a room comprised almost totally of windows?

Morning.

Our wedding night stretched far past midnight and into the early hours of the next day. I think we fell asleep around three a.m., so when I felt Arrow moving around beside me barely a few hours later, I was slightly grumbly.

"Hopp." The supple flesh of his lips brushed over my ear in a quiet whisper. The intoxicating sound of his voice, the sleepy quality to it, was the only reason I didn't fuss at being disturbed. "C'mon."

"Wha…?" I mumbled, reaching around to wrap my arm around him to pull him close.

Laughing low, he resisted my attempts to hold him. I cracked an eye open, the dull morning light intruding upon the night I didn't want to end. Arrow climbed over me, his naked body rubbing over mine.

I was pretty worn out from our marathon session, but not so worn out I still couldn't enjoy the way he felt.

Wrapping his hand around my arm, Arrow tugged. "C'mon, Hopp, we're missing it."

My eyes popped open. Concern for whatever he seemed so urgent about made me forget how comfortable this giant bed was.

"What's wrong?" I rumbled, sitting up.

Arrow just smiled, pulled the large fur throw off the bed, and let it drag behind him as he strolled to the windows. His bare ass was quite the sight.

"Look," he summoned, staring out over the strip. "The sun is rising over the strip."

Walking to him and taking the blanket out of his hand, I wrapped it around my back and stepped close to my husband. His bare body fit against mine as I enclosed him in my arms, tucking the furry fabric around us both.

Together we watched the early rays of the sunrise changing the horizon from light peach to vibrant pink until it lifted high enough the sky turned a beautiful shade of blue.

We had the perfect view of the new day as it dawned. I guess mornings weren't so bad after all. Especially when the night you didn't want to end gave way to a new day that promised just as much as the one before.

This was my life now.

Spending long nights in bed, exploring the body of the man I loved more than life itself. Getting up too soon, after too little sleep, to watch the sunrise with his naked body pressed close and my chin on his shoulder.

This life was amazing.

Once the sun was bright in the sky, I lifted A off his feet, cradled him against my chest, and carried him back to bed. The expression in his eyes was surprised, but he relaxed into me instantly.

Once we were both settled, I wrapped myself around him, letting out a contended sigh. "What time is checkout?" I wondered as the heavy blanket of sleep tried to pull me under.

"We have the room until tomorrow," Arrow replied, rolling so I was on my back, he was pressed into my arms, and his leg was tangled with mine.

I smiled because he always wanted to lie this way. I didn't mind. I liked knowing he wanted to have my arms around him.

A sound of appreciation filled the room when I kissed the top of his head. "Good. I'm not ready to get up."

"We have plans later," he informed me.

"What?" My fingers paused their perusal of his lower back.

Arrow looked up, propping his chin on his hand that was lying on my chest. His smiled turned sheepish. "Gamble is letting us use his private jet."

I blinked. "What do we need a private jet for?"

That shy look that always got me came into his brown eyes. "I booked us a honeymoon."

Lifting my head off the pillow, I stared farther down at him, surprised. "A honeymoon?"

Arrow nodded. "I cleared the time off for both of us through Gamble," he explained, nervous. "I hope it's okay."

I smiled. "How many more times am I going to have to tell you, babe? Whatever you do is okay."

He chewed his lower lip.

"Arrow," I intoned, "where are we going?"

"Seattle."

My eyes widened. Of all the places, that was the last one I expected, but really, I should have guessed because of how nervous he seemed.

"If you don't want to, we can have the jet go somewhere else."

I pushed up on the bed, leaning against the leather headboard. "So that's what my dad meant when he said something about us coming for a visit sooner rather than later."

Arrow nodded. "I thought maybe you'd want to see the rest of your family. I'd like to meet them… Your parents are really great, Hopp." He paused, glancing up. "They like me."

Ah, the innocence in his voice, the familiar awe he spoke with when he realized someone liked him.

Brushing the hair away from his face and smiling down at him, I said, "Of course they do. I always knew they would."

"You can show me around Seattle. I want to see if the coffee there really is the best."

"It is," I told him, nodding sagely.

He grinned, scooting up the mattress toward me. Welcoming him close, I lifted my arm, and he settled against my side, his cheek pillowed over my heart.

"I know it might be a lot… and I don't want to remind you of things…"

"Of Matt." I corrected, going right for it.

Tipping his chin up, Arrow looked at me. "Yeah."

"It's okay to talk about him now," I murmured. "Meeting you, the way we fought to be together, the interview, seeing my parents again… It's been good for me. I'm at peace with the past now."

"So you want to go to Seattle?"

"Yeah, sounds good. I miss my sisters."

"I know you do."

"It's not going to be much of a honeymoon, though. We can't be walking around my parents' house naked, and we can't be making all the noise we made last night."

Arrow made a sound. "We aren't staying with your parents."

"No?" I was surprised once more.

"Hell no. I want to get some on my honeymoon. You're too sexy to stay at the in-laws."

I laughed.

"I rented us an island."

The bed jolted with my shock. "You did what?"

He laughed. "There are some islands off the coast of Seattle, you know. We can have some family time, explore the city time… then boat back to our island for some naked, sexy husband time."

"An island," I echoed. "I like the sound of that."

"Me and you, a house in the center of a small wooded island, water all around…" He seduced me with the picture he painted.

"Now that's a fucking honeymoon."

"You like it?"

"I like it. But I love you." My chin dipped so I could claim his mouth in a gentle kiss.

"You really put some thought into that, into something that would be good for us but also something that might be good for me."

The fact that he singlehandedly reunited me with my family, gave me a piece of my life I didn't think I'd have again, and then added to it made me love him even more.

"I'm just glad you like it, 'cause renting an island for two weeks ain't cheap."

"Two weeks!" I exclaimed.

"I have to share you with your family, Hopp. One week ain't gonna cut it. I'm a needy bastard. I need my time, too."

"You're always gonna come first, babe. Always."

Arrow leapt up, bounding out of bed.

"Where do you think you're going?" I demanded.

His sexy, naked ass rushed out into the other room. Seconds later, he dove back onto the bed, still naked, but gripping his cell. "I have pics of the island and the house."

"Pull that shit up," I said, pulling him against me again. Sleep could wait; life could not.

Arrow settled back, leaning against me the way I leaned against the headboard. His email looked like a hoarder's den when he pulled it up to find the pics.

"Damn, babe. You need an intervention."

"Nah, I just use the delete button."

I groaned. "Babe, there may be work opportunities in there. Sponsorship shit."

"Aren't they supposed to go through you and the PR team at work?"

I groaned. "I love you, babe, but I'm gonna need your email password. You can't be trusted to run the account on your own."

He laughed. It vibrated through his back and into me. "It's your name and birthday."

I groaned again, this time louder and more dramatic. "You shouldn't use my shit. That's asking to get hacked."

"But it's easy to remember. And you're my favorite."

Pressing a kiss to his head, I smiled. "You're my favorite, too."

"Okay, let me find the pics the real estate place sent." He was quiet a second, then paused. "Hey, look. An email from *GearShark*."

"I don't work on my honeymoon," I muttered.

"It's your interview and cover shot." He sat up a little farther, glancing at me over his shoulder. "Holy shit, that was fast."

My voice was dry. "Yeah, well, when you pay someone two million for an interview, they're probably anxious to start getting an ROI."

"I still can't believe they paid that much," he murmured, opening the email and scrolling down to the attachments. Before I could answer, he made a sound, shooting up into an upright position.

"Holy fucking hairy goat balls!"

"Something wrong?" I asked, amused.

"Jesus," he muttered, lowering the phone and rubbing a hand over the back of his neck.

"Hey." I laid a hand over his back, concerned. "What?"

Arrow lifted the phone, extending it back to me without looking.

I took the phone and stared down at the picture filling up the screen.

Damn.

I looked like a fucking sexy beast, if I did say so myself. Which I just did. Clearly, A agreed, hence the colorful language.

No shirt, hands up behind my head, and the sweats riding low on my waist. The magazine went with a red and black color concept and a black-and-white picture. The coloring made it that much hotter… because I knew I didn't look like that all the time.

"Babe." Dropping the phone, I rubbed a hand up his tense back. "I can tell them to change it."

"You're so fucking sexy, Hopper." He almost sounded forlorn. I grinned at his back. "Don't you smile at me, you bastard. This is serious. One dude thinks he can hit on you, I swear I'll knock him into next week."

"I don't think it's going to come to that, babe," I remarked dryly.

Without turning toward me, Arrow felt around for the phone, sliding it into his lap, bringing the picture back up onto the screen. *"Fuck."*

"You're just as sexy as I am," I told him, thinking of his magazine cover. Secretly, I did admit to myself I was glad as hell he wasn't shirtless for it, though.

"I kinda wish our tattoo was across your chest like mine. Kind of like a brand. Assholes need to recognize."

I held in a laugh. "I'll get one on my chest."

"You already have one on your wrist. Which just happens to be behind your head on the cover."

I shrugged. "I'll have two."

Arrow made a sound. "I like it."

"Two tattoos?" I mused.

"No. The cover shot. You look amazing, babe. So amazing it makes me mad with possession."

Snaking an arm around his waist from behind, I pulled him across the mattress, back into my body. "I don't care about the magazine cover, but I do like being possessed by you."

He grunted, settling farther against me. The back of his head hit my chest, and he lifted the phone. "Wanna read the article?"

I shrugged. "I'd rather see the pics of our island."

"Article first, then island pics."

A yawn stole over me. "Any chance we might get some sleep before boarding the jet?"

"A few hours, then we have to be at the airstrip."

"Come here," I murmured. He wasn't close enough.

His sigh was heavy, the skin of his cheek smooth against my chest. "Looks like this will hit the stands next week. We'll still be in Seattle," Arrow informed me, still looking at his phone.

"Good. An island should be a pretty good way to keep the press away."

Arrow made a sound of agreement.

"Here's the article." He held it up, showing me the header. "Want to read it first?"

Wrapping my hand around his and the phone, I shook my head. "How about we read it together?"

Pushing up off me, Arrow climbed into my lap. His arm wound around the back of my neck and his lips brushed over my cheek. "I'm proud of you for doing this, getting it all out there and finally letting yourself have peace."

"I only did it because you gave me the strength and inspiration, babe. So I'm not proud of me… I'm proud of *us.*"

His lips rubbed over mine in a brief but very wanted kiss. "Let's do this thing," he announced, then held up the article for us to read.

presents

JAYSON HAMILTON

written by Emily Metcalf

© **GearShark Magazine**

Exclusive! **Exclusive!** **Exclusive!** **Exclusive!**

Nearly six years ago, the entire Motocross world was shaken by tragedy. At the center was rising superstar Jayson Hamilton, who placed among the top ten Ducati racers in the entire country. Not only that, he had just signed a deal that would launch his career internationally.

Unbeknownst to all his fans and the Motocross club owners, a deep-seated rivalry had rooted, one that ended in death.

Motocross racer Matt Lewis was also a bright star in the Ducati world, racking up wins and placements throughout the three years he drove for the division. The guy who always wore a smile was loved by everyone, even those who only knew him from his photo on TV.

Matt Lewis was involved with Jayson Hamilton, romantically. They lived together, drove together, and very rarely did the press see one without the other. Some hypothesized Matt sacrificed some of his own success to propel Jayson farther up the ladder, a rumor (or is it?) that only made him more likable.

The couple was never secretive about their relationship, but they didn't flaunt it either. They lived a low-key life based in Seattle and often described each other as their better half or best friend. Their same-sex romance never caused a splash in the media like Drew Forrester and Trent Mask's relationship or even the GearShark's recent cover model Arrow Ambrose. Perhaps because Motocross wasn't as popular as it is now, or perhaps because their relationship flew under the radar.

Until, of course, it ended in heartbreak that shattered their world and dominated headlines around the country.

Jayson's rivalry with fellow Motocross driver Roger Blaine came to a head when Blaine issued a challenge Hamilton couldn't refuse. A street race to be held at Pinnacle Ridge, known to the locals as a dangerous road filled with twists, blind spots, and danger. The road also boasts a lot of loose gravel, as it's an old road that has not been maintained well throughout the years.

The winner of the illegal street race would take Jayson's spot at MotoIntercontinental.

On that fateful morning, Jayson was hit in the head by a heavy metal door while getting his Ducati out of his trailer. With a possible concussion, he was unable to drive, but he was also unable to forfeit or his coveted spot would be lost. In a simple solution, Matt suited up in Jayson's leathers and mounted his Ducati to take his place in the race.

Blaine arrived at the race with friend, Josh Rockford, and unknowingly began the race with who he assumed was Hamilton. Jayson stayed out of sight in the back of their trailer, nursing his bleeding head with his partner's sweatshirt. The sound of Rockford unloading a second Ducati caught his attention, and soon Jayson realized Rockford planned to join in on what was supposed to be a man-on-man race.

Worried for Matt, Jayson jumped on his bike and drove off in the direction everyone had gone. What he found when he came upon the racing men was a nightmare. Blaine and Rockford had set up the street race, planning the entire time to manipulate it so Hamilton would lose. Their plan? Force.

The next series of events ended in Blaine and his partner Rockford running who they thought was Hamilton off the precarious road. Despite trying to stop what was happening, Jayson was too late.

When first responders arrived at the grisly scene, they found Matt's broken and mangled body on the side of the road, the Ducati he'd been riding totaled.

And Jayson? He was discovered unconscious, lying on top of Matt as if he'd been trying to resuscitate him before losing consciousness.

When Jayson woke in the hospital, he learned what the rest of the world already knew: Matt Lewis had died on Pinnacle Ridge that day.

The story was highly sensationalized and reported on for almost a year after Matt's death. But shortly after being released from the hospital and attending a massive funeral for his beloved partner, Jayson disappeared.

Not one interview.

Not one comment to the press.

The second the sentencing was over for Blaine and Rockford, Jayson vanished. No one knew where he went, who he became. It was as if he simply ceased to exist.

Some said he should have gone to jail. Some said he got what he deserved. Others passionately defended him against the ugly rumors and theories that swirled. But everyone wondered what had become of the man who was once on the path of international celebrity.

Fast forward six years. Jayson Hamilton is found! He sits in front of me today. He isn't alone, though, and he doesn't go by Jayson anymore. His longer hair and scruffy face make it hard to recognize him as the clean-cut young athlete we all knew.

His blue eyes appear colder than the pictures of the past— more piercing, more guarded. Even without speaking to him, I can tell you this is not the same man the world once knew. He's older, harder, and most definitely more private.

But even so, I have a feeling if I had met him just six months before, he would have been even more closed off. In fact, this interview probably wouldn't be happening at all.

We know what changed Jayson Hamilton all those years ago, but what changed him again? Who *changed him?* Where *has he been all this time, how did he elude the press for so long, and why did he never speak out and give his side of the story?*

GearShark *scored an* exclusive *interview with this ghost. For the first and only time, Jayson Hamilton has agreed to sit down and tell us the answers to all our burning questions.*

And I can tell you right now, his answers are going to rock your world. So much so, we've designed this entire issue around his exclusive. We've also been inspired to dig deeper, catch up with some of our past cover stars to bring you updates on where they are now. Settle in, turn the page, and read the interview the entire racing world has been waiting for.

Then head on over to the GearShark App (If you don't have it, be sure to download it!) and watch a short recording of a portion of this interview for an even more in-depth look at Jayson Hamilton... a man most of you already know as Hopper.

That's right. He's been right under our noses this entire time. And double yes, he's involved in a new relationship with hot up-and-coming NASCAR driver, Arrow Ambrose.

Once your curiosity thirst is quenched, turn to the back of this issue for the mini articles on all the race stars we love.

Without further ado, race fans, let us cross the #FinishLine of this introduction and veer off the racetrack to where the real story lies...

Jayson Hamilton

aka Hopper

GS: First of all, I want to thank you for sitting down with me today. It's quite the honor you have given to *GearShark* to trust us with your story.

JH: GearShark has been good to my family. Trust is earned.

GS: By family, you mean Arrow Ambrose, who is sitting beside you for this interview.

JH: His name is Arrow Hamilton now.

GS: Our entire staff noticed the rings on your fingers the second you walked in.

JH: <He looks at Arrow, and they smile at each other. The kind of smile I'm certain I would never get from this man.> We noticed.

GS: Let me backtrack for a few minutes before we get to the obvious exciting news.

JH: <Spreads his hands wide> This is your show.

GS: This is not actually the first time we've met. I met you on several other occasions for interviews with previous NASCAR and NRR drivers, such as Joey Gamble and, more recently, Arrow.

JH: <Smiles> Nice to see you again.

GS: <Now I see why all the stories from six years ago called him a heartthrob. Even with longer hair and

a scruffy jaw, this man is what some women would call sex on a stick. Just check out his cover image for proof.> Being the journalist I am, I have to admit it's a little insulting I had the hottest story of the year right under my nose and I didn't even know it!

JH: I wasn't trying to insult anyone. I was trying to survive.

GS: <His eyes are very piercing. Very hawk-like. It's slightly disconcerting, yet this reporter finds herself unable to look away.> You go by the name Hopper now. No last name, just one name.

JH: <Nods> You asked me at Arrow's interview why I only had one name. Now you know why.

GS: So Hamilton is still your legal last name? Is Jayson or Hopper your legal name?

JH: Legally, I'm still Jayson Hamilton. The only people that knew that was Ron Gamble and my accountant.

GS: No one else?

JH: <He leans forward.> You do now.

GS: This is a tell-all, you know. You're supposed to tell me all.

JH: <Wags eyebrows> Wanna know what color my underwear are?

GS: <I'm thoroughly charmed. I have to admit these racing boys, even the gay ones, have a way about them. Too bad they're all taken… Maybe GS needs a singles issue!>

AH (Arrow Hamilton, formerly Arrow Ambrose): She doesn't need the color of your drawers, Hopp. It's bad enough they took your picture with half your clothes off.

GS: <I'm looking at Jayson for this one.>

JH: <Grins, then whispers> Arrow isn't too happy about my lack of shirt for the cover.

GS: Okay, so forget backtracking. You boys make it nearly impossible. I need to know about your relationship. Then we'll get back to the past.

JH: <Raises an eyebrow> Boys?

AH: Men.

GS: I stand corrected. How did you meet?

JH: Through racing. Joey Gamble, who is a friend of mine—

GS: You managed her when she was with NASCAR, correct?

JH: Yes. Joey is dating Lorhaven, Arrow's brother.

GS: So Lorhaven introduced you?

AH: <laughs> My brother would have preferred I never dated.

JH: We met when he auditioned for Gamble for NASCAR.

GS: Did you hit it off right away?

JH: <Glances at Arrow, who nods> We avoided each other for months.

GS: Why?

JH: Because we were attracted to each other, and, ah… I wasn't ready.

AH: I wasn't either.

GS: You've both had painful pasts. Do you think that drew you together?

JH: In some ways, but mostly, I think it just made it harder.

GS: How so?

JH: <He shifts uncomfortably. You can tell he is a man used to his privacy.> Some pain is a lot to overcome.

GS to AH: Would you agree with that?

AH: Absolutely. I think it takes a lot to make a man want to move out of his comfort zone.

GS: And Jayson did that for you?

AH: I call him Hopper. <Looks at Hopper> But yeah, he did.

GS: How long have you been together?

JH: Long enough.

GS: This is the first time you've been seen in public with wedding rings. We are in Vegas… Did you just get married?

JH: Yes.

GS to AH: And you took Hopper's last name?

AH: Of course.

GS: Who was the one to propose?

JH: Me.

GS: Did you ever think you would be in another relationship, let alone get married, after Matt?

JH: <Swallows thickly> Honestly? No. I planned to live alone, in hiding, forever.

GS: But you weren't in hiding. You've been working at Gamble headquarters, managing Team Gamble NASCAR drivers all this time, haven't you?

JH: That's right.

GS: Did Gamble know who you really are?

JH: <Laughs> Do you really think Ron Gamble wouldn't know who I am? He was the one who found me. He offered me a job, a new life.

GS: Is he the one who helped you stay hidden all these years?

JH: Yes, but it was nothing sinister. Everything is legal.

GS: Of course. Everyone knows Ron Gamble is an upstanding businessman.

JH: He is.

GS: Have you been on a motorcycle since that day?

JH: <Looks away, a noticeable tick in his jaw muscle> Once.

AH: During my first pre-season race.

GS: Ah, yes. During the pileup on the track. You took the bike and pulled Arrow from his car.

JH: Yes.

GS: Is dating—excuse me—being married to someone who races difficult, given your past?

JH: <Sighs. Arrow reaches over and links their hands.> Yes, it is.

AH: I don't know how long I'll be racing. Not forever.

GS: You're willing to give up racing? So soon in your career. You know you are one of this season's to-watch drivers.

AH: Some things are more important than fast cars.

JH: He's here to stay for a while.

GS: Does everyone at Team Gamble know you are in a relationship? Given what happened last year with the hazing scandal with Joey Gamble, were you concerned at all about people knowing you're in a same-sex relationship?

JH: Yes, everyone knows. Of course I was concerned. What happened to Joey is unacceptable, and if I hadn't been so lost in my own pain over the past, I might have been able to stop it. I will always feel guilty for that. I will always have regret.

GS: And how has everyone in your camp been with your relationship?

JH: <The ice in his eyes cools about twenty degrees.> They're fine with it, and if they aren't, they'll be shown the door immediately.

GS: Does anyone ever accuse you of playing favorites?

JH: I treat all the drivers the same. It's business. I'm hard on all the drivers.

AH: He is. He's a real ass.

JH: <smiles>

GS: What would you say to anyone who says you got married really fast or that maybe you shouldn't have gotten married at all?

JH: You want the PC reply to that or the real reply?

GS: Both.

JH: I would say when two guys who have been through as much as we have, it's never too soon to grab on and hold tight to anything that makes us feel alive again. I'd also say everyone is entitled to their own opinion, and we ask for privacy for our private lives.

GS: And the non-PC response?

JH: Shove it up your ass. It ain't your life.

GS: I, for one, think you two make an adorable couple.

AH: You see all my tattoos? I'm not adorable.

JH: <Leans over to say quietly> You're kind of adorable.

GS: You disappeared for a long time, Jayson.

JH: Yeah.

GS: Did you keep in contact with anyone? Family?

JH: No one. I walked away from my life and pushed away everyone I cared about.

GS: Why?

JH: Because I thought it was what I deserved. I felt responsible for Matt's death.

GS: Do you still feel responsible?

JH: I always will.

GS: So what changed? Why come out of hiding?

JH: I didn't come out. People starting poking around in Arrow's life and started looking at me. Like I said, I am still legally Jayson Hopper, so the story broke.

GS: Do you wish it hadn't?

JH: I'm not upset it's out. I think it's time for some closure, time to move on.

GS: Because you're in love with someone else now?

JH: <Stiffens. I think my question offended him.> A part of me will always love Matt. And yeah, now that I'm married, I want to be happy.

GS: You know there are thousands of stories printed about what happened to Matt and then more stories later about you.

JH: I didn't read them.

GS: Never?

JH: No. I don't need to see theories or horror stories. I was there, and nothing the press writes can come close to the horror of that day.

GS: It was reported and then confirmed by Motocross that you were there that day to settle a rivalry, you hit your head, and Matt took your place.

JH: That's right.

GS: What else happened that day?

JH: After Matt and Blaine took off, I heard some noise outside. I was in our trailer. My head was gashed open and bleeding. So I looked out the window and saw Rockford suiting up and getting on a bike. I had a bad feeling and I was worried they were going to try and fuck with Matt.

GS: This race was to determine the MotoIntercontinental, wasn't it?

JH: I'd already secured the spot. I'd won it fair and square. I deserved it. But yes, Blaine was challenging me for it.

GS: Do you wish you'd walked from that challenge?

JH: <Pauses>

AH: It's okay, Hopp.

JH: Every single day.

GS: What happened after Rockford took off on his motorcycle?

JH: I got on Matt's bike and drove off after them.

GS: Did you have a concussion?

JH: Yes, but it didn't matter.

GS: What did you see when you caught up?

JH: <His eyes turn bleak and faraway.> They were trying to box him in on the inside… Matt never was strong on the inside. That was always my sweet spot. They were definitely trying to sabotage the race, run him off the road. The roads there… they weren't taken care of. There was a lot of gravel and dips in the pavement.

GS: Did they see you?

JH: Not at first, but they did when I got closer. It caught them off guard. They knew it was me right away. I wasn't wearing a helmet or any kind of gear. I was in my street clothes.

GS: What happened then?

JH: They went after Matt anyway. <His voice cracks.>

AH: I think that's enough detail.

JH: No, it's okay. That's what we're here for.

GS: You saw the accident?

JH: I tried to stop it! They wouldn't back off. Blaine wanted me to see. He nudged Matt right off the road. He lost control… I saw the bike flip, the way he bounced over the road and slid over the bank.

GS: You also wrecked. Is that right?

JH: Yeah, but I don't really remember… I woke up sometime after I was on the ground. Matt was there. He wasn't moving. I called out for help, but then I passed out again. I didn't wake up until the hospital.

GS: It was reported someone saw the crash and called the police immediately. Blaine, who also crashed, was picked up by Rockford, and the pair fled the scene.

JH: <His eyes flash.> They left us there to die.

GS: They didn't get away with it, though. The police picked them up several hours later, on their way out of town.

JH: I hope they both rot in hell.

GS: You aided the police in their investigation. I read reports that you cooperated and told everything you remembered. In exchange, you got a reduced sentence of reckless driving.

JH: My sentence wasn't reduced. I got a lifetime sentence of pain.

GS: You know Blaine and Rockford tried to blame you for Matt's death. They told the police you were the one who ran him off the road.

JH: Yeah, 'cause two men caught trying to flee town are innocent. <heavy sigh> But yes, they blamed me. I was questioned for hours. Spent a few nights in jail.

AH: You didn't tell me that, Hopp.

JH: <Glancing over at Arrow, his entire face softens.> Doesn't matter, babe.

AH: It does matter. <The hand not holding Hopper's cups the side of his face. I'm beginning to

think these two are what storybooks are written about.>

GS: I could keep telling you what the reports said, and you can confirm, but I'd rather hear the rest in your words, if you don't mind.

AH: <Frowns at me, and I admit I feel a little guilty.>

JH: Originally, I was looking at jail time. Involuntary manslaughter, reckless driving, reckless endangerment—hell, I think they were even throwing around gambling charges. Anything and everything they could think of, they were trying to pin on me.

GS: You fought the charges, got a reduced sentence?

JH: No. I was hoping they'd send me away for life.

AH: <Sucks in a breath>

JH: <No longer talking to me, but to his husband> The witness who called the police, he testified that I wasn't involved in the race, that I came out of nowhere, not dressed for a race, and yelled for them to get off the road. <pauses> I did gesture for Rockford to get off the road when he first saw me. Anyway, the witness testimony and his 9-1-1 call recording went totally against everything I was letting them pin on me. But they went a step further and called my mom down to the station. <clears throat> I hadn't seen her since… I told the hospital I didn't want any visitors once I woke up. She walked in, and I kinda lost it.

AH: Lost it how?

JH: I broke down and cried. It was all bottled up, you know? The image of Matt lying in the morgue. <He remembers I'm here and glances at me to explain.> I identified his body when I woke up from the brief coma I was in.

GS: That must have been very difficult.

JH: <Turns back to Arrow> I told her everything. Everything I said corroborated with the witness testimony.

GS: So they dropped the charges.

JH: I lost my driver's license for a couple years. I'm banned from Motocross for life. And I had some community service.

GS: What happened to Blaine and Rockford?

JH: <His voice hardens.> They went to jail. I hope they rot.

GS: And your spot for MotoIntercontinental?

JH: <shrugs> They gave it to someone else. I have no idea. I don't care.

GS: There are a lot of people out there who say you are responsible for Matt Lewis's death.

AH: <Jumps to his feet, angry> Say anything like that again and this interview is over.

JH: A, come on. Sit down. She's not accusing me of anything.

GS: I'm not.

AH: Don't even imply it. He would never intentionally hurt someone he loves. Never. He's not built that way. He's cut himself up into a million tiny pieces since that day. No one has suffered more than he has.

GS to JH: I can see why you love him. He clearly loves you.

JH: <Smiles>

AH: I'm not joking, Emily. I like you, but I *love* him.

GS: Duly noted.

JH: I didn't kill Matt. I shouldn't have been on that hill racing that day, but I didn't want him to die. I would have gladly taken his place if I could have.

AH: <makes a choked sound>

JH: I'm sorry, babe.

GS: Watching you two interact, it's both heartwarming and gut wrenching. Is it difficult, Arrow, to be so in love with someone who had a relationship before you?

AH: It would be more difficult to live without him.

GS: Do you plan to reach out to your family now that your identity and location is out?

JH: Maybe.

GS: Will you be going back to using Jayson instead of Hopper?

JH: No. I'm Hopper now, but I will be using my last name again.

GS: Since you're married now?

JH: Yes.

GS: Are you a different person now than you were six years ago?

JH: Completely.

GS: You two are the first married same-sex couple in NASCAR. Do you hope it gives other same-sex couples some sort of hope or makes it easier for them to be accepted?

JH: Sure, I mean, if A and I can fall in love, then anyone can find love. But honestly, we don't want to be poster children for gay marriage. We just want to live our life.

AH: I think Drew Forrester and Trent Mask make better role models.

GS: Think they'll get married anytime soon?

AH: Why don't you call and ask them?

GS: Maybe I will. Jayson, if you could say anything to Matt's family right now, what would it be?

JH: <A very somber look comes over his features.> That I'm incredibly sorry I lived and their son didn't. That I will regret that day for the rest of my life and that I'm so sorry he isn't there with them now. I would tell them that I loved him… and that he loved them very much.

GS: I reached out to Matt's parents before this interview. I wanted to see how they were doing six years later.

JH: I'm sure they blame me.

GS: They don't. Matt's mother, Rhonda, she told me she came to see you at the hospital, but they wouldn't let her in. She also went to the police and asked for leniency on your behalf because she says, to this day, she knows how much you loved Matt, and she believed you would never do anything to hurt him.

JH: <Jayson is visibly moved by this information. He bows his head. Arrow wraps an arm around his waist, hugging him, while resting his chin on Jayson's shoulder.>

JH to AH: I thought they hated me.

AH to JH: No one who knows you would ever hate you.

JH to AH: I missed his funeral. I was in jail.

AH to JH: You got a private good-bye that day in the hospital, babe.

JH: <whispers> I love you.

AH: I love you, too.

GS: <I feel kind of guilty breaking in here.> His mother said they miss him every day still, but they've learned to be happy again. She hoped you found the same. Looking at you now, I see you did.

JH: Thank you for telling me.

GS: How about we lighten it up a little now?

JH: Please.

GS: Does Lorhaven like you?

JH: <Laughs> Does Lorhaven like anyone?

GS: Where do you see yourself in five years?

JH: With Arrow. Hopefully in a house instead of an apartment. A house with privacy.

AH: A house with a wall around the property.

GS: Kids?

JH: <They look at each other, wide-eyed and surprised. Slowly, they both smile.> No. It's just me and A on this ride.

AH: Just me and Hopp. I don't want to share him with anyone.

JH: <laughs low>

GS: Congratulations on your wedding. I have to say I was surprised.

JH: You wanted an exclusive. You got one.

GS: Thank you for being here, for being candid. I know it wasn't easy.

JH: I'm beginning to realize the best things in life never are.

GS: One last thing before we end the interview.

JH: Yeah?

GS: What color are your underwear?

AH: <Groans> That is hardly relevant!

JH: What color are yours, Emily?

GS: Red.

JH: Black.

AH: I'm not wearing any.

JH: What? We're in public!

AH: <smiles slowly> Two can play at this game.

GS: Is there anything else you'd like to add to this very informative interview?

AH: I'm hungry.

JH: He's literally always hungry.

GS: Myself and the rest of *GearShark* wish you both the very best. Oh, and there is some chatter about you two having matching tattoos?

JH: <pulls off a thick leather cuff bracelet and holds out his wrist> These are the coordinates of where Matt died, a promise to him and to myself I won't forget. And this one <points below it> is an infinity sign with an arrow. Because Arrow shot an arrow right through my infinity.

GS: That's seriously romantic.

AH: <Pulls off his shirt> I have the same one here. <points to the area right above the heart where the same tattoo is displayed>

JH to AH: Put your shirt on! <Arrow glances at me and winks.>

Cleary, these boys—ahem—men have not always had it easy. To see they have found a way to carry on, even with the pain still with them, is very inspiring. It's also very refreshing to see two people who love each other so completely. I think we can all agree the world needs more of that type of love.

Another big thanks to Jayson Hamilton (aka Hopper) and his new husband Arrow Hamilton for being here today and for taking us beyond the #FinishLine to give us an all-access glimpse into their rearview as well as what's ahead.

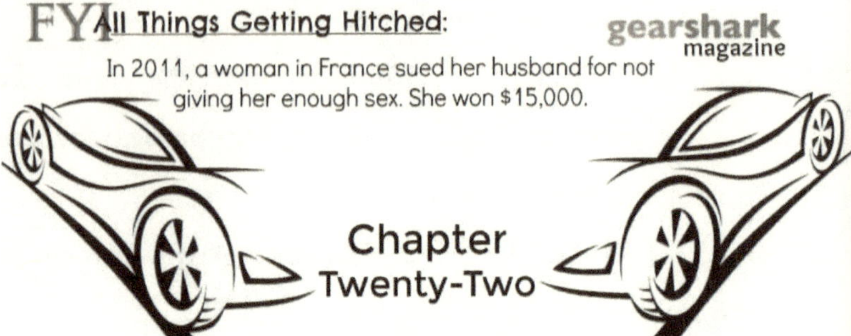

Life doesn't always give a man what he wants. Instead, he is given what he needs.

In my case, I got far better.

I was given a shitty, hellish start. A long, arduous walk through hell. But if I hadn't been lost in the darkness for so long, I might not have been able to totally appreciate the light I basked in today.

The exclusive interview with Hopper healed not just him, but us both.

We understood the deepest, most onyx parts that made us the men we were. Those parts would never go away, and that was okay. We loved each other for those parts and, sometimes, in spite of them.

To me, that was the definition of real love.

I didn't have to be someone anyone else thought I should be. And Hopper didn't have to pretend he didn't sometimes still tumble into the clutches of the past.

I'd come a long way from the days I sat inside the prison of my airstrip, behind locks and fences, living in the shadow of my brother's strength. It was okay to stumble, to even hurt. I could embrace that now, not try and run from it.

It was okay if I stumbled or maybe even fell. I no longer walked alone. Hopper would carry me, just as I would him.

Just like the article in *GearShark* said, every race had a finish line, but what happened once you crossed was what mattered most.

Hopp and I crossed our finish line. We joined our lives, our names, and everything beneath our skin.

But our story was far from over. Our race was far from finished.

Except we weren't racing; we were slowing down to embrace everything about our life. Even the messy parts and the parts when my sexy husband showed his goods on a national magazine cover.

(Someday I'd get over that. I would.)

I glanced up from his lap, the rhythm of his heartbeat steady and reassuring against my back, at the same time he dipped his chin to glance at me.

"Infinity is going to be good to us, Hopp," I told him, not a trace of doubt in my voice.

"Oh, babe," he purred, brushing the back of his knuckles over my cheek. "Our infinity is going to be one for the books."

FINISH
LINE
Joey & Lorhaven

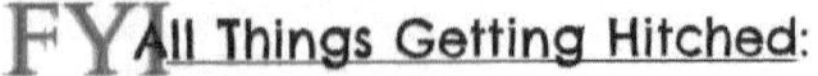

gearshark
magazine

Chapter Twenty-Three

Lorhaven

People were pissing me off.

I wasn't a hard guy to get along with, not really. Just don't fucking talk to me. Simple. I only had tolerance for a handful of people in life; the rest could take a flying leap off a bridge.

You'd think with my sunny-side-up persona, people wouldn't even bother.

People were stupid.

The questions were endless… or rather *the* question. At first, it was easy to brush off or give a simple reply. After all, I didn't owe people an explanation for the way I chose to live my life.

Except I did. To those handful of people I considered family. Hence, when they started asking *the* question, an answer became harder to formulate.

When are you getting married?

I felt those words up there should somehow shake this page, crack the world open, or at the very least come with a drum roll.

They didn't, but they were pretty close to giving me a rash.

Thing was I didn't dislike that question. I wasn't against marriage. In fact, I wanted to get married— something that, quite frankly, shocked the shit out of me. Yet when I glanced across my Lotus to the woman riding shotgun or woke to her skin sliding over mine like silk, I wasn't so shocked.

I loved Josie, and I knew in the deepest part of myself I would love her forever. My loyalty to the dark-haired, green-eyed vixen was unshakable.

I bought a ring. Something too flashy, probably too big, and one she probably would think I was nuts for. She'd get over it, and I'd get off every single time I saw it glistening on her finger, shouting to all the world (all the world = assholes who wanted to look at my woman) she was mine.

That over-the-top ring sat in the box for months. Sometimes in my pocket (a lot of times in my pocket), in my glovebox, at home in a secure hiding place. The secure hiding place being a closet we shoved the shoes we never wore, and Josie never went in there because she was convinced spiders bred in our old shoes. I asked her why, if she was never going to wear them again, we couldn't just toss them.

She looked at me like I had ten heads, and I never asked again.

Women.

I'd been waiting for the perfect moment, a time when I knew asking was absolutely right. Then people started asking the fucking question. Gamble wanted to know why I hadn't made an "honest woman" out of his daughter.

I felt if I pulled out the ring now, it would look like I was caving under pressure.

I did not cave under pressure. If anything, I thrived.

I didn't want Josie wondering if I asked because I thought it's what I was supposed to do, not what I wanted. Then Hopper announced he wanted to marry my brother.

Focusing on Arrow's happiness for a while seemed like the thing to do. I wanted him to be happy. He deserved it. And seeing him settled would make me feel less guilty for settling my own life.

Yeah, there it was. The guilt.

I thought only parents had that kind of guilt, but he did tell me more than once I'd been more like a Dad to him than a brother. Guess I felt the same.

I hadn't been able to fully settle into the life I wanted until he did the same. It was the reason I kept two houses, the one near our airstrip and the one with Josie on the other side of the state. I split my time between the two, never wanting to be away from Arrow too long.

It was fucking exhausting. But it was necessary, and I would do it for the rest of my life if I had to. I hadn't been there the night he needed me most. If I had only answered my phone… If only…

I shook off the thoughts. I couldn't change it. But I could make sure I was there from here on out.

When A moved down to Gamble Speedway, it was like a big fucking sigh of relief, even though I'd had my reservations about that, too. Still, he was growing. It was a fucking amazing thing to watch. I was so proud of my brother, the kind of pride that filled me up inside and left me sort of in awe.

I'd almost popped the question after that, but Hopper beat me to it. Arrow came first, his wedding and his future. Josie and I were happy, and she knew I loved her.

Enough was enough, though.

Arrow was married, and Josie's enthusiasm for their wedding was kinda adorable. And also kinda catching.

I was tired of waiting. I was tired of *the* question, and considering we had a phone interview with *GearShark* in the morning, I wanted to be able to give an answer, one they might not be expecting.

FYI <u>All Things Getting Hitched</u>:
In Ancient Greece, throwing an apple at someone was considered a marriage proposal.

Chapter Twenty-Four

Joey

Josie.

Where are you?

Jace.

Be ready in one hour.

Josie.

Are you bossing me?

Josie.

Be ready for what?

Read.

Jace.

Don't sass me, woman! Be ready.

Josie.

What should I wear?

Jace.

Something sexy.

Josie.

I'll be waiting.

What was he up to?

Slipping out of our room in Vegas, not saying a word… Was he trying to give a girl a complex?

He would argue obviously not. He answered my text after all.

Only to give me no solid answer and to boss me around.

This required some sort of payback. In the form of a red dress. Jace wanted sexy. Well, I would give him sexy. Then I'd tell him to keep his seductive hands off me until he let me in on whatever he was up to.

Marching into the large closet in the suite where our suitcases were up on large white dressers, I reached for the garment bag hanging on the rack. It was black and contained more than the dress I wore to Arrow and Hopper's wedding. I'd bought two dresses the day I went shopping, an unusual occurrence, but I couldn't decide.

I figured it would be a good thing to have something in reserve anyway, since I wasn't sure what else we'd be doing in Vegas. Now the wedding was over, my brothers were on their way to Seattle, and Jace and I were spending an extra couple of days here for a little R&R before real life resumed.

Pulling out a dress made of red lace, I smiled. *This will do nicely.*

I'd worn the silver dress to the wedding instead of this one because I thought it might be a little too sexy for a wedding. Plus, it was red, which seemed a little flashy for their big day (not that they were traditional).

This dress was sexy in a classy way. At least it was compared to some of the stuff I'd seen women waltzing around Vegas wearing.

The garment was a beautiful, true shade of red, sleeveless, and had a higher neckline that stopped right at the base of my throat. The bodice was fitted so it hugged my ample curves, but then the skirt flared out a little at the hips. The skirt itself was short. It showed almost all of my leg. What was sort of the saving grace for the tiny hemline was the way the lace overlay fell just past the red under-layer in a scalloped pattern.

It was a timeless dress really. The lace was thick, not dainty, and it zipped up the back. It didn't dip low and reveal my skin.

Of course, as was the case with almost every dress I bought (with the exception of that bandage silver number I wore to the wedding), this one had to be tailored. Curvy girl problems. My chest was big compared to my waist. I had to have this one altered so the zipper would close without making me look like I had a uni-boob.

Attractive, right?

I wasn't much into clothes, especially ones that had to be altered to fit my womanly body, but I was more into them this past year than ever before. What could I say? Jace brought out the girly side I apparently never knew I had. I wanted to look good for him. I wanted him to be proud to have me on his arm and to look like I belonged there.

Hanging the dress on the rod overhead, I grabbed a pair of red stilettos and set them nearby. I might not be much of a "girl," but I did love a good pair of heels.

To me, a woman looked powerful with high heels on her feet, and even more, they made me feel powerful. Plus, these things would do wonders for my legs in this shorter-than-short dress.

In the adjoining bathroom, I applied some makeup (something else I'd been getting a lot of practice at this past year), selecting a light cushion foundation for a natural look. But then I defeated the purpose of that "natural" look by smoking out my eyes with shadow and black eyeliner. Topping it all off, I chose a red liquid lipstick and coated my lips.

I didn't have to worry about it getting on him because, well, he wasn't getting any. Ha!

I'd found a blow-dry bar the day before, so of course I went there. I loved those places. They tamed my curls better than anyone. So today, my hair was long, straight, and glossy. I thought about curling it into beachy waves but decided against it. Mostly because I was lazy.

After brushing it out, I slipped on the dress. I felt a little self-conscious because it was so short and hugged the rest of me in all the right places (It better! I paid a lot to have it tailored!), but once I slipped the heels on and stepped in front of the mirror, I smiled.

For a finishing touch, I added the cuff bracelet Hopper and Arrow gave me, even though the stones were yellow and the dress was red. I didn't care.

It hadn't been an hour when a knock rapped on the door. Puzzling over who it was, I made my way over, my heels clapping over the tile. Jace had a key, so I knew it wasn't him.

I didn't bother looking through the peephole. I liked to live dangerously.

Pulling the door open wide, I gasped. "Jace!"

"Hey there, beautiful," he drawled.

He looked mouthwatering leaning in the doorframe in a pair of black jeans, black boots, and a white button-up. The shirt was untucked, and over it was his leather jacket… But there was a tie.

He was wearing a tie. Without me telling him to.

"Who are you and what have you done with my boyfriend?" I demanded, looking him up and down.

"Like what you see?"

Butterflies burst into flight in my belly. He was so arrogant, but damn, it was sexy.

"You're wearing a tie, with a leather jacket and an untucked shirt." I sniffed, tearing my eyes away.

"Bitchin', right?"

I laughed. "Something like that."

He gave me a look that said he knew damn well I thought he looked like sex on a stick, straightening out of the doorframe. A low whistle blew from between his lips. "Well, I made plans for us, but seeing you now, I think we should just stay in."

Reaching for me, I moved fast, lunging out of his grasp. "Oh no you don't."

His eyes narrowed. "Excuse me?"

I smiled, straightening so he could catch all of me. "You're letting me in on whatever secret you have going on." I waved my finger around in his direction as I spoke.

Jace's chuckle was warm and rich. "All right, baby, let's get this show on the road." He offered me his arm.

With a yeah right sound, I moved past him to strut to the door. I made sure to sway my hips a little extra just for him. The intake of breath behind me was my reward.

Inside the limo (yes, a limo), he turned his body toward mine. "You look absolutely gorgeous, Josie." He surveyed my body with great care, but it wasn't slimy; it was appreciative. "I'm a damn lucky man."

I softened a little. I mean, seriously, who wouldn't?

"Thank you," I replied softly, grabbing his black tie and tugging it toward me. "I like the tie with the leather."

"Only for you," he drawled, coming in for a kiss. I turned my head, his lips brushing over my cheek instead.

"Where are we going?" I asked, gazing out the window.

He laughed. "It's a surprise."

"I'm not much for surprises," I told him, though he already knew.

"Humor me."

Glancing back at him, all the lights of the strip fell away. "Only for you." I echoed his earlier sentiment.

Jace curled his hand around mine, and I entwined our fingers. Clearly, whatever this was, he'd put some thought into it.

Again, butterflies erupted in my stomach, making me feel slightly lightheaded. I wondered if perhaps tonight would be the night.

The night Jace would ask me to be his forever.

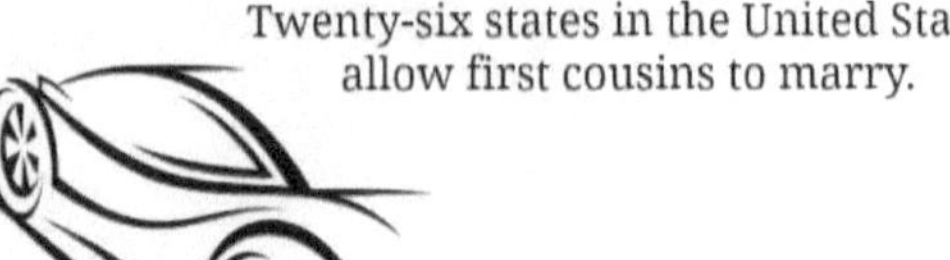

FYI <u>All Things Getting Hitched</u>:

Twenty-six states in the United States allow first cousins to marry.

Chapter Twenty-Five

Red hot.

Josie was red hot, not only in that fucking sexy as shit dress, but her attitude as well. Oh, she was pissed I disappeared, pissed I wouldn't tell her where we were going or what I had planned.

More than that, she was intrigued. It was obvious in the way her eyes scanned the strip, the way she crossed one long leg over the other, then reversed. The green in her eyes was glowing, suspicious but also excited.

I loved this side of her. Lucky for me, it was her most prominent side.

I had to admit I was sort of nervous. Asking a woman to marry me wasn't really ever on my lifelong to-do list. I never thought I'd find anyone I trusted or loved enough to take that leap.

Then Josie came literally speeding into my life in that damn yellow Skyline of hers and pissing me off plenty of times. She was everything I thought I despised yet somehow everything I always wanted.

The boxes in my pocket were burning a hole. I felt as if I were being branded by the promise of them but also the unknown. To me, Josie was a woman, all woman, and treating her any other way seemed wrong.

However, that woman side of Josie wasn't a side she showed many people. She was too proud, too strong, and too damn stubborn. Sometimes it was a fine line with her… But tonight, I was taking a chance.

I just hoped it didn't backfire.

"Isn't that so beautiful?" Josie murmured, a bit of whimsy in her voice as she stared out the wide window of the limo. She was fucking adorable like that, momentarily forgetting she was dressed all sexy, her nose literally pressed against the glass as she stared out.

"Even though it's half the size of the real one, it still has all the romance and presence."

Releasing her hand, I scooted across the seat so my body was pressed along hers. Resting my chin on her shoulder, I glanced out at the Hotel Paris and the giant replica of the Eiffel Tower.

"It's all right," I said, cheeky.

She gasped and elbowed me, light enough it didn't hurt and it didn't dislodge my body from hers. "You're stupid."

I laughed. The limo curved into the entrance of the Hotel Paris, gliding to a stop. Josie turned from the window. Light from the tower and all the other features outside glowed behind her, giving her a halo.

Without thought, I leaned in and kissed the tip of her nose. She smiled softly.

The limo driver was already moving around to open the door for us when she asked, "This is where we're going?"

"I guess even stupid people have good ideas sometimes," I quipped.

Excitement lit her eyes. "Really?"

The door opened, and a rush of warm summer air filled the interior of the car. "How about we get out and see?"

Her red-painted lips curled up. I wanted to tug them between mine and kiss her until all that red was on me, nothing left on her.

Josie scrambled out of the limo. I stared at her ass while she did it. That damn dress was so short I actually got a panty shot—or rather lack thereof.

Vixen was wearing a thong.

I almost grabbed her naughty ass and tossed her back in the limo.

My arm slid around her waist at the curb, tugging the hemline down as I went. Leaning close to her ear, my voice rumbled. "What the hell do you think you're doing romping around Las Vegas with no damn underwear?"

Glittering emerald eyes flashed up to mine. "I'm not romping anywhere. And I am wearing underwear."

"Newsflash, baby," I drawled, letting my lip rub over her earlobe, pausing to smile when she shivered. "If I can see your entire luscious ass, it ain't drawers."

"Just text me when you would like me to return," the driver said, interrupting my foreplay.

I nodded and thanked him because I figured snarling wouldn't inspire prompt service when I signaled later.

Josie's attention went back to the Eiffel Tower, which glowed with golden light. "Can we go up there?" she asked.

I scoffed. "Baby, we're having dinner up there."

It wasn't often she looked at me as if I'd hung the moon, but when she did, I felt I could.

Placing my palm to the small of her back, we went into hotel (which was pretty fucking impressive), and I steered her toward the elevator leading up to the Eiffel Tower Restaurant.

The gold double doors opened a few short moments later to a huge open dining room with sweeping views of the strip.

The carpet was red; most of the tables were round and draped in white cloths. There was a giant curved bar to one side, while the other was literally a wall of windows showing the illuminated night.

"Mr. Lorhaven," a man said, stepping up to us immediately. He was dressed to the nines in a black and white suit. "Right this way, please."

I felt Josie's gaze. I glanced at her and winked. Taking her hand, we followed along behind the man until he stopped at our special table.

I heard Josie's intake of breath when the man gestured for us to be seated.

The table was more private, in the corner of the restaurant, where two large walls of glass met. It afforded an even grander view outside. The round table was draped in white and set with red plates and lots of glassware. In the center were two dozen red roses arranged low so they didn't block the view. There were also a few flickering candles.

I pulled out a chair for Josie, and she slid in. Then I did the same right beside her. Both of us faced the window, the rest of the room at our backs.

I'd like to point out I don't normally sit with my back to the room, quite the contrary, but tonight I was willing to make an exception.

"Look at that!" Josie said, grasping my hand beneath the table and pointing with her other toward the floor-to-ceiling windows.

We had a perfect view of the water show outside. Both of us watched for long moments as the water shot into the sky, seeming to dance around and change colors all at once. The tall buildings and hotels behind it were also lit up, giving an even better show.

"I don't think anything will beat this view," I said.

Champagne was delivered to the table, along with a French appetizer, some kind of crepe. "Dinner will be out shortly," the server said.

"You already ordered?" Josie asked, looking at the food.

I nodded. "Sometimes a man just has to take control, baby."

Her eyes went back to the view. "Well, you definitely do it very well."

Using my fork, I cut into the crepe, which looked savory, not sweet, and held a bite up to her lips. She groaned when the flavors hit her tongue, and her eyes rolled back in her head.

She was practically indecent tonight. "Oh, that's so good."

"What is it?" I asked, trying to tell my dick to settle down.

Instead of picking up her own fork, Josie took the one out of my hand and fed me a bite. I was much less dramatic, but it was pretty good. It had artichokes in it.

We didn't have much conversation, really. It was hard to talk when the view was so spectacular and always changing. The food came out steadily (main course was steak), and the drinks were flowing.

The service was bomb, and the atmosphere was even better.

We did talk a little, some about Arrow and Hopper's wedding and the rest about everything I just mentioned.

"I've always wanted to see the Eiffel Tower. I know this isn't the real thing, but it sure feels like it right now," Josie said.

"You've not been to Paris?" That surprised me.

She shook her head, the long silky strands brushing over her bare shoulders. "Actually, no."

"We'll go." I decided.

She laughed. "When?"

"I might have something in mind." I hedged.

"Are you going to tell me?" she mused, propping her chin on her hand to stare at me, amused.

"I have something for you," I replied, hoping to redirect her attention.

Her eyes widened. "This isn't enough?" Gesturing to the table, the flowers, and the view, she raised an eyebrow.

"Not nearly," I whispered, feeling my heart start to pound. Reaching into the pocket of my leather jacket, I felt around, making sure to grab what I wanted. Josie's teeth sank into her lower lip, the white of them practically gleaming against the red.

Pulling out a black velvet box, I set it on the table between us.

Her eyes bounced between me and the box, and I smiled. "Well, go on," I told her.

Josie moved her body, spinning in the chair so her knees pointed in my direction instead of beneath the table. Without thinking, I put a hand over her knee, rubbing the velvety skin there. Picking up the box and holding it in her hand, she glanced at me again.

I smiled wide.

Watching her hold her breath, she popped open the box.

Her eyes rounded in surprise again as she nearly did a double take. Clearly, it wasn't what she was expecting, and she had no idea how to react.

Ah, my girl. I loved getting under her skin.

Lowering the box, the gift still inside, her eyes found mine. "A lock?"

I chuckled. I couldn't help it. "You like it?"

"Well," she said, glancing back down. "It's very pretty. I love that its red and shaped like a heart."

"But you still don't understand why I'm giving you a lock."

"Uh, no."

Pushing back the chair, I stood, offering her my hand. "C'mon. I'll show you." Once her hand was securely in mine, I reminded her, "Bring the lock."

On our way to the door, I nodded to the server, letting her know we'd be back. She gave me a knowing smile, and not for the first time tonight, my stomach knotted with nerves.

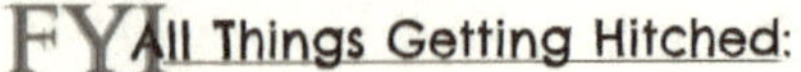

This entire night was totally unexpected. Right down to the velvet box I was holding… which had a lock inside.

Not a ring. A lock.

I couldn't even be disappointed because this was far too curious to be a letdown.

Jace led me through the Eiffel Tower Restaurant and pushed through a side door that seemed to come out of nowhere. When I stepped through, the summer air caught a few long strands of my hair and blew them out behind me like a flag.

"What is this?" I asked, looking around.

"It's a bridge," Jace explained, drawing me farther out onto the long bridge lined with streetlamps.

"Gee, thanks, Captain Obvious," I quipped. It was beautiful out here. Even down below, I could hear the water in the fountains from the light show.

He made a sound. "The Locks of Love Bridge to be exact."

I straightened, eyes flying up to meet his. "They have a Locks of Love Bridge here? I thought that was only in Paris."

Gesturing to the sides of the bridge filled with locks, Jace replied, "Not only in Paris."

Oh my goodness, this was incredibly romantic. "You got us a lock for the Locks of Love Bridge, Jace?" My voice was breathless and slightly awed.

He stopped walking, pulling me around so his arms could wrap around my waist. "Couldn't think of a better way to lock my lady down."

I rolled my eyes and groaned.

Laughing, his lips caught mine. I forgot all about his terrible joke and kissed him back, sliding my tongue over his. He tasted like champagne, but it was him who made me drunk.

"Thought it would be a good symbol of the way I feel about you," he whispered, his lips still upon mine.

I sighed. "I love it."

He pulled back abruptly and smacked my ass. "Good. Now come on. Pick a spot."

Taking his hand, we strolled down the bridge, looking at the thousands of locks already clipped here. Every single one of them symbolized love. All of them held a promise of forever, maybe even making something as great and intangible as love tangible.

Some of the locks were colored (like the red one we had) and some were just plain silver squares, but it didn't matter. All of them were beautiful because they represented something bigger.

"Here," I said, finally picking a spot and tugging Jace over to the railing.

"Looks good to me." He agreed. "You want to do the honor?"

Nodding, I took the red, heart-shaped lock out of the box along with the small key. Jace was quiet (and kind of fidgety) as he watched me open the latch. "Here?" I asked, slipping it onto a bare spot near the top of the railing.

"Anywhere you want, baby," he murmured.

I latched it closed, bending to make sure it was fully secure. "Hey," I said, noticing something I hadn't before. "There's something written on the back."

"Oh yeah?" he asked. "What?"

Holding it against my palm and turning the best I could to read it, I squinted at it.

Gasping, I straightened, totally letting go of the metal, spinning to look at Jace.

I gasped again.

He was standing there facing me, another black velvet box in his hands. This one was open, and it wasn't another lock.

It was a glittering ring.

My hand pressed against my chest, as if it were asking my heart to either restart or slow the hell down. I couldn't figure out which because I was so entranced by the sight of him standing there and the echo in my mind of the words I'd just read.

"What did it say, Josie?" Jace cajoled.

Tearing my eyes away from the ring and up to his dark, chocolate orbs, I sucked in another breath. "Jace…"

"Took you long enough to realize there was something written on that old, boring lock." He winked.

I recovered enough to smack him in the chest. "That was just mean, Jace!"

"Ah, but, baby, the look on your face right now is so worth it."

My lower lip quivered. Oh, he was getting to me. This was so incredibly sweet.

"What did the lock say?" he asked again.

The night air swirled around us, the lights glowed in the dark, and every so often, the locks would clink together to make a musical sound. "Will you marry me?" I whispered.

He nodded and actually dropped down on one knee. I started shaking, tears pooling in the corners of my eyes. I'd been hoping… but this was far more than anything I could have ever imagined. And Jace… down on one knee?

I'd never have believed it.

"I can't wait another day, another minute to ask you, baby." He began, holding the ring out. "I told you once I didn't own you, and I didn't want to. I wanted to be a choice, a choice you made every single day. I meant it then, and I mean it now. This ring isn't a sign of ownership; it's a promise, Josie. A promise that *I* choose *you*. Not just here and now, but always. For the rest of my life. Say yes, baby, but only say it if you know you will chose me for the rest of your life."

"Yes, Jace."

"You didn't even hesitate."

I scoffed. As if he expected me to hesitate. Yeah, right. "I'm a woman who knows who she wants."

Relief filled his face and body. Leaping up from the ground, he scooped me up, hugging me so tight my feet dangled above the concrete. "I love you so fucking much." I loved the growly quality to his voice.

Once he set me back on my feet, I smiled, feeling a little sassy. "And you might not want to own me, but you want this big-ass flashy ring to show I'm taken."

"How 'bout we slide it home so it can get to work?"

Holding out my hand, Jace picked up the ring and slid it onto my finger. Before allowing me to pull it back, he lifted my hand and pressed his warm, supple lips to the cool metal.

A small shiver shook my body, which made him smile smugly. I couldn't let his smugness go unpunished, so I responded by reaching out and cupping his cock right through the black jeans he was wearing.

Right out there in the open.

A couple walking by giggled because I wasn't exactly shy about the action.

Jace's eyes widened, and I gave him a little squeeze. A low groan slipped from between his parted lips.

Who was the smug one now?

Jace laughed low. "Life with you ain't ever gonna be boring, is it?"

I winked, then turned my attention to the ring on my finger. I had yet to fully appreciate its massive beauty.

It was too big. Too blingy. Totally gorgeous.

Maybe I was a little more girly than I thought. Jace always did seem to know that better than anyone, even me.

The ring was platinum and boasted a wide band. It took up quite a lot of space on my finger. It sort of reminded me of the cuff bracelet Hopper and Arrow gifted me, except this was a cuff for my finger. The width of the band had a scroll-like pattern. The design actually had a lot of movement, which I found beautiful. Inside some of the scrolls were inlaid diamonds, which caught the light expertly. The perimeter of the band on both sides was circled in small, round diamonds all lined up beside each other perfectly.

The design itself was cut out so the skin on my finger peeked through.

It was a gorgeous band. Made more so by the giant diamond in the center. The center stone was a perfectly cut round diamond set with four platinum prongs. It wasn't raised off the band too much, which I really appreciated. A ring like this had the ability to get in the way, especially when I was working under the hood of a car.

The center stone had to be at least one and a half carats, and the rest of the diamonds circling the band and filling out the scroll design had to equal another carat.

This ring was definitely more than I ever would have asked for, more than even I would have picked out on my own.

I loved it more than anything.

"Do you, ah, like it?" Jace asked, watching me study the design.

"Actually," I said, lowering my hand, "I'm in love with it."

He blew out a breath.

I lifted an eyebrow. "Could it be? Are you, Jace Lorhaven, actually nervous about something?"

His eyes narrowed. Then he muttered his reply. "Enjoying yourself?"

Stepping close, my arms wound around his neck, palms cupping the back of his head. "Am I enjoying the fact you love me enough to worry if I would like the ring you chose? Very much."

The sound of breath hissing out when our lips locked was all I heard. The sounds from the strip, passing footsteps, people nearby talking… all of it fell away.

In the moment, it was just Jace and me. Heat rushed up my neck, heating my cheeks, and the grip on the back of his neck intensified. A light breeze came out of nowhere, ruffling my hair, pushing it into his face as we kissed.

He moaned as if the feel of the silky strands was intoxicating. Meanwhile, his large, calloused palm reached around and cupped my ass. I stretched against him, leaning closer, and his hand slipped down and brushed against the bare skin of my upper thigh.

Breaking the kiss, Jace murmured, "This dress is too short, woman. Your fine ass is on display."

"You like it," I purred.

"Damn right." The husky quality in his voice made me smile, but my lips didn't hold it long, because he attacked my mouth once again.

Our tongues stroked together for a few more blissful moments before I pulled away to lay my cheek on his shoulder.

"Ah, Josie," he murmured, tucking me close.

We stood like that for a long time on the bridge, looking across the thousands of locks already placed there and out over the night lights and stunning view.

"I hope this proposal wasn't too… ordinary," he finally said.

Surprised, I yanked back. "What!"

He looked sheepish. "Vegas, the Paris Hotel, the Eiffel Tower… It's not cheesy, is it?"

I laughed. "Are you kidding? It's so romantic."

"You deserve romance, baby. I didn't want to do this at the track or at home… I've been waiting a long time, trying to figure out a way you deserved."

Surging forward, I took his face in my hands. "I love you, Jace. This is perfect, something I will never, ever forget." My eyes, which had been drilling into his, strayed to the ring on my finger.

Tucking me into his side, Jace led me toward the entrance into the Paris Hotel. "I'm thinking the real Eiffel Tower in Paris for a honeymoon," he said.

Paris in Vegas for a proposal, Paris in France for a honeymoon… It was perfect. "I would love that."

"Consider it done."

I gasped. "Wait!" I insisted and rushed back to where we hung our lock. "I need a picture of it!"

He laughed and patiently waited while I took too many photos. Then I made him smile for a selfie.

He secretly liked it.

"So you've been planning this for a while?" I asked after tucking the phone back into my red clutch.

Dragging his fingers through the long, straight strands of my dark hair, he sighed. "I've had that ring for months. It just never seemed like the right time. Guess you could say Arrow's wedding inspired me."

"You've been getting a lot of pressure to put a ring on my finger," I said knowingly.

"Not from you." He moved closer.

"That's because I know you love me," I whispered, rubbing my palm down the front of his chest.

Jace caught my hand, lacing it with his. "I do, baby. Always."

"Me, too."

"C'mon. We have dessert at the table." After a few steps toward the entrance to the restaurant, he said, "I'm assuming my punishment for bossing you around earlier is over and you're going to let me peel that sexy lacy thing off your curves later?"

My eyes rounded. He knew! What a dirty rat!

He laughed. "Ah, darling. Sometimes I just love to piss you off. So feisty."

I couldn't help it. I laughed. "You're definitely forgiven."

Before leaving the bridge, Jace lifted my hand and kissed the back of it. "Thank you for saying yes, Josie."

My skin tingled beneath his touch. "Thank you, Jace. Not just for tonight, but for all the nights I know are yet to come."

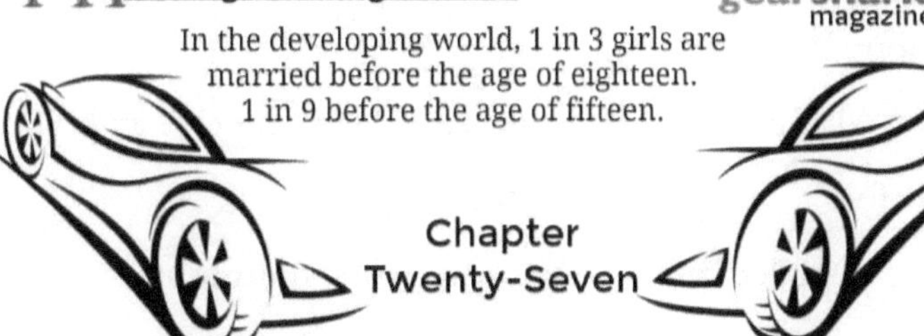

Larhaven

"Jace," her exhausted, sleep-rumpled voice moaned. I grabbed her hand, stopping her from hitting me in the chest for the fiftieth time. "Jace, the phone."

Snatching the phone off the nearby table while muttering an expletive, I practically snapped into it, "What!"

Someone cleared their throat. "This is the front desk, sir. This is your wake-up call."

"Already?" I moaned, wiping a hand over my eyes.

The voice on the other end of the line muffled a giggle. "Yes."

My eyes shot open, and I sat up. "Thank you." Before I could slam the receiver down, I thought better of it. "Any chance you can have coffee sent up to the room?"

"Of course, Mr. Lorhaven. Anything else with your coffee?"

I pulled the phone away from my mouth. "Baby, you want food?" I asked Josie, who basically looked like a pile of hair in the blankets.

She grunted.

"Eggs and bacon, please. And toast," I said into the phone.

"Of course. I'll have that sent right up."

After thanking her again, I hung up and dove on top of Josie, wrapping my arms around her and the blankets. She smelled good, like vanilla and something else. Oh, I knew the scent. It was me.

I loved it when my woman smelled like me.

"Wake that sexy ass up," I told her.

"Tired," she argued.

Messing around in her wild mane, I finally managed to find her ear, latching my lips around it to suck gently. "Did I keep you up too late last night?" I asked, rocking my hips into her.

"Yes," she moaned.

I chuckled. "You liked it."

With a heavy sigh, Josie rolled, pushing me off her to lie on her back. Her left hand flung upward into the air, turning so she could stare at the wide band there. "It wasn't a dream."

"Oh, fuck no. You're mine."

The hand and the ring curled around my neck, bringing me down for a good morning kiss. It ended too soon for my liking, and her attention went back to the ring.

"I didn't put that there so I could compete for attention against it."

"Should have bought me something smaller." She teased. Her voice was still throaty and deep from sleep.

"Hell," I muttered.

She laughed, letting her hand fall and turning to me. "Actually, it wouldn't matter. It could be a string around my finger and I'd still want to stare at it just as much."

I believed her.

"The *GearShark* interview is in like ten minutes."

Josie gasped and sat up. The blankets fell around her waist, exposing her naked body and velvety skin.

Her round breasts practically called my name, and the second the morning air brushed over them, they tightened into hardened pebbles. "I forgot!"

Palming the breast closest to me, I massaged the flesh, playing with the nipple, trying to nuzzle her neck. She yanked back and smacked me. "Are you crazy! We have an interview."

"It's a phone interview," I reminded her. "What did she call it? A flash round…"

"A rapid-fire round." Josie corrected.

I grunted. "Whatever. It's just a catch-up basically. We can do it from bed."

Without a word, Josie glanced down my body, realizing I was just as naked as her. "Wanna do it naked?"

"Don't we always do it naked?"

She rolled her eyes. "The interview, Jace."

"Giving an interview to a national magazine while naked?" I mused. "I like it."

Laughing, Josie began shoving the hair out of her eyes and brushing it back behind her shoulders.

There was a faint mark on the side of her breast from last night. I brushed a finger over it lightly. "Did I hurt you?"

She made a sound. "You know you didn't. I like it like that."

Last night had been all kinds of erotic. After we finished up at the Eiffel Tower Restaurant, we went up to the observation deck, a full story above where we ate dinner, and got an even better view of the city.

After that, I summoned the limo driver and told him to drive around for a while. I put up the privacy screen and proceeded to get some in the limo from my new fiancée.

Seeing that ring on her finger made me hornier than ever.

We went at it again when we arrived back to our room, finally passing out sometime in the early hours.

A knock on the door out in the other room had me banking the erotic thoughts. "Room Service!" someone yelled.

Damn, that was fast.

"Stay here," I told her, yanking the blankets up to cover her bare chest.

I was partway out the door when she yelled, "Jace!"

Glancing over my shoulder, I lifted an eyebrow. "Yes?"

"I'm all for a naked interview, but giving the waiter a show is a little much."

Flashing my teeth, I put on my best arrogant voice. "Maybe the waiter is a woman. Some tips don't require cash, baby."

Josie shot up so fast the sheet fell, putting both her beautiful, shapely breasts on display. It was an amazing sight.

"I will kick your ass, Lorhaven!" she all but roared.

Chuckling, I backtracked, still staring at her chest, to grab a pair of shorts, swiftly pulling them on. As I sauntered out of the bedroom, I told her, "That's Jace to you, sweetheart."

She was laughing when I closed the door behind me. Moments later, I shoved the door open wide again, wheeling in a cart of food that smelled like heaven.

"Mmm." She moaned, and I glanced up. Little minx dropped the sheets and was stretching her arms over her head, breasts on full display again.

Maybe doing the interview naked wasn't one of my better ideas. Talk about distracting.

Josie's cellphone, which was plugged in and resting on the bedside table, started going off. After glancing at the caller ID, she looked up at me. "It's Emily."

I motioned for her to pick it up as I poured some coffee. I was gonna need this shit to get through the questions. Why Emily Metcalf needed to follow up with us I didn't know, but as they say in business, any publicity is good publicity. I wasn't about to complain.

My sponsor for the NRR was thrilled when I let them know I got tapped for another interview. Might as well make the most of it. Besides, it wasn't every interview a man got to stare at a pair of perfectly round, perky breasts while he talked.

"Hey, Emily! This is Joey Gamble," Josie said, answering the phone. She sounded a hell of a lot more awake speaking to her than she did to me.

"Hi, Miss Gamble. Thank you so much for agreeing to this rapid-fire interview this morning. Is Lorhaven with you, or do you need a moment to get him?"

"Call me Joey," she insisted. "And Jace is here. Let me put him on speaker."

Josie motioned for me to say hi when it was done.

"Lorhaven here." I took a sip of my coffee and carried a mug to Josie, who was still in bed.

Darts shot from her eyes, so I figured that meant she thought I was being an ass. So I cleared my throat and tried again. "Thank you for calling this morning." I glanced back at Josie, and she smiled, so I figured she was happy now.

"Wonderful! And it's my pleasure. This is going to be such a fantastic issue for *GearShark*. The interview with Hopper and Arrow went so well, and to have you both a part of the issue along with Trent and Drew? Fans will devour this!"

"Trent and Drew are doing an interview?" I asked, drinking some coffee.

"A rapid-fire round like you," Emily replied. "I interviewed them via phone yesterday."

"That's great, Emily," Josie said. "We're glad to be part of this."

"Okay, so this is how it will work. I'll just ask you a few questions, you answer them, and then I'll write up a quick piece for the magazine. It's nothing crazy, and it shouldn't take too much of your time this morning."

I settled back against the headboard, drinking more coffee… I hated interviews.

Josie scooted closer, set the phone between us, and grabbed my hand. I moved over to grab her boob.

When I glanced at her, she smiled slyly.

"All right, Emily," I said, "ask away." Suddenly, I was feeling a lot more amenable.

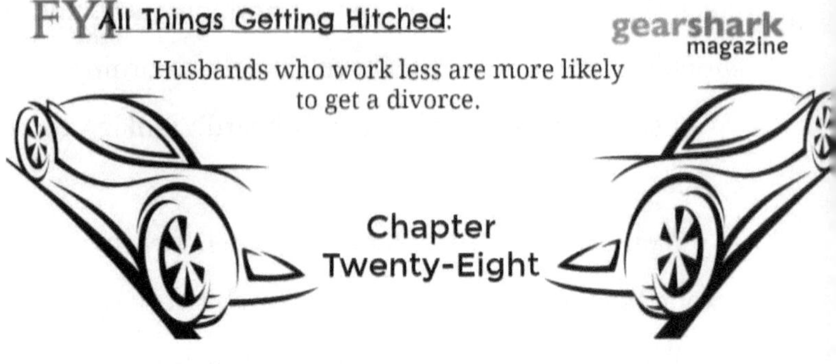

I think I made it weird.

Anyone who can make it weird with a guy while they're naked in bed, right after an epic proposal, while giving an interview to a national magazine is especially talented.

So how does one go about making things weird?

Tripping up over an answer that might have been easy but obviously wasn't. Well, it *was* an easy answer… Just not one I'd talked to Jace about and maybe one I was still mulling over in my own head.

Leave it to *GearShark* to go fishing for a story.

After the interview was over, we ate the room service and I distracted him with sex. Or so I thought.

Stepping out of the shower, toweling off, and making sure the bun I'd piled on top of my head hadn't gotten wet, I loaded my arms with clothes and went out to the bedroom to get dressed.

The ring on my finger sparkled as I moved and totally caught my attention. Wearing something this beautiful and large all the time was going to take a little getting used to.

"Want to go wander around the strip today?" I asked.

Jace didn't answer, so I spun, looking to where he sat in a nearby chair. The dark hair on his head was wet, so it looked darker than usual. It was combed back, the sides still short as they always had been. The defined muscles of his chest and arms were on total display because of the way he sprawled out in the chair, wearing only a pair of jeans, which were still unbuttoned.

"Jace?" I questioned. He was broody. I could tell just by looking at him.

Dark eyes flashed up to mine. The serious look on his face confirmed I wasn't going to put this off. "You didn't say anything."

I sighed, turning back to the bed and my clothes. "There's nothing to say."

He made a rude sound. "You want to have a baby, Josie."

This time I made the rude sound, glancing over my shoulder, hugging the towel a little tighter around me. "I thought you knew that. We always said we were going to have kids."

His eyes bore into me. I knew what he was thinking. "You want a baby now."

"I didn't say that," I argued, dropping the towel to dress.

"You didn't *not* say it."

Stupid interview.

I said nothing, instead focusing on dressing in a pair of wine-colored shorts. They were a silky material and tied at the waist, perfect for walking around the strip on a summer day. Over the shorts, I added my bra (of course), then a black tank top with wide straps. I felt

Jace's eyes as I slid my feet into a pair of black thong sandals.

"Josie," he intoned. God, it was delicious when he talked to me that way, even though it was his not-playing-around tone. "Come here."

Giving up to the conversation, I wandered over. He pulled me into his lap. Sighing, I rested my cheek against his bare shoulder.

I'd known immediately he picked up on the vibes bursting around me the second Emily asked the dreaded baby question. I hesitated, avoided his gaze, and then stammered out an answer that was pretty general.

Why couldn't she have pressured us about marriage? *Oh, that's right. 'Cause we already gave her the 4-1-1 about our engagement.*

"Why didn't you say something to me?" Both his arms rested on the chair. I didn't like it. He usually wrapped them around me. He was mad. I didn't like that either.

"Because I knew you'd react like this," I muttered, sour.

"Act like what?"

"Mad."

"You think I'm mad you want to have a baby?" Jace was choosing his words carefully. Something he didn't often do.

Lifting my head, I met his eyes. They were dark and unreadable, but mine still clung to his as if his stare were magnetized. "Are you?"

Suddenly, he sucked in a breath and just held it there in his lungs. After a few seconds, it whooshed out. "So you do?"

"I always figured I'd have kids, you know, like we both said we would someday. But I never really thought much about being a mother... To be honest, I'm not really sure I'll be a very good one. My own mother moved out when she and Dad got divorced and really hasn't looked back. I wasn't what she wanted. And then there's my father..."

"He didn't always make you feel too wanted either." Jace finished.

Shrugging one shoulder, I replied, "He's always been there for me, which is more than I can say for my mother. And I know he loves me. Our relationship has been a lot better the past year or so, but yeah." My voice quieted. "He didn't always make me feel like I was enough either."

"Ah, baby," Jace whispered, closing his arms around me.

My heart skipped a beat. My cheek went back to his shoulder and my world shifted back on axis. "You're so much more than just enough. And I know for a fact you're going to be a better mother than most."

"How can you be so sure?" I asked, vulnerability stark in my tone.

"Because you know exactly how you *don't* want to make a child feel. Because you're so good at love you made me, a guy who was pretty much a confirmed bachelor, change his mind and propose on the freaking Eiffel Tower, for Chrissakes."

Holding my hand out a little, I gazed down at the ring. "Last night was the best."

I felt his lips brush the top of my head. "It's nothing compared to what our future is going to be like."

I didn't say anything. I just sat there thinking.

"You should have said something to me," Jace said, not willing to let it go. "I shouldn't find out stuff like that during interviews."

"It's not like I told the world I'm pregnant," I burst out, looking up. "I didn't even say anything to that degree at all, just that we would have kids someday."

"I saw your face, Josie."

"It was a phone interview. No one else saw," I muttered.

His stare was stony. He was being a butthead. I sighed heavily. "Yes, okay. I've been thinking about it a lot recently."

"You didn't say anything."

"I'm beginning to think you're madder because I didn't tell you every single thought that goes on in my head versus the fact I actually want to have a baby soon."

His lips lifted on one side. "I am."

Well, that got my attention. Sitting up straight, I felt my mouth round in a little O.

Jace laughed low, rubbing his hand up my back. "I can't give you what you want, baby, if you don't tell me what it is."

I gaped at him. Nervous excitement fluttered around inside me. "I didn't think it was the right time. We weren't even engaged. You had enough pressure from my father and everyone else just to marry me. I wasn't about to come home one day and tell you I was getting a case of baby fever."

He lifted an eyebrow. "Baby fever."

I smacked him lightly in the chest. He was making fun of me.

Catching my hand, lifting it from his chest, and kissing the backs of my fingers, he said, "Tell me about this baby fever, Josie."

I shrugged again. "I don't know. Just one day I was out, planning Arrow's wedding, and I saw this woman… She had a baby and a stroller. The image stuck with me, kind of made me feel a type of longing I've never really felt before. We've been together a while now, Jace. It will be two years soon. During that time, I feel we've built a family around us. My father, Hopper and Arrow. Hell, we have family dinners now."

Jace laughed.

"I love it a lot," I whispered. It was kind of silly, but it made me feel shy to admit. I was always the strong woman, the woman who didn't need anyone. And really, I didn't. I could survive on my own.

I just didn't want to. Not ever.

"That's a good thing." He stroked his hand up my back.

"We have our house together, and I love waking up to you. It just feels like our life is so good. Hopper said something to me before about what our kids would be like." I pressed a hand to my stomach without thinking. "I just…"

"Just what?" he cajoled.

I met his eyes. "I want that piece of you. I want your baby growing inside me. I want more of us, more of our family."

"I like the picture you paint." His hand joined mine over my stomach.

I know he said he liked it, but this had to be a surprise. Geez, he just asked me to marry him. I never even planned to bring this up, not for at least another year. "I didn't tell you because it's just that, a picture. A thought… maybe a dream of what we might have in a few years. I'm so happy right now with you, *just* you." Laying my palm against his cheek, I went on. "I know we aren't really ready for a baby. I don't want to pressure you."

He laughed.

"Why are you laughing!" I demanded. I was trying to pour my heart out here!

"Baby, you know I don't succumb to pressure."

I rolled my eyes and tried to vacate his lap. He wouldn't let me go.

"I gotta tell you, though. I didn't see this convo coming. Not right now." He went on as if I wasn't trying to escape him.

I stopped struggling. "Why?"

"I thought you were loving the NRR."

"Why can't I love the NRR and want a baby?" I wondered.

He growled deep in his chest. "There is no way in hell I will let you behind the wheel of a race car with my baby inside you."

I slumped back against him, his arms loosely around my waist. "I'm not even going to argue with you."

His voice took on an edge he usually reserved for other people, manly people who thought he was an asshole. "Good, because this one fight you will not win."

"Let me finish," I demanded. "I won't argue with you because you're right."

Jace's body went rigid for a moment, as if he'd been stung by a giant wasp. *He's surprised I'm not arguing.* I smiled to myself. "I can't race and be pregnant at the same time."

"I won't have you or my child at risk."

My, my, he sounded like a grizzly bear. I liked it.

"The season is almost over. It's been a good season, but I don't know… Racing has kind of lost some of its spark for me."

Jace exhaled. "Because of the hazing and everything that happened when you were still in NASCAR?"

I nodded slowly. "But also because I don't really feel like I have to prove myself anymore. I've already busted molds and stereotypes. I've gone against the grain a long time. I'm tired, Jace."

He made a sound and stood, bringing me with him. When my feet hit the floor, Jace spun me so we were facing one another and pressed his forehead to mine. "I don't want you to be tired. And this seems like a much bigger conversation than just a baby."

I shook my head. "Not really. It's all connected. I just feel like things are changing inside me... I don't have to fight as hard now. I feel like I'm growing and I want more out of life."

"You didn't tell me about this, Josie." His brow furrowed, agitation back in his voice.

"I am now."

He scoffed. "Because I'm forcing it out of you."

"You would never force me," I whispered, wrapping my arms around his neck.

Dragging his knuckles down the side of my cheek, he whispered, "No, baby, I wouldn't."

I kissed him softly.

He lifted his head after. "If you quit racing, what will you do?"

Pulling back, pacing away, I said, "I'd like to become even more involved in the foundation I started with Dad. Maybe start a mentor program." I turned. The last thought kind of stuck to my tongue, not wanting to come out. It was sort of a leap.

"And…" He coaxed as if he sensed there was more.

Taking a breath, I spun. "I'd kind of like to write a book."

His face belayed his surprise. "A book? Like with words and shit?"

I giggled but then nodded. "Yeah, kind of like a tell-all, but more than that. Behind the scenes of racing, what it's like to be a female in a male-dominated sport. What it was like growing up as the daughter of a near billionaire, my mother leaving. How to be strong as a female without losing yourself."

He was staring, not saying anything.

I stammered. "I mean… I'm not an expert or anything. God knows I don't have it all figured out. I just thought it might inspire some women… It's stupid."

Suddenly, he launched across the space separating us, gripping my shoulders. "Don't say that."

"So you don't think the book is stupid?" I questioned.

"Nothing about you is stupid, Josie. You're so goddamn amazing. I'm so fucking lucky to have you. I love your strength, your drive. I love everything about you. I'd be fucking insane to not want my child growing inside you."

My heartbeat sped, making me feel like I'd just run a marathon. "What are you saying?"

He smiled slow. "Let's have a baby."

Emotion rose inside me, clogging my throat, making my chest feel tight. "But next year, right?" I asked, because this was crazy.

Right?

Lifting me off my feet so I would wrap my legs around his waist, he said, "How about right now?"

My mouth dropped open, and he took it as an invitation to kiss me into oblivion. My head was spinning when we fell back on the bed, him beneath me. Laughing, I kissed him again. Jace rolled, pinning me under him and reaching for the hem of my shirt.

"Jace!" Gasping, I pushed his shoulder back. Lifting his head, he gazed at me impatiently. "You mean, now *now*?"

"You got somewhere else to be?" he drawled, lowering his head to kiss the exposed part of my flat belly. Moaning, my fingers delved into the damp strands of his hair.

He circling his tongue around my navel, and I shivered a little as he kissed his way toward the waistband of my shorts.

"We should get married first." I panted, trying to pull his head up. "You should take some time to think about this."

Sighing, Jace crawled up my body, lying over me while balancing some of his weight on his elbows. "I don't need to think about it. I already know I want you forever. You and anyone else you might make me."

Oh my God, he was saying yes. He was totally willing to give me a child right now. Suddenly, nerves assailed me. Gazing up into his eyes, I chewed on my lower lip. "We aren't ready."

He grinned. "Who cares? I wasn't ready for you either, and that turned out just fine."

"You really want to have a baby?" I whispered.

His answer was to kiss me again. Fiercely. So fiercely when I pulled back, our lips made a suction sound.

Scowling down at me, he spoke, "I'm trying to get some."

"I have to go off the pill before I can get pregnant, Jace."

"Practice," he murmured, then dove back into my lips. "Nothing wrong with practice."

I surrendered to him, to the emotions swirling around us, and to practice. Practice was pretty fun.

Chapter Twenty-Nine

Lorhaven

I was going to be a husband. And a father.

Right now, I was arriving to a weekly family dinner.

This was a far cry from the streets I used to run. A giant leap from the street rats, fast cars, and fist fights. How quickly, how drastically life could change.

Josie totally caught me off guard with the baby thing. But once I looked in her eyes, saw the desire, heard her words… I wasn't about to say no to that shit.

Not when her desire made me desire it too.

Just looking at her now, at her flat stomach, and knowing my child could be growing inside her at any given time, it was the most satisfying thing I'd ever felt.

Seeing the giant ring on her finger was also a giant win.

These things also meant I needed to step it up. It was my job to make sure Josie was happy and had what she wanted. Starting with our wedding.

Which was why I was arriving a little early for Friday night family dinner. It was the first one since Arrow and Hopper got home from their two-week honeymoon. We were telling everyone about the wedding tonight (the baby plans were staying under wraps), but first I wanted to talk to Gamble.

I didn't bother knocking before entering his study. Family didn't knock. He looked up from behind his desk, a pair of black-framed readers perched on his nose.

"Lorhaven," he said in way of greeting. "Am I late to dinner?" He glanced at the Rolex on his wrist.

"I'm early," I said.

"Where's Joey?"

"She'll be here soon."

"Is something wrong?" he asked, abandoning the papers and stack of work in front of him.

"No. I just want to talk, avoid anything that might be wrong."

"I'm assuming this is about your engagement." Setting his glasses on the desk, he got up and went to the cart with drinks and crystal glasses.

I made a sound. "How'd you know about that?"

Gamble pointed to the newest issue of *GearShark*, the one with Hopper on the cover, lying on his desk.

"That's out already!" I burst out.

"I'm not sure if it's hit stands. I got early copies because of Hopper."

"And we told Emily about the engagement." I surmised.

"I'm a bit surprised to learn about it so impersonally."

"Yeah, I'm sorry about that. We planned to tell everyone tonight at dinner when we are all together. Joey wanted it that way."

"You didn't come to me, ask me for her hand."

I lifted an eyebrow. "You wanted me to ask you first? I thought I had your approval already. You pretty much gave it when I first came here to meet you.

You've been bitching about me putting a ring on her finger for months now."

"I don't bitch," he mused, drinking some of the dark-colored liquid. "Drink?" he asked.

I shook my head. "Are you telling me you don't approve?"

He chuckled. "Of course I approve. Congratulations, son. No one is good enough for my daughter, but you'll be okay." Stepping forward, he offered his hand, and I shook it.

"What a ringing endorsement," I muttered. Really, I could give a rat's ass what he thought.

"I expect you to make my daughter very happy." He went on.

"That's why I'm here," I said coolly.

"Oh?"

I took a seat near the fireplace. "Josie is excited to tell you about the wedding. But I want to make sure we're on the same page so she stays that way."

"Meaning what?" Gamble carried his drink back around to his desk.

"I'm not putting her through a big society wedding that's more like a show for all your business contacts. I want her to have the wedding *she* wants, not the wedding she thinks you want her to have."

He studied me a moment, setting down his glass with a distinctive thud. "I have no intention of turning my daughter's wedding into a business affair."

"Good."

"I'm not sure if I should be offended or proud that you came here to lay down terms on how I should approach my daughter's engagement."

"To be blunt, I don't give a shit if you're pissed. My loyalty is to Josie and making her happy. I'm not accusing you of anything. I'm just reminding you that your daughter always wants to please you, and you need to remember that when she starts talking wedding plans."

Approval showed in his eyes. It was nice to have, but like I said, I didn't need it. "What kind of wedding do you think my daughter wants?"

"I'm not entirely sure. I just know she had a good time planning Arrow's because they let her do what she wanted. It's going to be the same for this. And I know she's not going to want a dog and pony show."

Gamble nodded once. "Whatever she wants she'll have."

"I'm not asking you to pay for it. I'll take care of it. I just don't want her upset."

The first sign of that steely businessman glinted in his eyes. He sat forward. "I will pay for my daughter's wedding. Not you. It's a father's duty."

"Agreed." I relented. "So long as—"

"We're clear. I will be sure she doesn't do something she thinks I want."

"What do you want?" I asked curiously.

"For my daughter to be happy."

Pushing out of the chair, I nodded. "Then we both want the same thing."

The slamming of the front door and footsteps approaching caused us both to look toward the door.

"Dad!" Joey came rushing through, stopping when she saw me sitting there. "Jace, you got here early."

I shrugged casually. "My errand didn't take as long as I thought."

She smiled, crossed the room, and pressed a kiss to my cheek. As I was tucking an arm around her, she whispered, "Did you tell him?"

"Of course not," I said out of the corner of my mouth, noting Gamble was slyly covering the issue of *GearShark* on his desk.

"Tell me what?" he asked.

Joey stiffened. "You heard me?"

"Young lady, I'm not so old that I can't hear a conversation going on right in front of me."

"Jace and I have something to tell you," she said.

"Go on." He encouraged, rising out of his chair.

Josie lifted her left hand to flash the ring I'd put there. "We're getting married!"

Gamble smiled, surprise lighting his eyes. The old dog didn't let on even a millimeter that he already knew. "Well, it's about time!"

He came around his desk, and Joey rushed forward to hug him.

"Congratulations, my baby," he said against her ear while looking at me. I smiled. Joey pulled back, gazing at him. He cupped her face with his hands. "I'm very happy."

"You are?"

"Of course! Now I know the ring is a big deal for the ladies, so let me see."

She laughed and held it out. He lifted her hand to inspect the diamond. "Hmm, cut and clarity seem to be very exceptional. Platinum is a good choice."

I raised an eyebrow. "You know about jewelry?"

He drew himself up. "I'm a businessman. Of course I know about jewelry."

Joey glanced over her shoulder. "He owns a jewelry store chain."

"I didn't know that." I was surprised.

"I'm a silent partner," he said, glancing back at the ring. "Is this a custom piece by Clay Carver?"

I cleared my throat. "Ah, yes."

He nodded approvingly. "He's done a few pieces for me. He's very talented."

Geez, this man was everywhere.

"It's beautiful, Joey. Perfect for you," Gamble told her quietly, releasing her hand.

"Thank you, Dad."

"So when's the wedding?" he asked.

"Soon," I replied.

"We don't want to wait," Joey explained.

"I agree. Now you just tell me what you want and how you want it, and we'll make sure it happens."

"Really?" Her tone sounded slightly surprised.

Gamble glanced up and caught my eye. I smiled.

"Whatever you want. But nothing too flashy, huh? This isn't for the business pages. It's a family affair."

"Oh, I'm so glad to hear you say that, Dad!" Joey threw her arms around him again, hugging him close.

Our eyes met over her shoulder. He nodded imperceptibly.

You were right, he mouthed silently.

I know. I inclined my head. *Thank you.*

"Let's head into the dining room. I'm famished. I missed lunch because I was on a conference call," Gamble said, leading her from the room.

"Dad! I told you not to do that. You should have had Mary go pick you up something." Joey scolded him.

"Nothing ruins a business deal faster than chomping into the speaker like a man with no good breeding."

"Ugh!"

"Where are those boys?" Gamble mused as they got farther out into the hall. "They better not be late or they're not getting dessert."

"They're newlyweds." Joey excused them.

Gamble muttered something I couldn't hear, and Joey gasped.

I grinned and hurried to catch up. I was missing the good part.

Just as I stepped into the hallway, the front door slammed again. "We're here!" Hopper yelled. "We aren't late!"

"You're late!" Gamble yelled from the dining room.

"He better give me my dessert," Arrow whined loudly. "I'm starving."

"You'll get dessert, babe, even if I have to bribe the housekeeper." Hopper assured him.

"There will be no bribing in my house!" Gamble called.

I met Arrow and Hopper in the doorway of the dining room. Arrow came forward and hugged me instantly. My chest tightened just a little at his affection. I'd missed him these last two weeks.

When he pulled away, I studied his face. He looked good. Tan. Happy. Relaxed. His eyes were no longer shuttered as they used to be.

"You look good, A," I said. "Happy."

"I am," he replied.

"Sit down, you bunch of ingrates!" Gamble bellowed.

Joey and Hopper laughed.

My brother and I went to join the rest of our family for dinner.

PS: After dinner, I snuck into Gamble's office while Josie was talking everyone's heads off about everything she wanted for the wedding. Turns out she had the whole damn thing planned in her head already. For anyone who said she wasn't girly enough, clearly, they had no fucking clue. After unburying the new issue of *GearShark*, I flipped through to our rapid-fire interview and read it through.

It was a good article.

presents a...

RAPID FIRE ROUND

with

LORHAVEN & JOEY GAMBLE

written by Emily Metcalf
© gearshark magazine

What is a Rapid Fire Round here at GearShark? It's exactly what it sounds like! It's where I catch up with some of our beloved racers from past issues and find out what they're up to now! And since we here at GS love all things speed, why not have a rapid-fire round of questions? And what better issue to debut this new feature than this red-hot edition!

I recently caught up with NRR racer Joey Gamble and her ~~boyfriend~~ fiancé (Eek! I smell another exclusive! Keep reading for the deets!) Lorhaven, who were recently in Las Vegas for the wedding of our cover star this month.

Rather than sit down formally for this rapid-fire round, I dialed them up via phone so we could talk it out. And yes, they're still together and still as #swagalicious as ever. It's cheesy, I know, but I had to go there. This couple positively pours electricity, even through the phone.

This might be a quickie interview, but the news you're hearing here first will definitely put a slow burn in your heart.

So, race fans and readers alike, let's get firing!

GS: Joey and Lorhaven, it is so good speak with you again! It's been a while since your sizzling cover hit our stands, and I have to ask. You weren't a couple for that first interview, but you got together shortly after, so would you credit *GearShark* as your matchmaker?

L: Sure, yeah. We'll go with that. Or maybe it was my sexy, charming ways and the fact I know my way around a racetrack.

JG: <Groans> Clearly, Lorhaven is still as big-headed as the last time you spoke with us.

GS: If I remember, you two didn't get along too well in that interview.

JG: We've always had sparks.

GS: So besides burning up the NRR—congratulations on your impressive STATS this season—what have you been doing beyond the track?

L: I put a ring on it.

JG: <Laughs> He put a ring on it.

GS: Are you saying you're engaged?

L: Yes, and I plan to speed to the altar just as fast as I drive.

JG: <Laughing in the background>

GS: Another race-world wedding! Congratulations!

JG: Thank you.

GS: I have to throw it out there that we would love to have the first look at your wedding photos and maybe the ring you've got on your finger, Joey.

JG: I might be able to make that happen.

GS: <Side note: I scored a pic of the ring! You can check that out at the bottom of this article!>

GS: Usually we stick to racetrack talk, but for this issue, we're going past the #finishline to delve more into your lives beyond racing. You both up for that?

L: Depends on what you're asking.

GS: It will be painless. I promise.

JG: Ask away!

GS: In the spirit of the Rapid Fire Round, let's keep the answers short and sweet. First, favorite car?

L: I'm gonna have to go with the Corvette.

JG: I'm totally in love with Jace's Lotus.

L: And that's why I still drive it instead of a new Corvette.

GS: You call him Jace, not Lorhaven?

JG: Jace is his first name.

GS: So you do have more than one name! <Another exclusive!>

L: Sure do, but only two people in my life are allowed to use it.

GS: Who's the second?

L: My brother.

GS: What's in your pocket right now?

L: We're naked.

JG: Ohmigod! We are not! We're, uh, in our pajamas… so nothing in our pockets.

L: Naked.

JG: <Groans>

GS: <So tell me, *GS* fans. Do you think they actually did this interview naked?>

GS: Joey, do you like the NRR better than NASCAR?

JG: Yes.

GS: Lorhaven, what's your favorite word?

JG: It's probably not appropriate for print.

L: Josie.

GS: Josie?

JG to L: Really?

L: Of course, baby.

GS: <I think I may have swooned. Clears throat.>

JG: My name is actually Josephine. Joey for short… Or as Jace calls me, Josie.

GS: Do you live together?

L: Of course.

GS: Are you pregnant, Joey?

JG: <Makes a surprised sound>

L: What the fuck kind of question is that?

GS: Figured you might want to cut out any rumors about why you are engaged.

L: I asked her to marry me because I love her and for no other reason.

GS: So what about kids down the road? Think you two will have a few mini racers one day?

GS: <There was an awkward pause here. It didn't last long, but I feel it's my journalistic duty to mention the weird charge on the other end of the line.>

JG: I think kids are definitely part of the big picture. Someday. In the future.

GS: What do you like to do in your off time?

L: Have sex.

JG: Jace!

JG to GS: Don't put that in the interview.

L to JG: Who cares? Anyone who looks at you will understand my answer anyway.

JG: <mutters> Not my father.

L: BLEEP. BLEEP. <censored> Yeah, maybe don't add that.

GS: <Clearly, I have to add this.>

JG: I like action movies. And family dinners.

L: I like working on my cars.

GS: One last question before I cease fire. Who said I love you first?

JG: Pretty sure that was me.

L: But I said it back.

There you have it, race fans, my Rapid Fire Round with Joey Gamble and Lorhaven—who, by their own admission, are soon to be married!

If you enjoyed this RFR interview, be sure to check out our bonus RFR in the back of this issue with GearShark's favorite couple, Drew Forrester and Trent Mask!

gearshark
magazine

Chapter
Thirty

Joey

It only took me a little over a month to plan the wedding. I didn't want anything over the top, but I wanted something I would always remember.

My father was so supportive. When I offered to invite some of his business contacts, he shot it down instantly. He wanted our wedding to be all about family. I had to admit it surprised me, but it was a pleasant surprise, and I certainly wasn't going to question him.

Because Lorhaven didn't want to wait (I didn't either!) I chose a day in early September. The weather here in Maryland was cooling down but wasn't so cold we couldn't be outdoors for a beautiful fall ceremony.

The Gamble estate was the perfect location. The vast property my father's house sat on and the privacy it afforded was a no-brainer.

The guest list was small, just our family and close friends. Oh, and my mother flew in as well. It was the first time I'd seen her in several years. She was completely charmed by Jace, which annoyed me to no end.

All my life, she barely approved of anything I did, until she caught one look at my soon-to-be very attractive and rich husband and decided I was once again the daughter she always wanted.

Yeah. Don't think so, Mom.

Get your own man and keep your paws off mine.

Luckily, Jace was no fool. It was so terribly bitchy, but it gave me intense glee to watch him treat her so coolly and her get so flustered, unable to understand why.

I didn't have any close girlfriends, something I never really cared about until I was planning this wedding. My entire family was a bunch of men. I liked men… but let's face it; men were morons sometimes.

And they didn't care at all about weddings or gowns or bridal hairstyles.

I didn't think I much cared either until I started planning Arrow and Hopper's wedding and then my own.

I don't know how, but Trent knew. He always knew. He had some sort of deep, emphatic way about him, of anticipating someone's deepest emotions.

He and Drew showed up one day with their sisters in tow. Ivy Forrester was pretty much becoming a twenty-first century style icon. Rimmel was a self-proclaimed hot mess, but Ivy made a tsking sound and told her she was coming into her own.

I thought the tiny, dark-haired football star wife was pretty gorgeous, in an understated way. Even if she did some dress shopping in an old hoodie.

I'd met the girls before, of course, when I was "training" Drew for the NRR, at other races, and Jace and I had spent some time at their family compound because Arrow loved it there so much. Even so, I was too shy (Me, shy? Guess so.) to call and ask them to basically do girly stuff with me. Besides, I could do this on my own. I didn't need anyone to help me pick out a gown or makeup…

I kinda wanted someone, though.

Like I said, Trent knew. I didn't even have time to feel awkward when they all showed up, like I was pathetic for not having any girls as friends to rely on, because Ivy was like a tornado.

She swept into Dad's house as if she'd visited a thousand times and started girl talk as if we had every day for years. Meanwhile, Rimmel made coffee and gave suggestions, to which Ivy would gasp and proclaim to be the "best ever."

I sat at the giant island, a little overwhelmed but also kind of emotional. Trent caught my eye and smiled, which made me shove off the barstool and hug him spontaneously.

About thirty minutes into the visit, Drew announced he'd had enough torture and wanted French fries. Ivy called him a butthead, and Rimmel laughed.

Once the boys were all gone, the three of us put our heads together and came up with something I thought was perfect. During the weeks that led up to the wedding, I kept in touch with both girls, and to my surprise, they became real friends, not just girls who would help me with my big day and then disappear from my life.

The day of our wedding dawned. The sky was a perfect shade of blue and only the fluffiest, whitest clouds filled the sky. There was a cool breeze in the air, and as I dressed, I imagined it gently ruffling the petals of the sunflowers I'd chosen as decoration outside.

"You look absolutely stunning," Ivy said after adding the finishing touches to my makeup and stepping away. "Rim?"

Rimmel was standing nearby in a wine-colored, one-shoulder gown that skimmed the floor when she moved. The flowy fabric also did an expert job at concealing a barely-there baby bump. "Perfect." She agreed.

Butterflies danced low in my belly. I pressed a hand there and stepped up in front of the giant mirror leaning against the wall. We were in my old bedroom here at my father's estate, which I'd basically turned into wedding headquarters over the past few weeks.

"How in the world did you do it?" I asked, staring at my reflection, disbelief heavy in my voice.

"Do what?" Ivy asked, wrinkling her nose.

"Make me look like this in half the time it takes me to make myself look half this amazing."

Rimmel snorted. "It's her God-given gift. She does it to me all the time."

Ivy rolled her eyes. "It's hardly difficult. You two are beautiful to begin with."

Gazing back into the mirror, I took in the way I looked, noting I'd never looked so good. Which was so appropriate because I didn't think I'd ever been quite this happy.

"That gown is so beautiful. It inspired me to write an article for my column in *People* all about the designer," Ivy said.

My gown was the most stunning thing I'd ever worn, designed by Galia Lahav for the most recent fall collection. The gown was designed with a beautiful, classic silhouette that hugged all my curves expertly. From the waist up, the bodice was completely fitted, boasting a high, sheer neckline and lace cap sleeves. There was a wide cutout between my breasts, but instead of being open and too exposing, it was filled in with sheer lace and heavier 3D appliques that sparkled with fine beadwork.

The waist itself was also slightly sheer and made of the same material as the neck, which sort of looked like the fanciest kind of white, sheer netting a person could afford. From the waist, it draped over my curvy hips and fell to the floor in a white, sparkly curtain.

The entire gown was so white it was near icy. The lavish beading was so intricately done, on first glance, one thought it was the lacy fabric that shimmered so.

Because of the beading and appliques, the gown had some weight to it, but I didn't mind. It helped me feel grounded on a day I felt I was floating.

Due to the dress being such a showpiece, I went very simple on accessories, my only two being the cuff bracelet Hopper and Arrow gifted me and my engagement ring from Jace. I bucked tradition and chose a pair of wine-colored heels.

Ivy did my makeup in a natural, glowy way that gave me a "lit from within" look. My usually wild curly hair was blown out and pulled back into a simple twist with a few wispy pieces around my temples and ears.

"Just one more thing," Ivy said, pulling a small white box out of her bag. "For you."

My eyes widened. "You got me a gift?"

"You are the bride," Rimmel said, stepping closer.

"Yes, but you've already done more than enough. Just being here—"

"Are you kidding? We're friends now! Practically family. We don't work that way in our family," Ivy boasted.

Rimmel nodded sagely. "We like to give presents."

I laughed and took the box. "Seriously, though," I said, feeling all emotional. "The best gift of all is getting to know you both better. I've never had friends that were girls."

"That's because bitches be tripping," Rimmel quipped.

"Word," Ivy deadpanned.

I laughed. "Well, you two aren't bitches."

"Open it!" Rimmel insisted.

It was a pair of diamond earrings. In the shape of the Eiffel Tower. Tears flooded my eyes.

"Oh no you don't!" Ivy went into crisis mode and started fanning me with everything she could find. "Don't cry! You'll ruin your makeup."

Sucking in a deep breath, I forced back the tears. "They're beautiful."

"A little birdie told us you got engaged there," Ivy said.

Rimmel added, "And you can wear them on your honeymoon to see the original!"

Still holding the box, I threw my arms around them both.

"We need to go take our seats," Ivy said, sniffling. "Put those on and then meet your father downstairs."

I nodded.

When I was alone, a calmness settled over me. A bone-deep rightness. Suddenly, all I wanted was to make it to Jace and look into his deep, chocolate eyes.

My father was waiting at the back door when I stepped into his view. He straightened immediately, his eyes turning misty.

"You are the most beautiful bride I have ever seen, Josephine."

"Thank you, Dad."

Moving forward, I took his arm and gazed out the back door toward the wedding setup on the rolling lawn.

"Joey," he said before we stepped outside. "I just wanted to tell you how very proud I am of you. How much I love you. I know I haven't always showed it the best I could, but—"

I leaned over, kissing his cheek and silencing his words. "I know, Daddy. I love you. Thank you for always being here for me."

Blinking rapidly and adjusting his wine-colored tie, he cleared his throat. "I'm not sure this fellow is good enough after all. Maybe you should ditch him and just move back home."

I laughed, and the music started up outside. "I'm doing this," I said. "You coming?"

"Wouldn't miss it."

We walked together across a long white path that was laid just for this moment. It led up to a large white archway dripping in sunflowers and other greenery. On each side of the arch was a door. Old wooden barn doors that were weathered and opened as if they welcomed us into the wedding.

Beyond the archway and the doors were a bunch of white wooden chairs where all our guests sat smiling. I barely paid them any attention. My eyes went straight to the second archway that served as the altar. It too was draped in sunflowers and greenery. Huge pots of deep-burgundy mums flanked the wooden platform, defining the space where Jace stood.

He was dressed in a classic black tuxedo with a white vest and black tie. It's true what they say about men in suits.

Well, not all men—just Jace.

It was an aphrodisiac.

Our eyes collided instantaneously, as if they'd been waiting for the moment they would at last meet. He liked the way I looked. I knew because of the way his eyes widened and filled with awe when I first stepped into his sight.

Arrow stood behind his brother, also dressed in a classic black tux, and on the other side of the altar, on my side, stood Hopper.

When I glanced at him, he winked.

"Did you change your mind?" my father whispered.

I giggled and stepped through the doors beneath the arch.

Everyone stood as I walked down the aisle, arm in arm with my father, holding a giant bouquet of sunflowers. The autumn breeze stirred, spreading the scent of fresh-cut flowers t. I inhaled, knowing I would acquaint this scent with this day for the rest of my life.

I quickened my steps toward Jace, and the closer I got, muffled laughter filled the space. I glanced over and saw Romeo standing beside Rimmel. He was about four times her size.

"Young lady, slow down. Have some decorum," my father muttered mildly.

"No way, Dad. You know I like speed."

He laughed, and we powerwalked the rest of the way down the aisle.

Jace was grinning when I finally got there. "Took you long enough." He teased.

"Do you give this woman to this man to be married?" the minister asked my father.

"I guess so," he replied.

I elbowed him lightly in the side.

"I do," he said louder.

After kissing his cheek, finally, *finally*, I stepped up beside Jace.

The ceremony went quickly, and when we finally said I do, Jace wasn't shy about pulling me tautly against him, wrapping me in his arms, and planting the mother of all kisses right on my lips.

Everyone cheered, and we ran back down the aisle hand in hand as bird seed came flying from every direction.

The reception was in a nearby building my father had built just for this purpose. I thought it was a little overboard to build and entire barn just for the sole purpose of a wedding ceremony, but my father did what he wanted and that would never change.

The interior was rustic and chic at the same time. White lights hung everywhere. Sunflowers and white pillar candles wrapped in cinnamon sticks filled the tables.

We dined on lobster tail and steak, all the guys roasted Jace with their toasts, and our wedding cake was chocolate.

Yes, chocolate. Just like my shoes, I bucked tradition and went with what I wanted (and maybe I was kinda craving chocolate). It was five layers of rich, dark chocolate, and the side exploded with sunflowers.

Besides Jace, the cake was my favorite part.

Just after polishing off my second piece (It was my wedding; I could do what I wanted.), Jace pulled me outside, pushing me up against the side of the barn.

"I've been waiting to get you alone."

Lifting his left hand, I gazed down at the steel band on his finger. It had tire treads engraved around the band and my name on the inside. "The bad boy of racing wears a wedding band at last," I murmured, smiling.

"It's not nearly as painful as I thought it would be," he cracked.

Glancing down at the large engagement ring adorning my finger, which was now accompanied by a thin band of diamonds, I had to concur. "Doesn't hurt at all."

Sliding his arms between me and the wooden barn, Jace lowered his face to capture my lips. Music from inside filtered out and danced through the air, giving a rhythm to our kiss and making my body sway.

With one final stroke of his tongue, Jace lifted his head. "How much longer until we can blow this joint?"

Giggling, I shook my head. "We have guests."

Sighing, his forehead dropped to mine. "I'll share you a little bit longer, and then all bets are off."

"Deal." I nodded once, shoving my hand between us.

He knocked it away and claimed my lips again. This time the music faded away, and so did all our surroundings. It was just him and me… husband and wife.

Chapter Thirty-One

Lorhaven

The best part about a wedding? The wedding night!

Seeing Josie walk down the aisle was actually pretty freaking amazing, though. The second she stepped through the archway, I felt I was driving down a narrow two-lane road in the dead of night and a Mac truck came out of nowhere, blarring the highbeams right in my eyes.

Blinded.

She blinded me.

I actually lifted my hand to shield my eyes, still staring.

I'd think she somehow had some sort of witch make her gown to vex me, but I knew better. Josie was gorgeous. Seeing her walk toward me in an all-white gown of lace and some sort of sparkly shit was no exception. Shit, if anything, she was the reason the dress looked so fucking sexy. Her curves filled it out in all. The. Right. Ways.

Basically, the wedding was foreplay for me. A giant buildup to when I would finally get her alone in the honeymoon suite at the nicest hotel in town.

Which was right the hell now.

The elevator opened with a silent glide, revealing a set of pristine white doors with a gold plate in the center that read: PENTHOUSE.

The small space between the elevator and the entrance to the room was silent, hushed.

Barely noticing the way the doors whooshed closed behind us, I quickly pulled out the keycard, then whisked Josie off her feet to carry her over the threshold.

Before the door even shut behind us, I heard her breath catch. "Did you do this?" Her voice held a note of reverence.

"Wish I could say yes," I murmured, surveying the setup.

The suite was filled with lit candles and richly pigmented red rose petals. A little farther into the room, on a stone countertop, was a large gold bucket with a bottle of Dom sticking out the top. Two crystal champagne flutes sat waiting beside the bucket, along with what looked like a giant box of chocolates with an even bigger red bow.

"It's beautiful," she murmured, gazing over the path of red roses that led out of this room and into the next.

Holding out my hand, I wagged my brows. "Two guesses on where those petals lead."

Josie took my hand, but before we started across the carpet, she reached down and pulled off her wine-colored heels, tossing them near the door.

"Ahh," she sighed.

Following her lead, I kicked off my shoes as well, and then hand in hand, we walked over the silky petals. On our way by, I grabbed the bottle of Dom and the glasses, along with hte notecard sitting with them.

The petals led us straight into the bedroom, but they didn't stop. Instead, they bloomed out, scattered all around the room, even on the side tables and dresser. The all-white bed had a giant red heart in the center, made entirely of the flower petals.

"Wow," Josie said, barely inside the room.

Candles were lit around the space as well, their flames casting shadows over the pristine white walls.

Our bags were against the wall, having been delivered earlier, and from here I could see the darkened bathroom through the open doorway on the other side of the room.

"What's the card say?" she asked.

I slid it out of a sturdy white envelope and smiled. "Ivy and Rimmel."

"They're the best," she murmured, taking the card and tossing it on the floor.

"You guys have become really good friends, huh?" I asked.

"Uh-huh." She agreed, taking the bottle and glasses, setting them on the first available space. "I think we're going to be friends a long time."

"I've been waiting to get you alone all day," I confessed, pulling her into me.

"You're not the only one." Her hands slid beneath my jacket, pushing it off my shoulders and down my arms.

The fabric pooled behind me, and I started pulling at the tie, the vest, and all the other clothes that went with this monkey suit. Once I was down to just the pants, Josie's hands glided up my bare chest. I leaned down to claim her mouth, but she spun abruptly, putting her back to me.

I made a frustrated sound, and she smiled, looking over her shoulder with those wicked green eyes. "Help me get out of this gown? It's so beautiful. I don't want to rip it."

"Patience is not my strong suit tonight, baby."

"Once it's off, you don't have to be patient." She promised.

The gown unzipped all the way down to her ass. The white, heavy fabric fell open, exposing a huge section of her back. She wasn't wearing any panties. And from what I could tell, no bra either.

"Are you naked under that gown?" I partially choked, running a single finger down the center of her newly exposed back.

Her should shrugged dantily. "Only way to guarantee there would be no lines." Slowly, Josie spun, her arms crossed over her chest, holding the gown in place. Reaching out, I grasped the fabric at her shoulders, and she dropped her arms.

The weight of the gown helped it slide right down, revealing every inch of her perfect body from the waist up. The fabric still clung to the curve of her hips, requiring a gentle tug for me to slide it the rest of the way down.

Once she was free of the dress, she took it and sashayed her fine naked ass to the closet, where I assumed she hung it up. All I knew was I enjoyed the shit out of the view when she walked toward me for the second time today.

She was completely naked, completely bare, and completely mine.

Closing her fingers around the button, she freed my already hard and ready dick from the pants and boxer briefs.

Suddenly, I was the glad the room was all done up in romance because I wanted her right then. I didn't want to be romantic. I just wanted to bury myself inside her.

Her body wrapped around mine when I lifted her off her feet. The warmth of her core brushed over me, and I closed my eyes briefly. The brush of her lips brought me back, and I gave in with a moan.

As we kissed, she rubbed her naked breasts against my chest like she was a cat and I was a ray of sun. Her tongue was gentle but persistent inside my mouth, and my hands were filled with her lucious bare ass.

We tumbled on the bed, my body pressing her into the rose petals. Abandoning her mouth, my lips traveled over her cheek to her ear and then slowly down to lick up the curve of her neck.

Her body arched into me, her nails digging into my back.

Leaving a trail of hot desire as I moved down to her supple breasts, she whispered my name. I replied incoherently and kept on kissing, flicking my tongue over her already erect nipple.

"Jace," she said a little firmer this time.

"What?" my voice rumbled.

She shoved my shoulder a little, and I tipped my head, gazing up her body into glittery, green eyes. "I want to give you something first."

"I got all I need right here, baby," I murmured, closing my lips around her breast.

Josie moaned, filled her hands with my hair, and tugged me closer. "Deeper, Jace." She panted.

I obliged, sucking her flesh deeper into my mouth with the amount of pressure I knew would made her center throb.

"Oh, yes," she murmured, arching up into me.

I moved to the other breast, because I'm an equal opportunity kind of lover, and latched on without restraint.

Josie's legs wound around my waist and her hips began moving against me. She was already slick, already dripping with desire. And I knew just how sweet her desire tasted across my tongue.

Leaving her breast and licking down her stomach, I felt her body quiver beneath me. Pushing her thighs wide, I dropped onto my knees in front of the bed. Her ass was just a little too far away, so I pulled her down the mattress by her legs.

Rose petals rained off the edge of the bed around my knees, but I barely noticed because she was on full display. The already plump clit stood out at the top of her folds, and I practically salivated.

I dove right in, licking with one long stroke right up the center of her body. Josie shuddered and cried my name. I was beyond playing, beyond teasing. I just wanted her.

Spearing her with one thick finger, my tongue found her clit and began moving. Her hands hit the bed on both sides of her, crushing the petals between her fingers as the small of her back arched.

"Oh, Jace," she moaned.

I licked and sucked, pumping my finger in and out of her slick body. She tasted so incredibly sweet, but the way she whimpered my name was sweetest of all.

I knew when she was close because her knees started trembling. With one final push, I sank my finger deep and crooked it toward me, gliding it over her most sensitive spot.

Her breathing increased and a low moan built in her chest. Keeping up the added pressure with my mouth, I sucked her deep, and she exloded right across my tongue.

I drank her in deep, not licking, not removing my finger until she was totally silent and spent against the mattress.

Withdrawing carefully from her body, I stood and gazed down at her body lying limp across the bed. "You have rose petals in your hair," I said, my voice husky.

Josie's eyes slid down my body. Her pink tongue jutted out to lick over her lower lip. All of a sudden, she pushed up so I was standing between her legs and she was sitting on the foot of the bed.

Her hand wrapped around my rigid cock and her other cupped my balls. For long, blissful moments, Josie worked my dick with both hands. She had the skill of a magician.

My balls were drawn against my body when her mouth slid over my length. Fisting a hand in her hair, I held on as she worked my cock, bobbing her head up and down, pausing long enough to lick it from the base all the way to the tip like it was the biggest and best ice cream cone she'd ever had.

Eventually, raw need took over. My hips began moving, thrusting into her warm, wet mouth. Josie wrapped her hands around my ass, her nails digging into my cheeks as she urged me to fuck her harder and deeper.

I did, but only for a moment. I couldn't take much of her deep-throating because I knew I'd never last. Abruptly, I yanked free, my dick standing between us glistening from her mouth. Placing my hands beneath her arms, I lifted her up the mattress, settling her back in the center, among the roses.

She spread her legs wide when I came over her, brushing her hands lightly down my arms.

"I love you, Jace," she whispered, holding my stare.

"Ah, baby." I vowed, "I love you just as much."

With one long stroke, I went deep, filling her body and making us both groan. Josie started moving first, rotating her hips, teasing my cock until I pushed up onto my hands and began to pump.

"Harder, Jace," she begged, sinking her nails into my biceps.

I picked up the pace, and she literally purred. My body was shuddering, begging for release, but I held it off as long as I could. Until I felt her straining beneath me, asking for the same release my body was desperate for.

With one last push, I went deep inside her, wrapping both my arms around her body, holding her against me as my dick pulsed and released inside her.

She welcomed my orgasm with her own. Our bodies milked each other as we lay there tangled in each other's arms, spent.

I didn't know how much time passed before she patted my shoulder. I rolled sideways, onto the bed, pulling her along with me.

"You smell like roses," she murmured, inhaling deep against my chest.

"So do you."

We lay together a while longer before I carefuly slid out from beneath her. "You want some champagne, baby?"

"Not right now," she answered, sitting up.

"No?" I asked, setting aside the bottle and turning toward her.

In response, she climbed off the bed, padding to where our bags sat untouched. In seconds, she had her suitcase opened and pulled out a box with a white bow. "I have a wedding present for you."

"We said no gifts, Josie," I grumped. I hadn't gotten her anything because the agreement was to do some shopping once we got to Paris.

"But this one is special." She cajoled. "And I don't want to wait to give it to you." Her lower lip stuck out, and I caved.

"What is it?"

With a gleeful smile, she bounced back onto the bed, sitting naked in the center. Her cheeks were still flushed from the sex, but her eyes were alert.

"Come here." She beckoned, patting the space beside her.

Far be it from me to deny my sexy, naked wife.

As I joined her on the bed, she held out the box excitedly. Shaking my head, I took it, untied the bow, and lifted the lid. Josie was looking at me with wide, expectant eyes, a wave of nervousness flickering behind them.

Glancing back down, I pushed the tissue paper away and glanced in. The bottom fell out of my stomach. Looking between her and the item inside the box, my heart stuttered.

"Josie…" I began. She nodded and bounced a little on the mattress. Reaching in, I grabbed the small wand thing and lifted it up, gazing down at the two definitive lines. "Are you pregnant?"

"I'm pregnant." She confirmed.

Shock and awe rippled through my brain, robbing me of speech. After a long moment, Josie touched my hand. "Jace?"

My eyes went to her bare midsection instantly. "My baby is in there." I pointed.

She nodded, a smile playing on her lips.

Tossing the stick over my shoulder, I heard it clatter somehwere on the floor. I tackled her, and she laughed.

"You're having my baby?" I said, staring down into her beautiful face.

"Yes, Jace, I'm having your baby."

Fusing our mouths together, I kissed her long and deep. When finally I pulled back, I took her face in my hands and pressed our foreheads together. "You're pregnant."

"Are you happy?" she asked.

I laughed. "Are you fucking kidding me? I'm delirious."

Josie hugged me tight, joy bursting around her. "I found out a couple days ago. It was so hard not to say anything. I almost did a few times. But I wanted to wait 'til tonight."

Brushing the hair out of her face, I smiled down at her. "I'm never gonna be able to top this present."

She laughed. "I don't know. Paris is pretty good."

My eyes rounded. "You can't fly across the world in your condition!" I was straddling her body. My God, I cold crush her and the baby!

Literally vaulting off her, I bounced onto the side of the bed, giving her ample space to breathe.

She laughed. "You're being crazy!"

"Woman, don't you laugh at me. That's my kid in there," I ground out, pointing to her belly.

Josie's eyes softened. Reaching for my hand, she placed it on her stomach, resting hers over mine. "I already saw my doctor. I wanted to confirm it before I told you. I told him about our honeymoon, and he said it was perfectly fine to go to Paris. It's still very early in the pregnancy. I just can't travel when I'm further along."

"You're sure?" I questioned.

"I promise." She swore. "We better enjoy this vacation, because I have a feeling we won't be getting another one for a long time."

"A baby," I mused. The surprise was finally beginning to sink in.

"Yeah, a baby," she whispered, cuddling into my side.

So I became a husband and a father on the very same day. Seemed as if I didn't do anything without doing it all the way.

"Today has been a good fucking day," I announced.

Josie laughed. "I'll second that."

Glancing down, I pressed my lips against her forehead. "Stick with me, baby. I'll take you on one hell of a lifetime ride." Pausing and thinking of the baby growing inside her, I added, "With seat belts."

I felt her smile against me. "Now that's an offer I can't refuse."

Damn right it was.

Nine months later…

I didn't want to find out if I was having a girl or a boy. It didn't matter, and I spent far too much time in my life feeling I wasn't good enough because I wasn't a boy.

I would not do that to this child. No one else would either.

I knew it was a not-so-subtle message when I announced we wouldn't know if this new member of our family was a girl or a boy until he or she came out. I wasn't into subtle messages anyway. I was always stubborn and mostly defiant… Pregnancy seemed to exaggerate those qualities.

Jace was amused by it (which did not amuse me), often saying it was my momma bear mode. He was probably right. Being pregnant made me extremely protective over this baby and my body.

He wasn't any better, though. If people thought he was an asshole before, now they thought he was an outright bastard.

Personally, I thought it was sexy. I was picking up the protective vibes he was throwing down. Suffice it to say, our sex life was not hindered by my pregnancy. If anything, it kicked it up a notch… Something I didn't even know was possible.

So since I refused to find out the sex, we had a lot of neutral-colored clothes and maybe a lot of clothes that were more gender specific. I never thought I was a pink person until I walked into a baby boutique and saw it all. Ruffles, bows… sparkles.

You'd have to be a coldhearted dead fish to not think baby clothes were absolutely adorable. Even Jace's eyes would soften when I dragged him around the shops, holding his hand.

Half the clothes wouldn't even get worn. Maybe I'd save them, you know, in case we did this again.

I loved being pregnant, everything about it. In some ways, it made the fact I was a woman even more empowering. I fully realized pregnancy didn't always have that effect on women. For me, though—a girl who fought against being what I was born as and trying to prove I was stronger than—being pregnant was oddly humbling.

I'd been wrong all those years. Wrong to let anyone make me feel I wasn't enough. Men and women weren't created equal. We just weren't. But we were created to be equally amazing, sometimes for the same reasons and sometimes for gender specific ones. I was okay with that now.

Another contraction squeezed my midsection, and I sucked in a deep breath. Jace was half on the bed, leaning as close as possible, his hand gripping mine.

"Getting much closer," the nurse said, reading the machines beside me. "I think it may be time to push."

I nodded enthusiastically, and she went in search of the doctor.

"Next time you tell me you want to have a baby, I'm going to have to think long and hard about this shit, Josie," Jace demanded. His voice was harsh, but his eyes… they were worried.

"I'm fine, Jace." I assured him. After a few deep breaths, the contraction began to ebb. "I got this."

"You're in pain."

"Well, I didn't expect pushing out a baby to be pain free."

His hand covered my large, round belly. I liked being pregnant, but I would also enjoy seeing my feet again. "I don't like seeing you hurt."

"Will you like seeing me with your baby in my arms?"

With a soft sound, he leaned forward and kissed my stomach. "Oh yeah." His chocolate eyes found mine. "Maybe try and push him out real fast."

"I'll see what I can do," I muttered dryly.

"I love you," he told me.

"I love you, too." Right after, another contraction ripped through my stomach, and I winced, grabbing my belly.

"Josie!" he bellowed, shoving up out of his chair. It slid across the room, hitting the wall. "What's wrong?"

"I'm fine," I told him through deep breaths. "But… I really want to… push."

Racing to the door, Jace nearly ripped it from the hinges and launched out into the hall. "Someone better get me a goddamn doctor or I'm delivering this kid myself!" he shouted.

I giggled through the pain.

"'Bout damn time!" he hollered a few seconds later. "Were you on vacation?"

"Jace," I said, my voice not carrying as strongly as I wanted.

It didn't matter, though. He heard and came racing back into the room. "What is it, baby? What's wrong?"

"Stop being mean to the doctor."

He gave me a dark look, but I only held out my hand so he would take it.

"I hear it's time to have a baby." My doctor came striding in like he wasn't even bothered my husband was acting like a caveman. "Let's make sure," he said, lifting the blanket over my legs.

Beside me, Jace stiffened. He hated when doctors touched me. He hated it even more when they had to look between my legs.

He was an idiot.

Another contraction tightened my muscles, and I squeezed Jace's hand until he glanced at the doctor for help.

"All right, give me a nice, big push," the doctor said. Beside him, the nurse was there to assist.

I'd been in labor for almost twelve hours. Twelve long hours. I was tired, uncomfortable, and everyone was sitting in the waiting room, ready to come back and see the new baby.

But even so, the second he told me to push, I did. Poor Jace wouldn't last another twelve hours. I wasn't even sure he'd last one.

I pushed for only thirty minutes, and then the sounds of a crying baby filled the room.

"Let me see," I insisted, trying to sit up all the way.

A tiny, slippery baby was placed on my chest immediately. "It's a girl," the doctor announced.

A girl. I had a daughter.

She was crying and shaking a tiny little fist, as if she were telling everyone in the room she wasn't too happy with the way things were going.

I laughed. I liked her spirit.

The sound of my laughter made her cries quiet. She looked up at me, her eyes wide and green. Her head was perfectly round and had a light dusting of downy, dark hair.

"Hi," I told her, touching the fist she'd been waving around.

She made a sound, a cross between a cry and a yell. Grinning, I said, "She's just like you, Jace."

He didn't answer.

Tearing my eyes away from my new baby daughter, I found him standing a few feet from the bed, hands shoved deep into the pockets of his jeans. His eyes looked like wide saucers, the deep brown bottomless, and he was completely transfixed on me and his baby. His mouth was parted slightly, and the rise and fall of his chest was a little quicker than normal.

"Jace?"

"Dad, we need you to cut the cord," the doctor said at the same time.

Not tearing his eyes from us, he stepped toward the doctor, who put a pair of scissors in his hand and instructed him on what to do.

Removing his eyes from us only long enough to cut the cord, immediately, his stare returned.

I held out my hand. "Come meet her."

Jace came, moving cautiously, as if he were afraid to scare the still fussing baby wiggling around in my arms.

Tilting her up so he could see her better, I smiled. "This is your daddy," I told her.

Jace hit his knees right there beside the bed.

For the first time since I'd met him, tears glistened in his eyes. Working his throat, swallowing thickly, he reached out a hand, stretching a single finger toward his daughter. At the same moment, her fist opened, the pad of his finger brushed over her palm, and her fingers closed around it.

A tear rolled down his cheek.

Which made a fountain of tears roll down mine.

"You're so beautiful," he whispered to her. She stared at him as if he'd literally hung the moon, her eyes not leaving his face at all. "You have your momma's eyes."

She made a soft sound.

Jace nearly gasped. "Is she okay?" His eyes swung to the nurse. "What's wrong with her?"

"Nothing is wrong with her," the nurse replied patiently. "I think she likes you."

Looking up, I couldn't help but notice the way the doctor and nurse had stopped what they were doing to watch Jace with his daughter. I knew these people saw moments like this hundreds of times, but I knew just by looking at their faces they'd never quite seen a man as surly as Jace literally brought to his knees.

If I ever worried—even for a brief second—Jace might have wanted a son more than a daughter, that worry vanished. He loved our little girl instantly. Wholeheartedly.

And for that, I loved him just a little bit more.

"I'll need to see her." The nurse started forward.

"What do you think you're doing?" Jace demanded, swinging around between me and the nurse.

"I need to weigh her, wrap her in a blanket, put a diaper on her…" the nurse explained patiently.

"Mrs. Lorhaven, I'm gonna need you to push a few more times," the doctor said from the end of my bed.

Jace's body stiffened. I imagined his eyes were almost popping out of his head. "Is there another baby in there!"

I laughed. I couldn't help it.

"No," the doctor said, and I could tell he was slightly amused. "But we need to remove the placenta."

"How about you bring me the baby," the nurse said, moving just a foot away to her small station.

Turning, Jace glanced at me, his stare eating up the sight of us both. "Here," I said, offering him our daughter.

"She's naked," he whispered, horrified.

"Did you think she'd come out fully clothed?" I rebutted.

The baby started fussing and crying. I began to worry. "Take her, Jace. She's probably cold."

Without hesitation, Jace swooped in, and as if he'd done it thousand times before, he scooped her up, pulling her into his chest, both arms wrapped tightly around her.

"Hey now," he told her. "It's okay, sweetheart. Daddy's gonna take care of you now."

I sniffled. He was adorable. Absolutely heart-melting.

"Aren't you that bad-boy race car driver?" the nurse asked when he brought her over.

"And?" he barked.

"Looks like someone found his soft spot," she mused, taking the baby.

I watched them across the room as I finished with the doctor. By the time I was done, I was exhausted, but I felt sticky and gross. "I want a shower," I said.

"The nurse will help you with that," the doctor said. "But then it's right back off your feet. I'll send someone in and also have your bed changed so it will be ready for you."

"What the hell is that?" Jace said, pointing to the baby.

I jolted up, alarmed. "What!"

"It's a hat, sir. We put them on all the newborns."

"It's ugly," Jace announced, crossing his fingers over his head. "My daughter doesn't wear ugly hats."

"Oh my God, Jace, you are so rude!"

"It's a standard issue hat, sir,"

Jace wasn't listening. He was digging through the bag of baby items I'd packed—an entire bag. I'd brought pink, blue, gender neutral… basically way too much.

"Here," he said, pulling out something. The nurse moved to take it, but he made a sound, pushing past her.

"Here we go, sweetheart," he murmured, gently taking off the "ugly" striped hat and carefully tugging on a baby-pink cotton one with a giant red heart on it. When he was done, he made a sound of satisfaction and picked her up.

"Good luck getting a turn," the nurse told me slyly.

I giggled.

Jace carried her over to me. "Here's Mommy."

Halfway to handing her over, the nurse stopped him. "I need to take her to the nursery. I'll bring her back as soon as possible."

I made a face, and the nurse smiled. "She'll be back before you know it. Take the time to clean up. I'll have someone in to help you as soon as possible."

"I'll help her," Jace said.

"No, go with the baby." I insisted.

He frowned. Glancing between me and our daughter, I could tell he was torn. Placing a hand over the bundle in his arms, I said, "Go with her."

He nodded once. "I'll be right back."

"I know."

About an hour later, I was cleaned up and dressed in a pair of sweats and a T-shirt. They offered me a clean hospital gown, which I politely declined. Did people actually like wearing those things?

My hair was pulled up into a smooth bun on top of my head, out of the way. It was straight. I'd been wearing it that way a lot because I could go and have it blown out, something that didn't require any effort for my large, pregnant butt.

After I was settled in the bed, pain meds swallowed, and fresh water at the bedside, the nurse left me in the room alone. The second she was gone, I pushed out of the bed, grabbed the baby bag I'd brought, and set it on the mattress so I could dress the baby when she came back.

Then, impatient, I went out into the hallway to find my daughter.

Feeling kind of like a cup of Jell-O as I walked toward the nursery, I knew I should be in bed, but I'd just been there for twelve long hours and I wanted to see my daughter.

Jace hogged her, and it made me grumpy.

About halfway down the hall, a familiar figure came around the corner, along with a clear baby bassinet and a nurse.

Everything inside me brightened. Pushing away from the wall, I started forward, stumbling just a bit.

"What the hell are you doing?" Jace demanded, rushing to my side and lifting me into his arms instantly. Even though it was embarrassing, I let him have all my weight.

"I wanted to see the baby."

"I told you I'd bring her back."

"You really need to stay in bed." The nurse chimed in.

I ignored her, glancing instead at the little bundle wrapped up in the bassinet. My heart fluttered just seeing her. Warmth burst inside me. She was utterly beautiful and so tiny.

"I don't know what kind of place this is," Jace spoke very quietly against my ear. "Look at that blanket, Josie. It's just unacceptable."

I laughed. Since when did he become so concerned with fashion?

"She weighs seven pounds, six ounces," the nurse told me as we went toward our room. "And is perfectly healthy."

"She likes to cry," Jace told me.

"She's hungry," the nurse said. "You'll need to feed her right away."

Once the nurse was confident I'd gotten the hang of feeding her, she finally left us alone. I held her, mostly staring at her. Jace sat on the side of the bed, his arm around me and his daughter the entire time.

"She's so pink," I whispered, brushing a finger over her chubby cheeks. "So little."

"Kid's got a set of lungs on her, though. Did me proud. Every time that dragon nurse touched her, she let 'em have it."

"You must be so proud." I teased.

He didn't seem to realize I was joking. "Damn straight. This kid isn't gonna take shit from anyone."

"You can't say shit in front of a baby." I scolded.

He made sound, and I leaned into him, resting my head on his chest. The baby was sleeping in my arms, breathing soft and steady. I loved her so much… in a way I'd never loved anyone before. I loved her when I was pregnant, but the second I saw her, I loved her ten times more.

Jace kissed the top of my head. "She's beautiful, Josie."

"I can't believe we have a daughter," I mused. Tilting my head back, gazing up, I said, "Thank you, Jace. Thank you for giving her to me."

"You have to share."

I laughed. "I think I can handle that."

"The nurse asked me her name," Jace said as I gazed back down at her. "I didn't know what to say."

We'd tossed names around my entire pregnancy, but one never felt just right. We had a few that were our favorites, but as I looked down at her now, none of them fit.

"Sophia," I said, adjusting the pink hat on her head. "I think she looks like a Sophia."

"That's a new one," he mused.

"I like it. It can't be shortened into a boy name. It's very feminine but also beautiful."

"Sophie for short?" he asked.

I nodded. "How about Sophia Jacqueline Lorhaven."

I felt the slight change come over him, the way his arm tightened just a little around me and our baby. "After my mother."

"Jacqueline is a beautiful name," I said, knowing it would mean so much for him to be able to give a piece of his mother to the daughter she would never meet.

Jace pressed his lips on the top of my head. Beneath me, I felt the thundering of his heart.

"Is it okay?" I asked after a moment.

"God, baby, it's perfect."

A few moments later, there was a knock on the door before it opened and Arrow poked his head in. "Can I come in?"

Jace motioned for him, slipping off the bed. Arrow entered, followed closely by Hopper, my father, and Donna.

Donna and my father were holding hands. It was nice to see them happy.

All eyes went to the baby in my arms. "It's a girl," I said quietly.

I couldn't help but look right at my father when I announced it. Part of me was worried what he would say.

Leaving Donna's side, he came right over, leaned close to her, and kissed her cheek. Sophia yawned. Dad smiled.

Clearing his throat, he straightened, sweeping his eyes around the room. "I should make it clear here and now she's my favorite. All you others can just get in line behind her."

I laughed. "Dad!"

"She's just beautiful," he said, gazing down.

"What's her name?" Arrow asked, leaning over the foot of the bed like that would help him see. I motioned for him, and he came around reluctantly to peer down into my arms.

"Sophia Jacqueline," I said, holding her out toward him.

"You want me to hold her?" He faltered.

"Well, she is your niece."

His eyes went round, glancing around at Hopper for help. Hopper came forward to stand at his back.

"Support her head," I instructed, passing her into his arms.

"Don't drop her," Jace intoned. I shot him a look.

Arrow straightened, holding her tight into his chest. Hopper stared at her from over Arrow's shoulder. Seconds ticked by. Then Arrow gasped. "She's looking at me!"

"Tell her hi," I told him.

"Hi, uh, Sophia…" he said. She made a sound, and he smiled. "Oh, she likes me," he announced.

Hopper rolled his eyes.

"I'm your uncle. I'm going to teach you about driving fast and—"

"No!" Jace cut in. "No freaking way."

Arrow looked at me, and I winked.

She started fussing, wiggling around in Arrow's arms. "Oh shit." He worried "What'd I do."

"You don't say shit to a baby!" Jace muttered, stalking over to push between Arrow and Hopper. "Give me my daughter."

Sophie was surrendered to Jace, and she stopped crying immediately.

I watched him with her, marveling at how natural he was without even realizing it. He knew exactly what to do with our daughter, and he made sure he ordered everyone around as they all took turns holding her.

After a while, he shooed them all out, and I fed her again. Afterward, I changed her diaper, outfit, and blanket. Even though I had an abundance of clothes in the baby bag, everything we put on her was pink. Even the soft blanket we swaddled her in.

Snuggling her close, I yawned. My eyes were so heavy. I was so happy, but I was exhausted.

"You need to get some sleep," Jace said, watching me.

"I wish I didn't have to."

"You'll be up soon enough to feed her again."

Nodding, I let him gently take her from my arms. "Go to sleep, baby," he whispered, kissing me on the forehead. "I got this. I'll watch over you both."

Settling into the pillow, I smiled as my eyes grew heavy. Jace dragged a big rocking chair over by the bed and sat down in it to gently rock Sophie.

I watched him with her as I drifted off. My husband and my daughter. I had not one regret about giving up racing to pursue a family and empower women. Doing those things empowered me in ways I never knew possible.

I loved my life now. More than I ever had before.

Sophie made a noise, and my eyes sprang open.

Jace tucked the blanket around her a little tighter, kissed her tiny head, and smiled. "Don't be waking up Mommy, Soph," he whispered. "She's grouchy when she's tired."

"I am not," I argued.

Looking up at me, he smiled.

My heart constricted. He was perfect. She was perfect. Life in this moment was absolutely flawless.

One final thought drifted through my mind before I finally succumbed to much-needed sleep.

Who knew life could be so much better beyond the #finishline?

The End

But turn the page for more…

Turn the page for a BONUS *GearShark* article featuring Trent & Drew!

Drew Forrester and Trent Mask made GearShark *history when they announced not only the beginning of a brand-new indie racing division, New Revolution Racing, but also when they announced their relationship.*

Same-sex relationships aren't uncommon in today's society, but they are in the racing world. In the overall sports world. So to have two men come right out and admit they're in love and ask for respect was groundbreaking here at GearShark.

They also happen to be very easy on the eyes, charming, and very successful at what they do. Because of all this, it comes as no surprise that the magazine still gets emails and phone calls about these two men.

They are quite arguably our most popular cover models, which makes them a no-brainer choice for a bonus Rapid Fire Round in this red-hot issue. I caught up with these boys via phone just after they were guests at Jayson Hamilton (AKA Hopper) and Arrow Hamilton's (formerly Ambrose) wedding in Las Vegas.

It didn't take them long to remind me why it is they're everyone's favorite.

GS: Our readers are going to be very thrilled about this interview. We get asked for more articles about you both constantly.

DF: We're pretty boring guys.

GS: Something tells me that isn't exactly true.

TM: Well, if it's not, we'll never tell.

GS: <I can actually hear him grinning through the phone.>

GS: You ready for this rapid-fire round? You're gonna have to do some telling.

DF: Bring it on.

GS: Who has the best French fries?

TM: He's never met a French fry he didn't like.

DF: It's true. I like 'em all, long as they have ketchup.

GS: No favorite type at all?

DF & TM: Waffle fries.

GS: It's well known you live on a family estate, behind a wall and a gate, with Maryland Knights stars Romeo Anderson and Braeden Walker, plus their wives and children. What's it like living with so many other people?

TM: They aren't people. They're our family. And we wouldn't have it any other way.

DF: T and I have our own place on the property.

GS: Do you see your family often?

TM: Every single day.

GS: Everyone wants to know if you're getting married.

DF: Why does everyone want us to get married so bad?

TM to DF: They can't understand why you wouldn't want to put a ring on all this.

DF: He's gesturing to himself.

TM: You're looking.

DF: I like what I see.

GS: <Obviously, they need help staying on track.> So is that a no to the wedding?

TM: It's not a no. But it's not a right now either. We're happy how we are. We have a great life, great jobs, a great house, and a big family. I don't need a ring to make me happier.

DF: I don't either. T makes me happy, and I know he's not going anywhere.

TM to DF: You're stuck with me, Forrester.

DF to TM: Hells yeah.

GS: Do you think if you were to get married, it might cause unwanted drama.

DF: What kind of drama?

GS: In the media? With family members who might not understand?

TM: How about we skip to the fun questions?

GS: You'll have to forgive me. Our readers are very vocal. I had to ask.

DF: Hopefully they'll understand we like to keep our private life private.

GS: <Clearly, these two are still insanely protective of one another and their relationship.>

GS: Who hogs the bed?

TM: Drew.

DF: I don't hog the bed.

TM: He totally hogs it.

GS: Do you share clothes?

TM: Always.

GS: Drew, you're currently ranked number one in the NRR. Do you plan on bringing home the championship trophy again this year?

DF: Of course.

GS: How is the rivalry with Lorhaven going?

DF: He's a good driver. Doesn't make it easy to stay ahead.

GS: Do you like kids?

TM: Of course we do.

DF: We have two nephews, a niece, and there's another munchkin on the way.

GS: That would be Romeo and Rimmel Anderson who are expecting, correct?

TM: Yes.

GS: Ever think about adopting?

DF: We just adopted a dog. Our sister won't stop bringing them home from her shelter.

GS: I meant a child.

TM: He acts like a child, always wanting to eat, and I think he might need a diaper. He won't stop peeing on shit.

GS: The dog?

DF: He's brown. His name is French Fry.

TM: <Muttering> We are not calling that dog French Fry!

DF: French Fry is a good name for a dog. Don't you think, Emily?

GS: I'm going to have to go with Trent on this one.

TM: I told you, Forrester. It's terrible. Not even Rimmel was on board, and she named her dog Ralph!

GS: Ralph is better than French Fry.

TM & DF: <Laughs>

GS: Coffee or tea?

TM & DF: Coffee

GS: What is your favorite month during the year?

TM: October.

DF: My birthday is in October.

TM: That's why it's my favorite.

DF: Aww, frat boy.

GS: What's your favorite movie?

DF: Terminator.

GS: Any chance I could maybe get you to talk more about marriage and kids?

TM: No.

GS: Can't blame a girl for trying.

It's not exactly the answers I think all our persistent readers were hoping for, but it does give everyone a little inside look at our favorite couple. Perhaps in the future, GearShark will be lucky enough to have a special wedding issue featuring Trent and Drew.

Until then, let's hope those boys pick a name for their "brown" dog that isn't French Fry.

Author's Note

Did this book surprise you? It did me. I thought *#Blur* would be the #finishline for the *GearShark* series, but when I finished, I realized I had more to say. Arrow and Hopper are hard characters to let go of. They were still in my brain, talking, telling me things.

When I realized I wanted to do a wedding book, it took me by surprise. I never intended to marry off any of these characters. I always felt right with their happy endings, and in my heart, I know all these couples will be together forever. A wedding didn't seem so important to me… until Hopper made it important. He just popped up in my head and wouldn't let it rest that he wanted to marry Arrow. So I started it in secret. Didn't tell anyone I was writing it because I had no idea how it would go. Originally, I thought it would be three sections: Arrow and Hopper, Joey and Lorhaven, and then a third section for Trent and Drew.

Obviously, having just read it, you know there isn't section for Trent and Drew (except the bonus interview!). Hopper and Arrow had a lot to say, and I felt Joey and Lorhaven's happily ever after fit really well. They kind of coincide, you know?

Trent and Drew, not so much. I wouldn't be able to condense anything into a small section, so I didn't bother trying. I realize Trent and Drew are HIGHLY requested for a wedding book and a baby book. I know, guys. LOL. Here's the thing. It's just like they said in the book. They're happy. *#Junkie* and *#Rev* are my favorite books. I will not add another one until/unless I have something that will live up to those two books. I have a couple ideas, but nothing concrete, and I won't put a book together and put it out there just because it's highly demanded—UNTIL I have it the way I really want it.

So this is it for now. I'm not ruling out a revisit to Trent and Drew. I'd love to do it. I love them. But not right now. Maybe sometime later this year. We'll see.

Until then, I hope you enjoyed *#FinishLine*. Hopper and Arrow are so special. I love the way they love each other.

What's next for me? I'm really not sure. My entire life has been *#Hashtag* and *GearShark* for a couple years now. I think it might be fun to write something else. I just hope you all will read it.

As always, thank you for the enthusiastic and unwavering support for this series. It means so much to me. Thank you for all the shares, reviews, and beautiful comments. I appreciate each one.

See you next book!

XOXO,

Cambria

Cambria Hebert is an award winning, bestselling novelist of more than thirty books. She went to college for a bachelor's degree, couldn't pick a major, and ended up with a degree in cosmetology. So rest assured her characters will always have good hair.

Besides writing, Cambria loves a caramel latte, staying up late, sleeping in, and watching movies. She considers math human torture and has an irrational fear of birds (including chickens). You can often find her painting her toenails (because she bites her fingernails), or walking her Chihuahuas (the real rulers of the house).

Cambria has written within the young adult and new adult genres, penning many paranormal and contemporary titles. She has also written romantic suspense, science fiction, and most recently male/male romance. Her favorite genre to read and write is contemporary romance. A few of her most recognized titles are: *The Hashtag Series, GearShark Series, Text, Torch,* and *Tattoo.*

Recent awards include: Author of the Year, Best contemporary series (The Hashtag Series), Best contemporary book of the year, Best book trailer of the year, Best contemporary lead, Best contemporary book cover of the year. In addition, her most recognized title, *#Nerd* was listed at Buzzfeed.com as a top fifty summer romance read.

Cambria Hebert owns and operates Cambria Hebert Books, LLC.

You can find out more about Cambria and her titles by visiting her website at: http://www.cambriahebert.com

Sign up for her newsletter: http://eepurl.com/bUL5_5